On the wall outside, three se  railing of Isadora's balcony scuttled to the sides, and up. Firs balcony to press against the wa two on the balcony, hesitating to seen or heard. There was nothing from within, and the third, the taller leader, dropped lightly from the railing and crept to where he could glance into the room.

Isadora stood within, whirling slowly like a dancer and making her skirts billow. He watched with no indication that the sight affected any particular change in his emotions. He waited until Isadora turned toward the door at last, showing him her back, and then he moved. The others flowed in behind him, and before Isadora was fully aware that she was not alone, a silver glitter marked the arc of thin metal chain over her head, and her arms were gripped tightly, holding her steady.

The first intruder's arms snapped to either side, and with a grimace of surprise, her lips parted in a silent "oh," Isadora's head flew neatly from her neck. The two holding the arms of her decapitated body released her, and the three turned, moving swiftly back to the balcony. It would not take Alfonzo long to wonder why she hadn't joined him. The tallest of the three, the leader, stooped and gripped Isadora's hair, lifting her head easily.

His cowl fell back, just for a moment, revealing a strong, Slavic face framed by wild black hair. His eyes were piercing, perhaps ice blue, perhaps silver-gray. He gazed into the lifeless eyes of the head gripped in his hand. Bowing his head, he closed his eyes for a moment, and his lips moved in silent prayer.

CLAN NOVEL

LASOMBRA

BY DAVID NIALL WILSON

WHITE WOLF

Dark ages
LASOMBRA ™

David Niall Wilson

MORTE ASCENDO

AD 1206
Fifth of the Dark Ages Clan Novels

Acknowledgments

This book is dedicated to Trish, who makes all things in my life possible, including insane deadlines and creative darkness. I would also like to gratefully acknowledge Mr. William Hartman for his interest in the World of Darkness, his creative addition to this volume, and his amazing generosity.

Finally, I'd like to dedicate this to my little brother. It was a long time coming, but when he started reading, he did me the extra honor of loving my writing, and the vampire Montrovant from the Grails Covenant Trilogy. Here's another one, bro.

What Has Come Before

It is the winter of 1206 and almost two years have passed since the misguided Fourth Crusade sacked and looted the golden city of Constantinople. The Franks and Venetians—called simply Latins by the local Greeks—have carved up the fallen city and empire, founding their Latin Empire of Byzantium. Already they face threats from the Bulgars in Thrace and various Greek successor states, but for now a Frenchman sits on the throne of the Second Rome.

Away from the eyes of men, in the benighted world of vampires, things are no less chaotic. Michael, the powerful predator who ruled as patriarch of the Byzantine undead has been destroyed, and none have stepped forward to succeed him. Among Greek vampires, all hopes rest with Malachite, a member of the Nosferatu clan. He is said to be on a quest across Anatolia to find the Dracon, an ancient who had a hand in founding Byzantium. Among the Latins, members of Clan Lasombra—an ancient line of Mediterranean schemers and kingmakers—vie for power. Alfonzo, a bishop in the macabre Cainite Heresy, represents Venetian interests, while the Lady Gabriella is an agent of rival Genoa. No one has any real handle on the Latin Empire or the bands of vampiric refugees gathering in Adrianople, only a few nights' ride away.

The young vampire Lucita of Aragon is afloat in these troubled political seas. Far from her Iberian home, she can either sink or swim.

Prologue: Ten Years Ago (AD 1196)

Alfonzo the Venetian moved smoothly through the alleys of Constantinople's Latin Quarter. At his side, laughing and leaping occasionally to a low ledge, or flipping over a portico, Juliano and Adrianna accompanied him. It had been an amazing night. They'd attended a local festival, slipping through shadows and mingling with the crowds. Blood had pulsed all around them, hot and heady, and they'd dragged several into the darkness, feeding until they were gorged.

The blood had energized them, and Alfonzo, sire to the others, was feeling powerful. Invincible. He liked to get out and away from the affairs of his position. He was a bishop in the Cainite Heresy, a church unknown to popes and patriarchs but potent nonetheless. He was the childe of Narses, the Archbishop of Nod himself, who counted on him in many things. But the moments he cherished were those on the hunt. It was best when shared, and he had none others he preferred to share it with. Juliano was young and bold, dark of hair and eye with the body of a Greek athlete. Adrianna, in contrast, was slight, her perpetually young features, those of a girl just entering the nunnery, but the wicked twist of her grin belied the deception of her appearance.

Ahead, his estate spread out between two important avenues. They hurried their approach. The dawn would soon soak over the skyline and bring the cursed sun. They had precious little time left, after their revelry, to reach their places of rest.

As they approached the walls of the mansion, rising tall and majestic, Alfonzo could not help himself. He raised his arms and called on the shadows that resonated in tune with his dark, dead blood. He gathered them and flung them to the wall, using them first as a stair-step to leap and then snaking his way up the wall in a sinuous dark mass that resembled a giant serpent, or a wave of darkness. Juliano stopped, crouching low and watching his sire taking his leave with a dark smile.

"Always the showman," Adrianna commented with a laugh.

Juliano nodded. "Always *the* showman," he corrected.

Then, feeling the oppressive weight of the approaching dawn, the two hurried to a ground-level entrance. Their own quarters were beneath the main level. Alfonzo had sealed off an upper chamber, preferring the heights.

The first sensation that something was wrong assaulted Juliano and Adrianna as they entered the hall. None of the movement they associated with the place was there, no servants bustling about to prepare the day-face of the bishop's home. Nothing. Juliano glanced at Adrianna, not nervous, but questioning. She shrugged, and they hurried down the hall.

A stair led down to the left, and they took it, several steps at a time, ready now for their rest. The sluggishness was kicking in, drawing them toward the embrace of the earth. They knew it was time to be away from the open halls and chambers and tucked away safely behind thick, iron doors.

They reached the door to their chambers and Juliano grabbed the huge iron ring, dragging on it. Nothing happened. He frowned, gripping more tightly and yanking harder, but the door didn't budge. It took a second to register, then he hissed.

"It's been latched. Someone is inside, and it's locked."

Adrianna only had time to blink at him, wondering if a joke was being played, or if he were teasing her. She started to speak, but was cut off.

Steps pounded on the stairs behind them, and the two whirled. Men poured out of the stairwell, eyes wild and arms upraised with swords and crosses. At their head, a white-haired madman pranced. He waved his cross over his head and began to shout over the tumult.

"As your father Caine bows before Satan," the man cried, "so shall you bow before Calomena."

"Who in the seven hells is Calomena?" Juliano hissed, backing against the wall and looking wildly for an escape. Adrianna did not answer. She was busy pressing into the opposite wall, protecting her back. There was no way out. The passage dead-ended beside the now impassable doorway to their chambers. The only way out was through, and if they won through, they would find the daylight waiting.

The mortals banded together behind their aged leader, and he continued to speak, intoning the words as if he were reading them from some sacrament, though his gaze was locked to those of his two prisoners.

"Dark Caine has a sister," he said solemnly, "and she has a purpose. A destiny. She is the heart, and we are her limbs."

Juliano sprang. He had no intention of listening to this gray-haired lunatic preach. The sun was rising, and the strength was draining from his limbs too quickly. He reached the line of mortals just as he heard Adrianna's scream behind him. She had attacked, as well, striking the mob on the far side of the leader. Blood washed the floor as Juliano lashed out again and again, drawing the last of his strength into that bolting run. He nearly made the stairs when the whistle of a blade caught his ear too late, and he was cut nearly in two. He spun madly, careening off the wall, fighting to remain alert. Crashing into the stone, he found himself facing off with a huge, bearded man.

Eyes wide and mouth literally foaming, the giant lunged, crying out. Over the sound of the battle, Juliano could still hear the strong, resonant voice of the leader.

"Take this offering, Calomena, toward the day when you shall rise, and the children of Caine will be washed from the face of God's earth in a river of stolen blood."

Juliano sank toward the floor, and the blade sank into his flesh again, half-severing his head from his body. He choked, coughing out a final word before a last stroke severed his neck completely.

"Adrianna."

She lay in final death, far beyond hearing him, the remnant of her flesh decaying quickly, ravaged by the boots and blades and spittle of the mob, praying now in unison.

Praying to Calomena to wash the evil from the earth.

Far above, safely behind walls of stone and doors of iron, Bishop Alfonzo rested. In his rest, he stirred, nearly crying out, but he did not rise. The sun was high in the sky, washing the shadows down ditches and sweeping them under doors. Below, his childer lay slain. On the ashes that remained, he would find only a silver medallion for each. In relief on that trinket, the profile of Calomena, glittering coldly, would mock him.

Chapter One

Lucita of Aragon stared off into the deepening darkness and wondered if the city would ever shake off its drifting shroud of smoke and death. The "Dream," the Greeks' romantic notion of their city's glorious past, was a giant monument to destruction and decay, and Lucita had never enjoyed mourning.

Beneath the balcony where she stood, the clatter of carriage wheels echoed through the night. Hooves pounded the pocked remnant of the road. Lord Brexiano's entourage was the only thing moving within sight of the balcony. The carriage bounced precariously, a rider to either side, their mounts skittering sideways to avoid the jostling coach. Lucita momentarily entertained the hope that one of the wheels would snap, unceremoniously pouring the sniveling, useless ambassador onto the earth. It would be a good way to remember him.

Brexiano would crawl back to Castile and Archbishop Mongada, tail between his legs, and whine about the death of the city and the ensuing chaos. It was expected of him. He had been placed in a position of power, and he had failed. Much of what had happened would already have been relayed to Madrid, and Mongada would be angry. When one ruled the confessionals, one owned the truth. This was a lesson Lucita had learned early and well. Brexiano would hear the bad news in his official capacity, and he would bear the brunt of Mongada's wrath.

Lucita knew better than to put herself in that position. Byzantium was rife with possibilities, chaotic and without leadership. Brexiano was a fool, and in such a climate he would flounder, or worse yet, ally himself with some power beyond Mongada's influence. Brexiano was weak, so Lucita had sent him away. If he'd had a backbone, he would not have allowed it, but the back of his departing carriage spoke the truth. There was only one who could be trusted to handle the current situation in Constantinople, and she stood watching the rest depart, aching for the moment they would leave her sight, and her mind. Lucita turned and crossed the room quickly. The home she currently inhabited had supposedly been magnificent before the crusaders broke through the walls in 1204—was still magnificent, after a tortured, crumbling manner. There was rubble on the stairs, tapestries hung crooked on the walls, the stains of blood and spilled wine splashed on the walls and floors, much of the furniture had been overturned or destroyed. Lucita's people had begun the restoration of the building, but it was slow. Only the skeleton remained. The city was a giant structure of bone and death, and through those bones, powers moved silently.

The bones nearest to the mansion Lucita had claimed were lower to the ground. They were dirty and overrun by vermin, both human and otherwise. The Latin Quarter stretched out like a human garbage heap, interspersed with pockets of power, infested with factions that should have been banned from the city, a serpent's nest of intrigue. Still, it had weathered the storm of conquest better than many other quarters. There wasn't much you could do to squalor to make it worse, and there was little, on the surface, to plunder. It was all an artifice of magnificent design, and at its center lay Alfonzo the Venetian.

Lucita moved about her room, sliding her sword-belt about her slender waist, beneath the long cloak she wore, the thin blade camouflaged by trailing silk. She did not want to appear as an assassin, or a warrior, but as neither would she enter the unfriendly darkness unprotected. At times her seeming lack of years and slight figure were an asset, at other times a burden. She could count on men to underestimate her, but all too often this led to attacks and unwanted advances, and always with the worst timing.

There were those she needed to see, places she had to visit. On every side the delicate balance of power was shifting from one house to the next, whispering through the alleys and teasing at the ambitions of the strong. The city was in chaos, but the outcome of such chaos would be order. The structure of that order would set the stage for long years to come, and Lucita did not intend to be left in the wings, watching as other played out their parts.

Alfonzo ruled the streets directly beyond her balcony, and Venice was stretching long arms out to claim prizes long denied. Constantinople. New Rome. Riches and power, magnificent temples, and dark trenches. Worse still, Alfonzo and his Venetian masters were heretics, vampires who professed the union of Christ and Caine and the primacy of bloodlust and any number of vile practices. Her own sire, Archbishop Mongada, reserved an especial hatred for this Cainite Heresy, but she had never been quite sure whether his ire stemmed from their differences in belief, or from the fact that the heretics had their claws deep in many mortal churches—just as he did. A combination of both, she imagined. Mongada believed vampirism to be a test of the mortal soul, not a reward as the heretics claimed.

That orthodox view was foundering in Constantinople and elsewhere, and those who would see her topple pushed from all sides. The only thing that prevented the fall was the warring forces lined against one another. They forced a fragile balance, and it was along the sharp ridge that Lucita intended to stride.

The door opened, and she turned. Anatole entered the room, eyes downcast, steps slow and deliberate. He was maddening in his intricately contrived stoicism. Lucita knew the wild dance of those down-turned eyes. She knew the back-beat of his words, the subtle way he could twist a moment into a vision, and back again without the slightest indication he was aware of that shift. He and Mongada shared many things, both were fervent, and both saw the Curse of Caine as a test from God. But where Mongada represented all the opulence and wealth of the bishoprics, Anatole was a simple monastic brother, affecting the pale robes of an ashen priest.

All this flashed through her thoughts, and more, before the Malkavian spoke.

"The carriage is waiting," he said softly. "There is little time if we expect to arrive on time. All about us, they watch—they hover at the gates and mill about like pigs in a sty. We must go."

Lucita didn't answer immediately. She continued to check her weapons, moving about the room slowly. She knew, of course, that she was ready, but she did not like to give the appearance that any moment of her existence could be scripted. Anatole, of course, would be smiling beneath the shadows of his cowl, and waiting. The two had traveled together too many times, shared too many intimacies, for her contrived indifference to affect him.

"Brexiano has gone," she said at last, turning to face Anatole, and the door beyond him. "He will run back to Madrid, no doubt to report on my insubordination and the horrible ways I have undermined his authority. I am certain he expects me to fail here—that is why he departs so easily. If I banish him in Mongada's name, then prove less than worthy of this responsibility, it will deflect attention from his own inept actions."

"There is a saying," Anatole intoned. "You cannot build a temple with no foundation."

Lucita laughed softly. "Brexiano builds no temples unless he is directed to build. He tells no tales unless he feels they will support his feeble ego. I do not care what he says to Mongada—I only care that he is gone. Can you feel it? The freedom?"

A soft sound issued from beneath Anatole's cowl. Not exactly a chuckle, but what might have passed for one in a noisy room. The monk was impossible to read, his emotions a chessboard where the pieces never moved the same way twice. Lucita didn't know if Anatole was glad that Brexiano was gone, but she believed that he was. He had always supported Lucita's desires, and her desire to be rid of the weak-kneed influence of Brexiano had been a palpable presence since they'd arrived in the winter of 1204 to find the crusaders camped outside the city.

Brexiano had wanted to withdraw, to wait out the storm and then deal with the crusade when it moved on. Then, when the attack came that April, he'd suggested retreating to the makeshift refugee camp forming outside Adrianople. The Crusade they'd wanted to shape was over and the great Dream of Constantinople—the Constantinople they'd known—was dead. Brexiano had accepted this and moved on, already worrying over the position he might weasel his way into once they returned to Madrid, and to Mongada's side.

Lucita dreaded such an end more than anything in her existence. There was a weight hanging in the air between herself and her sire. She would not have been surprised to find that he scourged himself in front of an altar dedicated to the moment he could draw her fully back into his clutches, and she had no desire to take up residence near enough to allow his fantasies to ferment. She respected his power, but she had enough sense to fear it, as well.

As long as she remained where she was, furthering Mongada's goals through her words and deeds, she knew she needn't fear his interference. Mongada was many things, but stupid was not one of them, and he had already realized that she was more valuable to his cause as an ally and ambassador, than she would be as a slave to his own dark desire, no matter how strong that urge might be. As long as Lucita remained distant, they were a partnership of power.

These last two years had been a constant effort to keep Brexiano from pulling up camp, using the threats of Assamites, Ventrue lords, Bulgarian armies, and anything else that presented itself to put off their departure. Now, she'd sent him away and she would have to deal with the consequences.

Adjusting her sword belt a final time, and checking the small bejeweled dagger in its scabbard at her side, Lucita motioned toward the door.

"Let us leave this place, then," she said. "Time, as always—is our enemy."

"Time is no enemy," Anatole chided her, turning to the door without once meeting her gaze. "Time is simply time. After all, we invented it to judge our own progress through eternity, why should it not humble itself to us, in the end?"

"You speak in riddles more fluently than most men speak their mind," Lucita laughed.

Anatole did not offer an answer. He stepped through the doorway to the hall beyond and moved toward the stairs leading to the lower levels, and the stable beyond. In the shadows, to either side of them, Lucita sensed his followers gathering. Anatole never traveled alone these nights, but from the silence and intensity of those who mirrored his steps, one might have thought him very solitary indeed.

Lucita had servants—enough to see to immediate comfort and important needs. The carriage would be hitched and ready to move out. Even if her own people had not seen to it, Anatole's would have, or the monk would have handled it himself. He was the most efficient creature she had ever met, for all his madness. There would be no wait, once they reached the gates.

"Have you sent word ahead?" she asked softly.

"Of course," Anatole replied. "They are expecting you."

Lucita nodded. She knew there were dozens of others she would have to speak to, cajole, and manipulate to reach the end she sought. Anatole knew, as well. They had spent long hours going over it, she pacing and speaking her thoughts aloud, as if to the wind, and he nodding, tossing out arcane insights and seemingly nonsensical phrases that would haunt her, itch at the back of her mind, and eventually manifest themselves as truth, no matter how obscure their initial trappings.

Anatole was mad. There was no doubting it. He could appear as a quiet, unassuming presence, or whirl off like a dervish, eyes widening to the whites and beyond, lips pulled back into a feral snarl and words hurled to the heavens and the earth in random patterns that were never truly random. For the most part he was lucid, and Lucita had come to learn his ways, accepting the moments that seemed meaningless in return for those where he saw to the center of her heart and held it out for her to examine. Less than ten years ago, when she was barely a fledgling, the two of them had traveled through Hungary and Transylvania, and their bond was forged by their experiences there.

Even more than in those years, Anatole's was now a dark vision. He hunted like a wild animal, feeding and destroying what stood in his path, but his was a controlled fury, for all of that. His beliefs were deep, and those who followed him were held to his own standard.

"Who is driving?" she asked, as they descended the stairs. "I don't want anyone who will cause a scene. This is to be a quiet visit. As little stir as possible. I need to know what is going on in the camp. Rumor has it that, though it seems to be the same place it was a year or two ago—tents, shacks, unorganized and filled with fanatics—it has stretched new roots into Adrianople itself. I need to know who is there, who has departed the city and who will stay. I need to know who has wandered in from the east or west, what they are doing and saying, and who is listening. In short..."

"You need to be their Goddess," Anatole finished. Lucita felt the smirk soaking through his robes.

"You blaspheme, Anatole," she replied, trying for a harsh tone that did not quite succeed. More softly she added, "I need to be everyone's Goddess, but that is a matter we can discuss on the road. I need information. I need to know the lay of the land, so to speak, before I can own it."

This time there was no mistaking Anatole's chuckle. "I have good men to drive us, child," he said in his soft, melodious voice. "We know the roads, and they can drive through day and night. We are less likely to attract attention this way, than if we risked using the inns and relays. The last leg, the two of us will take alone. Others will be with us, near enough if we need them, but in the shadows. None will see them as we pass. The Roman road is not what it once was, and no shadow is exactly as it seems. Best to make as small a ripple in the darkness as possible, and concentrate on the journey's end."

Lucita laughed. "Does the journey ever really end? Power shifts, patterns rearrange, and nothing really changes."

"We have several nights in which we do little else but discuss such things," answered Anatole.

The two continued in silence, making their way to the lower levels and through the door leading to the stable and the street beyond without further conversation. The city, and the night, awaited them, pregnant with possibilities.

Chapter Two

Their fifth night on the road was still young when the lights of the camp at Adrianople came into view. They'd turned from the main Byzantium-Adrianople road soon after dusk and Lucita now sat beside Anatole, her cloak pulled about her to mask her features and to disguise her slight, girlish figure. She swept the landscape, eyes dark with concentration, as they passed, alert for anything out of the ordinary. The roads had not been safe since Constantinople had fallen and there seemed to be a constant effort to take Adrianople as well. Though she and Anatole were both well-able to protect themselves, Lucita had no time for foolishness.

They passed a few straggling bands of refugees, either coming or going, but few eyes rose from the road to mark the progress of their carriage. The steps of those they passed were slow and weary, and they showed the cowed obeisance of those long accustomed to punishment. If they did not acknowledge her, they had less chance of offending her. Lucita frowned at the irony of it. Many of those they passed were damned, yet they moved and walked without purpose. They were defeated, only looking for a hole to crawl into, and it angered her to think of all that had been lost.

Of course, it was not all a loss. The fall of Constantinople and its ancient vampiric master Michael were not considered a bad thing in all circles, and Lucita was quick to see the advantages the current chaos offered. Over the past two years, things had shifted again and again, among mortals and undead alike. The Cainite Heresy was growing in power and support, though the more orthodox were reluctant to give ground. Mongada had made his own wishes clear—but there was always room for innovation. Difficult times call for creative politics.

It was unlikely that her sire would soon fall under the sway of the heresy. The notion that history was falsely recorded, and that Christ was actually Caine was not an easy one to swallow, even in light of the belief that this made Cainites superior. Besides, even those who claimed full belief in the heresy seemed, at times, less than sincere.

Rumors had reached the city from the camps that worried her more than any direct threat to the orthodoxy. There were reports of sightings in and near the camp, Caine, Lazarus, the insane Nosferatu doomsayer Kli Kodesh, even dark Calomena, Caine's sister, were claimed to either walk the streets or enter the dreams of those present. Rumors of Calomena were especially strong these nights. Reportedly she called from the depth of the night, whispering that the time had come to drive back her brother's followers and claim the foundations of the new dream in her name.

Lucita did not believe in these visions. Not directly. Despite her associations with holy men of all sorts, she'd not received any grand revelations. It was much easier to believe that there were those who used such stories to their own ends. She would have no qualms about spreading such a rumor, if there were something she might gain from the deception. The present whirlwind of belief and legend, fiery fanaticism and desperate defeat was a challenge. She saw it as a puzzle to be laid out, considered, and pieced together as she wished.

Anatole did not speak as he directed the horses past dark structures that no longer held the living or the damned, the rubble and ruin of huts and larger dwellings, the skeletal remains of what had once been a bright, cheerful inn. A stable, the fence fallen and broken, its gates swinging on shattered hinges and dust blowing across dead grass where nothing grazed.

The camps were worse than she had feared. She had not been here since May of 1204, when Hugh of Clairvaux, a zealous vampire in Templar's tabard, had stirred up the refugees with word of a crusade into Egypt. She'd seen that one destroyed by the Assamites, vampiric warriors from the lands of Islam.

Assamites were not unknown to Lucita. Many of their number fought hard in Iberia to push back the Christian Kingdoms of the north, including her beloved Aragon. She knew well the danger they could pose. Still, Sir Hugh's destruction had been masterful, carried out at the peak of his power, when he was ready to launch his crusade of loyal templars and lost Greek vampires. Seeing him fall had stolen all the wind from the crusade's sails, sending his followers back to Adrianople to await their next savior. She'd even heard that some of them claimed he would rise from his scattered ashes and lead them again.

Lucita told herself that some night she would have to find the Assamite who had engineered this masterstroke. A warrior of that caliber could teach her a great deal. That was a matter for another time, however.

Finally, Lucita turned to her companion. "Do you think there is truth to what they say?" she asked softly. "Do you believe that Caine himself might have come among us?"

Anatole did not look at her when he answered. He concentrated on the reins in his hands and the steady clatter of wheels and hooves on the road rolling away beneath them.

"The Dark Father is mysterious in His ways," he said quietly, "but I doubt revelations that do not lead to action. And the stories claim any number of messiahs wander the night. If you were Caine, would you come to Adrianople?"

Lucita laughed at that. "If I didn't have pressing business, I wouldn't go there now," she answered. "What about the Dracon? Or even Malachite? I won't be surprised if I hear that Jesus and the Holy Mother are walking the streets at night, looking for the two lost thieves to drag their souls back to heaven."

"Rumors are always with us," Anatole answered dismissively. "I will admit that the idea of meeting any of those you've mentioned on the road at night is intriguing, but until that happens, I'll spend my energy on the moment."

He shifted topics. "Mongada will not be pleased that you sent Lord Brexiano," he intoned solemnly. "He will wonder what you are up to, and why you don't come to him. He will wonder if he has made a poor choice in trusting you, and Brexiano will be quick to fan the flames of doubt. It might even be that it would have been wiser to kill him and send the body back with your deepest sorrow as a guide."

"My actions will answer for me," she replied. "Brexiano is a fool, and Mongada knows this as well as I do. He will see through the surface of my actions and understand the truth. There is only one he can trust to watch over his interests in Constantinople as she rises from the dust, and that one is certainly not Tommaso Brexiano. The rubble he left behind him will haunt his steps. The city burned two years ago. He should be among its lords by now."

Anatole grew silent again, and Lucita watched him for a while. His long, thin blonde hair was escaping the cowl of his robes, blowing about his head in the breeze like gold tassels. His mind seemed miles away, yet she knew he was acutely aware of all that surrounded them. She wondered if the others could sense it as well, the touch of his mind.

They were nearing the outskirts of the camp proper. Low slung tents lined the sides of the road. Many buildings, half-destroyed or crumbling with the weight of years had been fashioned into makeshift lean-tos. Eyes marked their progress as they passed. Nothing stirred. *Have they done nothing,* Lucita thought, *since Hugh's downfall?* But mortal armies had been over this ground many times, the city besieged again and again, so no existence here could be permanent.

The camp was strung out along the outer walls of Adrianople, divided by powers that slunk here and there, coaxing new followers from those who joined the exodus from Constantinople. It had begun further from the city, and once the sieges lifted, migrated inward, drawn by the need to feed, and the instinct to rebuild whatever life was most comfortable, or profitable.

Groups whose leadership was intact were the most vocal, but there were others. Obscure sects and dangerous pockets of death and destruction stained the streets and alleys. There were social structures, but these were precarious. Temples had risen in warehouses and barns, and the churches of the shantytown teemed with those of every belief and dream. The streets were lined with those whose dreams had been shattered, and could not be retrieved. Much like the Latin Quarter, the camp was both a reality and a facade covering deeper truths.

The carriage rolled steadily through the outskirts and closer to the city, where the buildings rose a little taller, with a sensation of semi-permanence. The streets there were more forbidding, and the shadows deeper. They passed a low-slung structure that served as a church, walls of piled white stone capturing the glow of the nearly full moon in brilliant contrast to the deep shadows of the surrounding streets. There were few torches, fewer still of the dwellings they passed showed candles, or lamps lit. They might as well have been walking through a mist that gave only the impression of civilization.

Further in, the glow was brighter. There were neutral grounds in the camp; there had to be. In such a tight group of the damned, thrown together by shared tragedy, the rules shifted slightly. Belief systems were bent and ideals were ground to dust. Greed would force some to try and profit from the gatherings and hungers of the lost.

From the darkness to their right, a lumbering figure staggered to the street. He reached out as the carriage passed. Lucita glanced down and caught the gaze of yellowed, rheumy eyes. Lips parted, the ghoul favored her with a smile that more closely resembled a crooked smirk and reached out, trying to grip the side of the carriage as it passed.

With a grimace of disgust, Lucita lashed out, her booted foot crashing into the thing's face and pounded it back and away from the carriage as it passed. She did not look back to see the result of her blow. She had felt the satisfying crunch of bone.

"What do you suppose he wanted?" Anatole almost chuckled.

"I thought you were known," she replied. "Isn't that what you said? Less trouble?"

Anatole's smile widened. "You should see the trouble we'd have if they didn't know me."

Lucita shook her head, managing not to smile, but barely. The camp was depressing, and that aided her efforts. So little had changed since the immediate aftermath of the crusade. For so many, of such power, to have come to this. They rolled on a few more minutes in silence, and Anatole pulled the carriage up beside a tent that was less frayed than the others. They dropped easily to the ground and stood for a moment, staring. The doorway was hung with dark curtains. Several layers, Lucita thought. The daylight would be blocked quite thoroughly, and she suspected that there would be tunnels, holes leading down and back into the walls of the city itself. The appearance of poverty was often a powerful shield.

"You're sure this is the right place?" she asked, still not moving closer to the tent.

Anatole nodded. "I have been here before. Many times."

She didn't dwell on his answer. The fact he had been conferring with others who might or might not share her best interests was a matter for another time and place. Tonight, she had a mission to fulfill, and she needed the Malkavian by her side. Even with Anatole's assistance, the night would have its dangers.

Behind them, figures melted from the darkness to take the dropped reins of the carriage. The horses shied, then settled, and Lucita felt the ground shake slightly as they reared and stomped in distrust.

Anatole stepped forward and reached out for the canvas, but before he could touch it, it was pushed aside from within. A long, slender arm stretched from the interior of the tent, gnarled fingers beckoning them to enter.

Lucita glanced at Anatole, then stepped forward into the darkness.

The interior of the tent belied its outer appearance. Tapestries lined the walls, adding to the ambiance, and at the same time insulating further against the heat and sun of the day. They moved inward, passing one, then another screen, as the space around them shrank, and the layers of material increased.

They ended in a hallway, still moving forward, and Lucita realized suddenly that they were within the great stone wall circling the city. Or beneath it. There had been a subtle slope to the floor when they entered the tent, but now it was more pronounced, leading downward.

Their guide remained silent, and neither Lucita nor Anatole pressed him—or her—for speech. They were not here to deal with an underling, and it was either a very good sign, or a very bad one, that they were not being addressed at this point, but simply led inward.

Marcus Licinius, the Roman-era Lasombra who'd made Adrianople his domain, still ruled the night here. Although he did not affect the Christian dogma of Mongada or Anatole, he considered the Cainite Heresy a danger as well and was a respected elder of the clan. Lucita guessed that as the refugees remained after Sir Hugh's death, Prince Licinius and his circle had had stretched out their influence. A skilled leader was never stagnant.

In the nights before the crusade came to Constantinople, there had been Lasombra who used the Orthodox Church as Mongada did the Roman Church. Under the patronage of the Toreador Methuselah Michael, the Lasombra Magnus had sat like a spider in the center of a holy web. Now, Magnus was destroyed and the heretics under Bishop Alfonzo had grown fat on the great city. Rumors were, however, that Lasombra from other Orthodox cities were slipping into the region, seeking shelter with princes like Licinius.

Orthodox Lasombra were seeing the very roots of their belief in jeopardy—and so they had come. Beneath the walls, it seemed, and of course, by other means, steadily working their way into the society of the camp, listening, learning, and bending those who could be bent back to the truth. Lucita was an expert at such bending. It was a shame they so often broke, but such were the pains of true faith.

Mongada had given her letters, and he had spoken with those in Madrid, who had spoken with those in Rome, and in Constantinople herself before the fall. In turn, the clan elders in Adrianople were aware of her presence. They had not sent word to her, nor had they welcomed her upon her arrival. There had been only silence. Still, she knew that they would support her, at least on the surface. Archbishop Mongada was a dangerous enemy, and it was well-known that he favored Lucita above most others of his followers.

Now there were powers moving in the ruined streets of Constantinople, as well. The Lasombra orthodoxy was only one faction flexing broken muscles and preparing for the world to come, and Lucita knew she would need the resources and contacts that Prince Licinius and his guests could provide. She was, to put it shortly, going to have to rely on Mongada's influence and the fear of his anger to get her in the door. Beyond the door, she was on her own, and that door now stood about six feet in front of her.

Solid wood, embedded in stone, the door was ludicrous in the face of the tent and its layered descent. It would have been appropriate if the door had opened into Hell itself, or some deep, subterranean vault. It did not. Their guide reached out a withered, bony hand and rapped on the wood in a short rhythm that must have been a code. Lucita tried to catch it, but hadn't been prepared or paying enough attention, and it slipped away. She glanced at Anatole, but his features gave away nothing. No way to know if he'd caught the password, or even already known it.

There was an extended silence after the knock, then a heavy grating sound as wood scraped on stone. The door swung open, and Lucita saw that beyond it was a stairway, wide stone steps leading steeply upward. So, they were either beyond the wall, or somewhere just past the center, moving upward to the far side.

The trio mounted the steps in silence. It wasn't a long climb, and Lucita noted that there were no torches. There were no sconces for lighting, indicating that whoever had designed this entrance had not designed it with mortals in mind. This was not, then, an entrance for ghouls, or servants, but only the damned. It was a secret, and knowing another's secrets always came with a price.

Anatole had moved closer, matching her step for step, half a pace behind. Lucita didn't know if he sensed something she'd missed, or if he was concerning himself with appearances. The monk was still a mystery to her after years of association—he was never the same twice, but eternally unchanged.

They rose quickly, and it was not long before they reached another doorway. This was a double door, and the wood stretched up and up, showing that the ceiling of the stairwell, lost in shadow, was much grander than she had first imagined. They seemed to have moved from the tunnel they had climbed through into a room where the stairs continued, as if they'd burst through into another world.

The doors opened slowly as they approached. Lucita found herself wondering who had opened the wooden door below, and who opened these now. There had been no sign of another on the stairs, and though she stretched her senses, she could detect no sound or motion now, other than that of the doors. She knew it was a calculated effect, one that was supposed to put her at a disadvantage. She steeled her gaze and moved through the doors as though she were returning to her own home after a long journey. As Anatole passed through behind her, their guide dropped back, turning to close the doors behind them. They continued, and he did not follow.

They had entered a large chamber. Marble floors glittered with pools of deep color as moonlight filtered in through massive stained-glass windows. Columns rose to impossible heights around them. This church was grand. An empty cathedral. Silent save for the soft echoes of their footsteps. Entering that chamber, Lucita stopped and cocked her head to one side, as if curious. Anatole stopped at her heels.

As they waited, a sound rose from the shadows. Then, the shadows themselves began to whirl, slowly circling the room, rising and thickening, until they spun like a shroud about the interior of the room. The whisper of silk. The flutter a thousand moths' wings. Lucita glanced to the side, but realized at that moment the sound came not from one side, but from all sides. The soft scuff of slippered feet. The shadows parted to either side, then fell away

"The Bulgar tsar is open to counsel, child, and it is obvious that he has the ability and strength at arms to extend his influence. And, of course, if he extends his influence, he extends mine as well. Ours."

The correction was late—and telling.

Lucita remained silent for a moment, then continued as if she'd noticed nothing. "Things are not as they once were in Constantinople," she began. "You know this, of course, but the thing that troubles me is that our mutual enemies—the Cainite Heretics who are like a pox on our clan—grow in strength with each passing day. Very little harm came to those in the Latin quarter, and Bishop Alfonzo stretches his influence daily. Others have darker motives, wanting only destruction and chaos, and they flourish as well. It is a very difficult time, and I believe that we must act quickly."

"What does Mongada say?" Basilio asked with interest.

"I have heard nothing detailed from Madrid," she answered carefully. "I act in Mongada's interest, and he wishes the Heresy stymied here. Brexiano thought only to weaken various players, but that is a fool's agenda. Without more decisive action, the city will fall to the Heresy, or worse, and there will be nothing left for us here."

Basilio smiled at her in a manner that showed he did not share her pessimism. Bulgaria was another world from the Byzantine. Still, he was a powerful leader, respected by her sire. Lucita waited quietly.

"You want to know how you can push back heresy in a city trapped in its own death throes, how to bring the truth to those who seek only to bring the world to flames." Lucita remained silent. Basilio was playing her, waiting to see if any of his words would bait her into a hasty comment, or a denial. She did not play.

"You say," he said at last, "that the bishop Alfonzo grows in strength. Do you believe he will stretch his influence beyond the Latin Quarter?"

Lucita thought for a moment, then nodded. "If not checked, he will certainly increase his power," she said. "That, or he will be killed."

"Alfonzo is of our blood," Basilio commented. "He is powerful, and he is Lasombra. Do you believe it is in your best interests to hinder his growth?"

Lucita's answer was swift. "Alfonzo is a heretic," she almost spat. "Mongada despises him, and all he stands for. Narses has him on a puppet string, and he plays his part almost too well."

The elder Lasombra smiled, and the smile was deep and dark. "Narses may have made him, but Narses is not here. He is not as close as you or I, and he can only wield so much influence in a situation like this. For example, you speak to me of power and of intrigue, but you speak far from the lips or ears of Mongada."

"I support Archbishop Mongada in all things," Lucita snapped, her eyes blazing.

Basilio was not impressed. "You speak for yourself. Mongada will benefit from what you do, of that I have no doubt, but do not speak to me of loyalty. You would not be speaking to me if you believed the only counsel that mattered came from Madrid."

Lucita said nothing, and Basilio continued.

"You must find a way to sway Alfonzo," he said at last. "He is the key. Of our kind, he is the most powerful in the city, and it is far easier to bolster the support of one in power than it is to bring another from the dust. You must find a way to drive the Heresy from his mind and drag him back into the fold. The Friends of the Night are not without power and influence. Narses may not seem as tempting a guide with you close at Alfonzo's side."

Lucita considered the elder's counsel in silence. There was an odd harmony to it, as if it had found some spark in her own mind she'd been ignoring and fanned it to flame. Turning, Lucita drew Anatole into the conversation with a glance.

"What do you think?" she asked him.

Anatole did not meet her gaze, nor did he meet that of Basilio, who was eyeing him keenly. He stared into the depths of the church, then at one of the circle of Basilio's shadowy followers. It seemed, at first, that he would ignore her question, but just as she began to lose patience, he spoke.

"There is truth in your words," he said at last, turning to Basilio. "You would take control of Constantinople if you could, and you still may—time is a fickle mistress. Still, I believe you would see the clan orthodoxy regain control. Alfonzo has been a puppet for long years, and more than one master can manipulate the strings of a puppet. The key, of course, is in getting him to believe it is in his own interests."

"There will be opposition," Lucita mused. "Alfonzo is strong, but he is neither the only power in the city nor the oldest. There are others, even among our own blood, who will contest any move to assume power."

"What is life without its contests?" Anatole said softly. "What is death without companionship? What is the value of anything gained too easily?"

Basilio was staring at Anatole, his eyes warring between confusion and anger. "You are never without your riddles, Malkavian," he said at last. "But it is another truth you speak. Does the Bible not teach that there will be trials? Persecution. It would not be the first war fought in God's name, and certainly it will not be the last. If you want to hold sway over others, you have to be willing to exert your hold on them. You have to be willing to watch the final death steal over their features. You have to be strong."

"Never doubt that I am, milord," Lucita said softly. "Nor should you doubt my sire. Don't let your own strength cloud your sense."

"You would threaten me?" the elder asked, his voice very low, his expression unreadable. He stared at Lucita, ignoring Anatole completely.

"No," Lucita replied, "but I would not fear you either. I came to you for counsel, not to threaten or be threatened. I ask only the same consideration."

Basilio watched her for a sign of weakness, or treachery. Lucita met that gaze with a haughty pride. It was the elder who broke the contact with a wave of his arm. The shadow-figures that circled them, silent and stoic, began to move again, backing away and seeming to grow toward the walls and the vaulted ceiling far above.

"Go, then," Basilio said. He moved backward, but he did not seem to be taking steps. It was as if the space that Lucita and Anatole occupied was retreating from the old Lasombra, rather than the other way around. The voice that floated to them whispered like wind over crackling parchment.

"Find Alfonzo. He is the key."

Then a deeper darkness descended. Lucita turned to Anatole, who stood silently by her side. He did not seem affected by Basilio's sudden departure. He gazed into the depths of the chamber, as he had done before, expressionless and centered. There was a soft thud to their right, then another…and another.

One by one Anatole's followers dropped silently to the cathedral floor.

Lucita watched, not truly surprised, but curious. "How did they get in?" she asked softly. "And, more to the point, old friend, how do we get out?"

Anatole did not answer, but he smiled, turning back the way they'd come.

The slender, robed figure that had guided them beneath the wall stood a few feet behind the pair, waiting. Eyes like glowing coals watched from beneath that hood as the others gathered around, slipping in behind Lucita and Anatole.

Without a word, he turned and stepped back into the shadows. Mind whirling with plans and possibilities, Lucita followed.

Chapter Three

Vast walls rose against a darkened sky, stark and angry. Alfonzo's mansion, very nearly a palace by standards beyond the city, was a marvel. There were gardens hidden in shadowed alcoves, dark terraces overlooking every angle of the city, and towers stretching like dark fingers into a sky filled with stars.

When it was lit up, as it was this night, the dancing candle light and raucous music and laughter made the palace into a giant version of some child's music box gone mad. There were battlements, as if it were a castle, though the appearance from the street was deceptive. The design of the building made it largely indefensible. It was not designed for war, but as a wonderland of debauchery.

Alfonzo stood on one of the balconies, the music floating out beneath him and wafting up to tease at his senses. His hair blew gently in the night wind, and the moon had risen to her full stature in the midnight sky. On the lower floor of his estate, a party awaited. There would be dancing, music, and—entertainment. Alfonzo had seen to this himself, because it was an important night. There were a great number of influential guests milling about his lower levels, a few who might actually be dangerous, if not watched carefully.

Something was in the wind. He couldn't put a finger on it, but his senses were keen, and he could feel it. Glancing out over the Latin Quarter, his personal kingdom, he sensed it even more strongly. There were forces moving over the city, through the alleys and down the grand roads. The vampiric lords who'd come with the Crusade—the Ventrue Lanzo von Sachsen and

Caesar Valerian, his own clanmate Tommaso Brexiano—were at last withdrawing, but now there was the danger that some other Cainite would rise up from the ruins and try to proclaim some sort of dark new Byzantium grew more intense. That wretch Malachite was still out there somewhere, searching for the ancient Dracon to be his new patriarch.

Alfonzo fixed his gaze on the starry sky above as though waiting for a sign. When nothing was forthcoming, he turned his gaze to the city gate, not far down the road. There was movement—a carriage returning to the city. He stared at it for a moment, then spun away. It was too far to make out a face, but something itched at the back of his thoughts. It wasn't a night for such distractions. In the hall below, several powerful leaders awaited his arrival. It would not do to keep them waiting too long.

The ballroom was filled with motion and color. There were several local groups in attendance, hanging close to one another against separate walls and in small cliques. They were under the peace of Alfonzo's house, but no one took that any more seriously than it warranted. In matters of safety and power, it was best to trust only your own. You weren't really safe there, either, but at least you had an idea from which direction an attack might come.

Alfonzo's people moved through the crowd, serving rare delicacies, looking after the needs of the various groups, and working quickly and silently to prepare the entertainment to come, careful not to let details slip, or to give away their master's secrets. Alfonzo was a showman, and the details of the night's party had been worked out long in advance. It was important that they follow his instructions exactly if they intended to continue their service—or their existence.

The main room was huge, but what the guests only suspected, or caught hints of, was the vast number of alcoves, rooms, halls, and gardens that led off of the central ballroom. The layout was complex, and it eased the task of working behind the scenes. It had been designed for a Byzantine lord, a place his guests could be entertained and his future secured.

Over the decades, additions and wings had been added to the structure by a variety of personalities and architects, and to one not accustomed to the chaos, it was overwhelming. Alfonzo had relieved the man of both home and life just after the city had begun to crumble. He'd had his eye on the place long before, but the attacks on the city gave him the opportunity he needed to act without fear of calling too much attention. If friends of the deceased owner came to call, they were turned away with stories of flight or death. If they persisted, they became the main course at the next feast, and were not heard from again in the hours of daylight. Not many had come, after the first week or so.

To one side of the ballroom, Gabriella of Genoa stood calmly, surrounded by a large entourage of Genoese and locals. She watched everything in the room with distrust. She did not take the offered refreshments, though she allowed those who accompanied her to do so, and she did her best to ignore the music and the servants hustling about their chores.

Gabriella had the air of one held against her will, as if her presence were not a voluntary thing, but an obligation. She appeared ready for the end of festivities that had yet to begin. She also appeared considerably less than comfortable with the others who were present. Her gaze swept the room constantly, never lingering on any one guest or object.

The vampires of the Toreador clan, inheritors of the felled patriarch Michael, had for the most part, declined the invitation, with the exception of a small group of musicians that had been sent as a token of their esteem. Alfonzo was far too canny to believe they held him in much esteem, but the music was superb, better than any that his own people might have provided, and he'd accepted the offer graciously. He'd set two of his followers to watch the group, keeping an eye not only on what they did, but also on who they spoke with, and what they watched. They were spies, as well as musicians, and it might come in handy before the evening was over to provide them with a few selected events to report back to their leaders.

"Always show them what they expect to see, but never show them what they need to see," Alfonzo was fond of saying. "It is one thing to allow a spy into your home. It is expected. The trick is to manipulate what is spied upon. Disinformation in the hands of your enemy is sometimes more valuable than their ignorance could ever be."

Myca Vykos had been invited, but in his stead had sent a few retainers and his apologies. The Tzimisce monk kept largely to himself, supposedly seeing to the reconstruction of the Obertus monastic order, which had seen its monastery burned and its leader destroyed during the city's collapse. Vykos was a power in Constantinople, however, a sign of the old order rising from the ashes. His absence tonight was somewhat of a blow to Alfonzo, though he'd never admit or show it. The Tzimisce's influence might prove critical in the nights to come.

There were lesser lords too, and also those so unsavory they stood out like blemishes against the brilliantly colored attire of the main body of guests. These were more of Alfonzo's people. They had strayed from their holes and dens in the Latin Quarter to attend the party. Their presence was a show of power, a way for Alfonzo to let his guests know that his influence was strong, and his vision wide. They were here to keep people from quite letting go of their inhibitions, to keep them on edge as Alfonzo walked among the crowds, completely at ease. It was an advantage, however slight, and everyone moving through the ballroom was looking for an advantage.

While Alfonzo descended the stairs toward his guests, others moved through one of his exterior gardens, and these were not his followers. Keeping low to the ground and sliding from shadow to shadow, they moved in toward the building silently. Their cloaks contrasted with the silver glow of moonlight that lit the approach of midnight. There were three in all, one taller by a head than his fellows, all moving with the grace and speed of warriors.

They spoke no words, pressing to the stone wall and moving stealthily along the edge of the garden. There were no servants or guests near them, and no one had been set to watch. It was a night of truce, when many factions that normally avoided all contact came together, drawn by two common bonds: curiosity over what Alfonzo might have up his sleeve and hunger.

The three moving along the base of Bishop Alfonzo's wall

were not paying any attention to the music from within. They were focused, synchronized shadows slipping from darkened wall to darker alcove, ever watchful for sentries, or errant guests. Alfonzo had been entrenched in this place for some time, and there was every indication that the other factions were respecting this night, in particular, so precautions were at a minimum. Though he would never have left his home completely defenseless, neither had he wanted a great show of arms to be the first sight that met visiting eyes. Better they should wonder how strong he was, and where his assets were hidden.

There were a few separate apartments around the perimeter-wall of the mansion. Most were not on the ground floor, but watched out over the city from balconies and terraces, lit from within and recessed, so that their inhabitants could easily step onto the wall itself and command a view of the city below, but when in their rooms, only shadows would be visible beyond the mansion's walls.

It was beneath one such room that the three stopped, huddling close against the wall, just inside a small flowered garden niche. They stood like ebon statues in the shadow, waiting and listening. There was no sound save that of the musicians from within, and after a few moments of absolute motionlessness, the taller of the intruders turned and reached up to the wall, feeling for a grip in the stone and mortar, and finding it. Without a sound he drew himself up, pressed tight to the stone wall, like a great black insect, climbing easily. One after another, the others followed.

Isadora sat before a grand, gold-leafed and unmirrored vanity, contemplating her entrance to the party below. Though still quite young to the night, she was the current favorite of the house, slender and tall, sharp features and deep eyes that bored through and beyond a person, and a perpetually bored smirk painted across her lips. It wouldn't do for her to be seen milling about with Alfonzo's lackeys and lieutenants. Not if she aspired to move up, and that aspiration was the center of her being.

So, the entrance was important. She could sense Alfonzo moving about above her, and she knew the moment he turned from the wall and exited his own chambers. It was nearly time.

She would wait until the ripple had subsided from Alfonzo's own entrance, and she would follow behind, making her way to his side, and drawing every eye in the room to her. It was to be an event. Though her growing relationship with Bishop Alfonzo was important, he was still a means to an end. If he rose to greater power, Isadora would be happy to walk that road at his side. If he faltered, she'd not hesitate to step on his head for a boost to the next level.

There was a hesitation in the music below, and she knew that Alfonzo had entered the party. Isadora rose, whirling once to catch the lamplight on the shimmering folds of the silk gown she wore, watching as it slipped over the long curves of her legs and smiling. Isadora had been twenty-five when she met the darkness, and her muscular body was that of a dancer. She would attract attention in almost any crowd. Tonight, she wanted to dazzle.

On the wall outside, three sets of strong hands gripped the railing of Isadora's balcony. Spider-like, the three figures scuttled to the sides, and up. First one, then another slid over the balcony to press against the wall. They waited, one on the rail, two on the balcony, hesitating to be certain they had not been seen or heard. There was nothing from within, and the third, the taller leader, dropped lightly from the railing and crept to where he could glance into the room.

Isadora stood within, whirling slowly like a dancer and making her skirts billow. He watched with no indication that the sight affected any particular change in his emotions. He waited until Isadora turned toward the door at last, showing him her back, and then he moved. The others flowed in behind him, and before Isadora was fully aware that she was not alone, a silver glitter marked the arc of thin metal chain over her head, and her arms were gripped tightly, holding her steady.

The first intruder's arms snapped to either side, and with a grimace of surprise, her lips parted in a silent "oh," Isadora's head flew neatly from her neck. The two holding the arms of her decapitated body released her, and the three turned, moving swiftly back to the balcony. It would not take Alfonzo long to wonder why she hadn't joined him. The tallest of the three, the leader, stooped and gripped Isadora's hair, lifting her head easily.

His cowl fell back, just for a moment, revealing a strong, Slavic face framed by wild black hair. His eyes were piercing, perhaps ice blue, perhaps silver-gray. He gazed into the lifeless eyes of the head gripped in his hand. Bowing his head, he closed his eyes for a moment, and his lips moved in silent prayer.

At that moment, one of his companions turned back to the body, transfixed. A very slow, tepid flow of dark blood leaked into the lavishly woven rug. He stared, unable to drag his gaze from the sight. Just for an instant, it seemed he might slink back, fall to his knees and drink, but the leader's eyes snapped open then. Barking a quick command, and eyeing his companion coldly, he moved, trophy in hand, to the rail and slipped over. He descended the wall as easily with one hand as he had climbed with two and disappeared into the night.

Alfonzo paused as he entered the ballroom. He sensed something, a tingling at the nape of his neck. He swept the room with a searching gaze, but though there were a dozen in the crowd who would benefit from his own destruction, he did not sense anything out of place. He had planned for each of those who might wish him harm. He had been careful.

There were many in the crowd who appeared to be doing no more than mingling, laughing, serving, or dancing, but this was deceptive. He had planted those who were faithful to him in the crowd, revelers and servants alike. Everything was watched, but his plan had not allowed for the impression that he was mistrustful, so those who watched were planted subtly. Still, something did not feel right, and he entered the room more slowly than he'd planned.

"Milord." A young man, dark-complected with a thin nose and close-set eyes materialized before him.

"Yes, Matteo. What is it?"

Others had spotted him and were already in motion, crossing the room in patterns that led from one small clique to another, not too obviously moving in on him, but inexorable as a tide.

"The others are all in place," Matteo said softly. More loudly he added, "Something to drink, Milord?"

Alfonzo nodded almost imperceptibly. "In a bit. I believe it is time for me to welcome my guests, and if I don't do so quickly, I'll be hemmed in and trapped in discussions of the city and the new empire for hours."

Matteo nodded and backed away.

Alfonzo stepped forward, skirting around the boy and making his way toward the center of the room He wanted to be on the far side, where a slightly raised space held a single table with two chairs. A glittering red chalice sat on the table, glistening in harmony with the brilliant flickers of light reflected by the matching goblets. Alfonzo wanted to reach his seat before anyone headed him off and tried to divert him down roads he had no intention of following.

There would be time for speeches and discourses. There would be time for the rebuilding of the city. This night was his and the intent was pleasure. His pleasure. Their pleasure. Pleasure such as had been missing since the city had been sacked and the damned turned into the streets and driven to the camps. It was a show of power, and of understanding. It was a peace offering to many, and a sign to others that Alfonzo was coming into his own. The crusaders and leftover Greeks had failed to act in the interim and it was long past the bishop's time for watching, or thinking.

Alfonzo also wanted to be seated when Isadora entered the room. She was a prize, a beauty beyond any he'd known in the long, long years of his existence. As a bishop in this city, he was her master. In public, she was his student and most ardent supporter. In reality—understood by all—she was simply his. Isadora was a headstrong, conniving, multi-faceted companion who kept him watching his back. This was a talent one honed at every opportunity, and with Isadora, the benefits of such an arrangement far outshone the possible dangers. In her own way, she cared about him, but Alfonzo wasn't naive enough to believe that this caring outweighed her own ambitions.

Her ties to the elders in Rome were strong. Combined with his own roots, that made them a formidable pair when they were on the same page. Of course, he couldn't let on to his own people that she was linked to the Lasombra in Rome—no more than Isadora could let her own people know of her arrangement with Alfonzo himself. His roots in Venice were well known, and there was no love lost between the two cities. Right now, Alfonzo was thinking only of the two of them, seated at the raised table and sipping slowly at deep red wine, laced with the blood of a young girl harvested that very afternoon.

Somehow, with a grin and a shrug or two, Alfonzo navigated the teeming masses spread across the room and mounted the steps to his table. He smiled as his foot landed on the first step. Nearly there. Nearly perfect. So much was riding on this night. His reactions to every conversation would be measured, his words would be sifted and judged. For days and nights his name would he on every lip. It had to be perfect.

He found himself wishing that Isadora would hurry. He had made it to the table unmolested, but he could not put his guests off indefinitely, and he preferred to meet them with her on his arm. She was the perfect accessory—the perfect partner. Young, yes, but wise beyond her years. It would not do for any, Alfonzo included, to underestimate her.

He glanced at the stairs, frowned, and leaned down to catch Matteo's attention as he passed with another tray of drinks.

"Has anyone seen Isadora?" he asked under his breath. "She should be here by now. We can't keep them waiting all night."

Matteo glanced around the room. "I haven't seen her," the young man said uneasily. "I expected her to follow you down."

"As did I," Alfonzo replied, eyes narrowing. "Go to her quarters. Find out what is taking her so long and get her down here. I will do what I can to divert my guests until she arrives."

He hesitated, then continued. "I don't need to tell you, Matteo, what this night means to me. I should not have to tell her either. Make certain that she is swift."

Matteo nodded and ducked away into the crowd. Somehow, he did not spill the drinks balanced on his tray, or collide with any of the milling guests moving ever closer to Alfonzo's table. The only thing that prevented him from being suddenly overrun by the crowd was the raised platform, and the frown knitting his brow. It was only a matter of time.

Across the room, Gabriella stood to the side of a wide window, overlooking the city. She watched him carefully, not exactly staring, but never concentrating her gaze too far to one side or the other. The musicians were in full swing. Since Alfonzo had entered the hall room, the pace had speeded, reaching a frenzied pitch, then dying back to a steady backbeat.

The music was contemporary, but there was more to it than that. It had a manic quality, as if there were something behind the notes, lurking and waiting to strike. Alfonzo shook his head and swept the room with a lingering gaze, memorizing faces and locations, mapping out his route through the crowd. There were a great number of people to be spoken to, some to placate, others to feel out on certain issues. Still others had been invited solely to allow them to see Alfonzo's strength. The entirety of it was intricate, and his mind shifted quickly about the room, trailing his gaze and filing away information.

Suddenly, there was a commotion at the stairway, and Alfonzo turned. Matteo had reappeared, crashing into the crowd and rushing toward the main table. Alfonzo set his glass on the table, half-rising, eyes blazing. The crowd had parted, and Matteo staggered toward him. Things were falling apart, somehow. Something was wrong.

When Matteo crashed against the platform at his feet, Alfonzo leaned suddenly, so quickly he did not seem to move at all, but to materialize a few feet in front of where he'd been sitting. He had Matteo by the hair, lifting his servant's face to meet his gaze.

"You little fool," he said softly. "What are you doing? Where is Isadora? I set you a simple task, and you..."

Matteo's eyes were clear and wide. Too wide.

"She..." His voice choked off. His eyes closed. Alfonzo gripped Matteo's hair more tightly and snarled, shaking the hoy roughly.

"What?" he snarled. "What? Where is she?"

Matteo gulped, blinked, and spat the words too quickly. His eyes remained closed, his back arched, as if he expected Alfonzo's reaction to be swift, and deadly. As if the words he spoke would be his last.

"She is dead, Lord," Matteo breathed softly. "Her body...
most of her body...is on the floor of her quarters. Her head..."

Alfonzo didn't wait to hear more. He released Matteo,
and the boy fell, suddenly bereft of support, striking his head
sharply on the stone floor. Alfonzo had leaped over him, hitting
the floor at a dead run and making his way through the now
humming crowd like a bull, pushing guests to either side with
such strength that they fell and crashed through whomever
stood near them. Drinks splashed and voices raised, cursing
and crying out. Alfonzo saw and heard nothing.

He hit the stairs so quickly that it seemed he sat at the table
one second and had disappeared the next. Those left below
watched, dumbstruck, as their host burst from their midst and
disappeared up the stairs.

Alfonzo heard the sounds behind him, the voices, some
crying out, others muttering but none of it was sinking in. His
mind was filled with Matteo's voice—his words: "Her head."

Cursing, Alfonzo burst into Isadora's room, ready not to
believe what he'd heard, what he'd read in Matteo's glazed eyes.
He was ready to berate her, whatever the problem she might be
facing, and to drag her down to the party—*his* party—to make
things right once more. He opened his mouth to speak—then
closed it again. Quickly.

Isadora's body lay on the floor, already beginning the slow
fall to ash that signaled her final death. The wind blew softly in
from the balcony, and Alfonzo crossed the room at a run. He
stepped onto the terrace, leaning out to glance down the wall,
then stretching his gaze further, scanning the shadows beyond
the building's base. He glanced up and down the streets, but
nothing moved. Nothing made a sound. He concentrated, forcing his senses beyond their normal limits. He could hear voices
two streets away, an argument in an alley—the creak of axles
as a cart passed. Nothing he could equate with the nightmare
that shared that room with him. No sign of any who might have
been intruders.

Turning back, Bishop Alfonzo moved to the center of the
room where Isadora's inert, decomposing body rested. He
watched for a moment, something near to regret showing at the

corners of his eyes. Then, without warning, he drew back his leg and lashed out, kicking the bones of his lover furiously, then again, and again. He kicked, and he cursed, and he kicked some more, until her skeleton had begun to bow and crumple. Then, without a word, he turned and strode from the room, his face dark.

From the balcony behind him, which was open to the night sky, a breeze blew in, teasing the soft silk of Isadora's torn gown.

Chapter Four

Alfonzo's exit from the ballroom had thrown the night into confusion. The guests were no longer milling about, but had divided themselves and moved apart defensively. No one was certain what had taken place, though rumors began to circulate immediately.

Isadora had left, leaving nothing but a note.

Isadora's elders in Rome had found out about her liaison and taken measures to prevent its continuation.

It was all a ruse, calculated to catch the guests off-guard in some plan of the bishop's own creation.

Everything but the truth. Alfonzo strode down the stairs, steps steady and bold, eyes focused on some point on the far side of the ballroom. His servants moved aside as he passed, scurrying into the shadows. Guests parted slowly, none wanting to fall within his reach. It did not escape the notice of any that his boots and the lower folds of his robes were coated in blood, or that he did not appear to acknowledge those he passed.

Alfonzo did not hesitate. As he moved through the crowd, he seemed to grow taller—darker. His eyes blazed, and for a moment it was not their elegant host who walked among them, but a beast, tall and eerily handsome despite the darkness. He mounted the steps to his table once more, and he whirled.

No one spoke. The musicians were silent. Whispers slipped softly around the room and died. With a great effort, Alfonzo opened his mouth to speak. He closed it again, hesitated, then raised his hands. He gestured to the troupe of players, and his gaze compelled them, one by one, to grasp their instruments and begin a new melody. They might have prevented him, but for the moment, no one was willing to break the spell his mood had cast.

Seating himself without a word, he grabbed the carafe from the table. He reached for one of the crystal goblets, then thought better of it, swiping both from the table with a crash of his fist, sending them arcing through the air, glittering like whirling bits of ice. They shattered on the wall behind him sending sharp shards scattering across the floor. Alfonzo seemed not to notice. He upended the blood wine, letting the deep red liquid cascade over his lips, only about half of it reaching its target, the rest pouring over his hands, his face, his robes. He leaned his head back and poured until there was nothing left but glittering crystal, and then with an almost maniacal scream, he held the solid crystal decanter in trembling hands.

Backdrop to his insanity, the musicians had picked up a deep resonant dirge. It might have been a staged tragedy, over-acted and dark, had it not been for the sudden wrongness of it all. The overpowering sensation that something had been broken or lost, and that it had nothing to do with shattered goblets. The music reflected and amplified the shadows that gathered around the bishop, driving them into the brighter corners of the room to snuff the light with the finality of the tomb. Had any of the mortals who knew the bishop only from dark mutterings in the shadows of confessionals seen him in that moment, they would have believed themselves tossed into the final days, facing off with Beelzebub himself.

Alfonzo's hands pressed together with impossible pressure, so quickly that the motion was a soft blur, and the crystal exploded. White powder plumed, then fell, capturing torchlight and dusting his body, his legs, and the floor at his feet. The wine and the blood gripped the dust, clinging to it, making the glitter a part of the whole. There were cuts on his hands, but Alfonzo ignored them. He ignored everything, head back, leaning over the back of his chair like a martyr, transfixed.

Then, as suddenly as his rage had begun, it ended. He sat up straight, brushing bits of crystal from his lap almost absently, and rose unsteadily to his feet. He turned to the room, noticing for the first time that every eye was upon him. He felt his clothing matted to his skin, felt the sharp bitter pain in his hands and the fire burning through him as the blood wine flooded his system. He stared at them for what seemed an eternity, neither speaking, nor backing off. Then he turned and glanced down. Matteo cowered, just to the side of the table in a small mound of crystal shards, his knees planted in puddles of spilled wine, shaking like a leaf. The boy was a thrall, but even the call of the blood could not drive the fear of what Alfonzo had become, if only for a short moment, from the front of his mind.

"More wine," Alfonzo said. He spoke softly, but his words carried. They echoed through the room, caroming off the walls and reverberating about the vaulted ceiling to whisper down the walls and back again. "Bring me more wine. If we are to have our party," he continued, "then I must offer the benediction."

Motion trickled back into the room. First Matteo skittered off along the floor, picking his way carefully through the broken glass and crystal, skittering around the legs of those guests and servants who stood most closely to Alfonzo's table. The moment the young man was beyond the first wall of people, he rose with a choked sob that echoed through the room and crashed through the crowds toward the kitchens and wine cellars.

Alfonzo watched him go, marking the boy's course through the crowd, fighting desperately against the pounding rate threatening his sanity. Everyone watched him still, and their very lack of motion added to the surreal impression of moving through a slow-motion world. The clarity of the moment was astonishing, worth standing and contemplating, but he knew this was not possible.

Others were moving now, first Alfonzo's servants, then the guests, milling in small circles, whispering among themselves. Alfonzo knew that he would have to speak now. He would have to exert every tiny scintilla of control remaining to him, or all would be ruined and lost. It might take years, centuries to begin again after what he had done. This was a defining moment, and his reaction to it would mark him throughout eternity.

He closed his eyes for one last moment. He saw Isadora as

he'd last seen her whole—tall, regal, eyes blazing with inspiration, strength, and ambition. He felt the thrill of her touch, the
graze of sharp ivory across his skin, felt the twining of their
bodies—and he clutched those images tightly. Then, with a great
effort, he allowed them to slip deeper, drawing those images
inside and gaining strength from this until he opened his eyes,
and he smiled.

Some were already moving toward the doors, and Alfonzo
held up his arms to quiet them.

"Please," he said. Again, his voice seemed soft, but it echoed,
slipping in and out of the corners of the room. "Please allow
me to apologize for this interruption. It appears that not all of
tonight's guests were invited. This is a matter that I must attend
to myself, but it need not completely distract us from our time
together.

"I must go," he glanced down at his robes with an apolo-
getic smile, as if the damage to his clothing, and to the area near
his table, had been the slightest of accidents, and not the spec-
tacle that would be spoken of in hushed tones for a hundred
nights. "I must go to my chambers and make myself presentable once more. There are festivities planned that you would
be sorry, I think, to miss. Allow me this moment of delay, and I
shall return."

Again, he gestured to the players, who'd grown silent at the
crushing of the crystal carafe. They watched him uncertainly,
then one young flautist stepped forward. He seemed young, no
more than eighteen years, but his eyes belied this. They were
fixed on Alfonzo, and the musician's face, framed in deep red-
gold hair that flamed about his features wildly, was lit by light
that flickered both down from the walls, and from somewhere
deep inside. With an almost imperceptible nod, the silver flute
was brought to pale lips, and the musician dropped his head,
closing his eyes and allowing the long hair to cascade forward
over his features, covering his hands and the flute. He began to
play.

There was something in the song, something deep and powerful. Alfonzo smiled thinly and turned toward the stairway
once more. As he moved, servants flocked about him, following

as he moved from the ball room and bustling about him, whispering to one another. Two ran ahead and scurried upward to Alfonzo's chambers to prepare new robes and arrange for the blood wine that Matteo had been sent in search of, then forgotten.

As Alfonzo disappeared upward, the music flooded the ballroom once more. Servants swarmed over the broken crystal and spilled wine and it disappeared efficiently and quickly. The tension, very slowly, and never completely, drained from the room.

With this, the voices rose once more, and the music of the single flautist rose, piercing and deep, and the night deepened perceptibly.

"Who did it?" Alfonzo snapped, holding his arms out impatiently as his soiled robes were removed and replaced efficiently. "When I knelt and touched her robes, I got the impression of violence, but no more. There was no face, no recognition. I felt incredible darkness, but heard no sound." The bishop bowed his head, as if trying to drag something free of some inner pit of darkness, but a moment later he shook his head and looked up once again. "I could sense nothing of use."

To his right stood a small group of swarthy, dark faced Cainites, fronted by one sallow-faced, man with a too-thin beard and close-set eyes. These were Ricardo and his own men, outlanders who'd found their way to the central roads of the Latin Quarter before the fall of the city and gravitated naturally to Alfonzo's service. They were hardened, part of no clan, but loyal to the final death. For a price.

"There is no sign," Ricardo replied darkly. "The mother-loving bastards left not a mark in the room, and they were down and gone before she was discovered."

"This was more than just a simple raid," Alfonzo said, whirling so his arm would shoot into the sleeve of his clean robe and whipping it the rest of the way around his body in irritation. "Bandits have many things they are fond of, but they do not, in my experience, make off with the heads of those they rob. There is more to this than we know, and I need to know *everything* here, Ricardo. Everything.

"Get to the streets. Pass the word. I will pay well to find out who has done this. I must return to those below and try to undo the damage this night has done. I will have to send word to Rome, somehow, and that is another matter for care. It is important that they not believe we are responsible for Isadora's death."

Throughout this short speech, Ricardo stood silent, nodding slightly at each instruction. His men remained still and perfectly motionless behind him, grubby shadows against the elegant tapestries and brilliantly polished silver candelabra that ornamented Alfonzo's personal chambers. This was an outer room, where he received others. At times, when things were properly cleansed, he entertained elders of the church in this chamber, seated on a polished mahogany throne that overlooked all below in such a manner that you could not help but look up if you wanted to meet his gaze. Games. Power and play, always.

This was no night to think of mortal clergymen, or of Isadora's elders in Rome, or any of the other thousand things that whirled through Alfonzo's mind. The preparations for the night's entertainment would he reaching their nexus, and that nexus was his place. He would stand at the center of it all, controlling the puppet strings of the night. He had planned this entertainment for his guests, but now... now he needed it himself.

"Go now," he said, waving a hand in the direction of his balcony, and the city beyond. "Find out who has done this thing, and report to me immediately."

Ricardo turned, and within seconds left Alfonzo alone among his bustling servants. With an angry wave, the bishop dispersed them. He grabbed the goblet of wine Matteo held by the door, sweeping past and down. As he came abreast of Matteo, he softly ordered.

"Prepare the hunt."

The ground floor of Alfonzo's mansion was not the lowest. Beneath the kitchens were labyrinthine corridors and branches, lined with storage rooms and wine cellars, roots and herbs, and cells. The deepest, most central branch of the tunnels that ran beneath cut into the rock of the building's foundation. Barred doors separated the pitch black of the passageway from the equal darkness of the cells that lined it.

Matteo hurried along this passage. Two of Alfonzo's clan followed at his heels, making the young thrall nervous and eager to please. They were young to the blood, these two, embraced less than a year earlier. Twins. Bishop Alfonzo had presented them to Isadora as a gift, their embrace not intended at the time, and she'd been so fascinated by their similarity of appearance, and their soft, young skin, that she'd insisted, and he had acquiesced. Arturo, almost imperceptibly taller than his brother, had been embraced by Alfonzo himself. His twin, Leonid, had tasted Isadora's kiss.

They moved as a single unit. When one slid to one side, the other moved as his polar opposite. The effect was mesmerizing, and the two made Matteo's own blood run cold. He yearned to be through with this task and to return to his master's side. He had been in the bishop's service for so long that he felt any separation deeply. Now, deep beneath the stone floors, where dozens of the undead milled and danced and conspired behind his master's back, he felt that separation very acutely. Being in the presence of the twins magnified the sensation. They were like serpents, wrapping in and about one another with eerie precision.

The three came to a bend in the corridor, and just around this, Matteo reached up to the wall and drew down a torch. He lit it quickly with the small tinderbox he carried, and replaced the torch in the sconce. The flame guttered, caught in a subterranean gust, almost extinguishing, then grew slowly to a life of its own. As the illumination grew, fingers gripping the bars of a door set deep into the stone walls became visible. Wide, frightened eyes stared out at him from the shadows within, and he felt the sharp hiss of sudden hunger escaping the thin lips of the twins.

"Not yet," he said softly, knowing he could not allow a hint of command to enter his voice with such as these, but knowing, equally, that they would abide the bishop's instructions. The twins were powerful, when together, swift and deadly, but

they were not intelligent. They had been brought up by peas-
ants with barely the sense not to walk into stone walls, and
this had followed them into darkness. They did as they were
told, but there was no light behind the dull silver-gray of their
eyes. Oddly—this placed them among Alfonzo's most trusted
followers.

Matteo fished a ring of keys from the pocket of his tunic,
and moved to the cell door.

"Get back!" He cried harshly. There was a shuffle of feet,
followed by dry whispers and mewling cries, but the fingers
retracted from the bars of the cell, and the eyes, now framed by
pale young faces in the flickering torchlight, slid back to the far
wall, away from the door. Away from the leering countenances
of the twins, and Matteo's own stern glance.

Within the cell were at least three dozen young women,
ranging from ten or twelve years in age to their early twenties.
All wore only the ragged remnants of the clothing they'd worn
when captured. All of them, despite their circumstances and the
fear that leaked from them in palpable waves, were beautiful.

"We must move quickly," Matteo said, breaking the silence
once more. "We will get them to the outer kitchen. Others
are waiting. Once they are in place, they will be stripped and
cleaned. Do you know what it is that you are to do?"

He turned to the twins, bracing himself for the intensity of
their gaze.

They nodded. The motion was one, not two, as it might have
seemed with any others. Their heads bobbed as though bound
by hidden wires.

Matteo nodded in return and slid the key into the lock,
drawing the door open slowly. He stepped into the cell and
stood, facing those within with a cold, even stare. He had long
since learned to steel himself against their pain. He knew their
fate, far better than any of them knew it. That fate sang through
his veins and called to him. It was his destiny. He was certain it
was his destiny, but in time only, and only when he was found
worthy.

"You will come with me," he told them. "You will walk in a
single line, and you will be chained. The first of you will hold

my hand, the others will join hands behind until you have made a string. If you break that string and falter, or fall behind," he hesitated, "you will be killed."

He glanced at the twins, who had moved uncomfortably nearer to the cell door. Their eyes glowed, and their hunger was obvious. The girls made soft mewling sounds and backed more tightly against the wall. One of them began to scream, but Matteo stepped forward and slapped her, hard, and the sound died to a soft, bubbling whine.

Slowly, caressing each calf, and several thighs, letting their hands and their lips press to soft flesh at every opportunity, the twins fastened the slender chains to the girls' ankles, binding one to the next. They seemed to move with interminable slowness, but the process was over in moments.

Without another word, Matteo grabbed the first girl, a blonde-haired beauty in a torn peasant blouse and skirt, barefoot and wild-eyed. She could not have seen her sixteenth year. Matteo took her hand stoically and turned to the door, leading them off and down the corridor, feeling the gentle tugs as each was grasped, and pulled, and drawn into the line. The night was passing too swiftly, and Alfonzo would not want to be kept waiting. Not this, of all the nights of eternity.

Behind him, the twins slid from side to side, guarding the rear of the line against stragglers and allowing their presence to strengthen Matteo's control of the "herd." That was how they saw the women, Matteo knew. Food. They hungered, and it was only the strength of Alfonzo's will that held the two back from a monumental feeding frenzy. Matteo's heart pounded more swiftly, but he held his fear in check. For the moment, he was safe enough, as long as he did exactly as he was told, and nothing more was allowed to go wrong.

Above him, guests were growing a bit restless, and Alfonzo was descending the stairs a second time. Despite all that had happened, there was still half an hour before the midnight hour would strike. It was almost time for the real party to begin.

They reached the kitchens, and the women were taken away by dozens of sets of hands, some mortal, most not. The women were unchained, turned, and teased, tossed between those who

worked around them as clothing was stripped away and water
was tossed. Hands moved over each, cleansing and caressing,
teasing and pinching soft, rosy skin. Matteo slipped from the
center of the room and watched, just for a second, as a vampire
with long dark hair leaned in close, one hand holding a sponge
that soaked the front of a young woman's flesh. He cleansed
the filth and grime of the cells below, as a flickering tongue slid
over the girl's ear, unheard words whispered and tears stream-
ing steadily down young cheeks, even as the flesh that was so
coveted recoiled from the unwanted touch.

Matteo tore his eyes from the scene and bolted into the hall.
There was more to be done. He gestured to a group of young
thralls who'd been awaiting his approach, and they moved off
down the halls, each in a different direction, closing windows,
and lower-level doors. Securing them tightly. Closing off all
escape. None of this would hold against an onslaught of the
damned, but for their prey the building was being sealed as
tightly, and with as much finality, as a tomb.

Chapter Five

Lucita and Anatole reached the gates of Constantinople before midnight, moving swiftly on the nearly empty road. She knew that most other Cainites would be off the roads that night. She knew of Alfonzo's gathering—had, in fact, timed her trip to Adrianople so that she and Anatole would he returning to the capital on the very night of his fete. This allowed her the double-advantage of being able to legitimately beg off the bishop's pro forma invitation by citing pressing business while still being nearby for the festivities' aftermath. Such ribald and macabre festivities, although distasteful, did tend to set matters in motion. Pressure as existed in Byzantium had eventually to be released and Alfonzo was providing an opportunity for a metaphorical dam to break.

Bishop Alfonzo had not actually expected her to attend, of course. There was no love lost between Archbishop Mongada and him. Narses had his talons deeply embedded in Alfonzo's throat, and he worked the vocal cords from afar with ease and quiet malice. Alfonzo appeared to be very much in control of himself, his people, and his dark, ratty corner of the city, but Lucita knew how precarious that control truly was. All part of the dance.

Anatole steered through the gates of the city and turned inward, toward the central squares. It was early, and their intent was to return the carriage to Lucita's servants and see what the night might bring. There would be rumors, by now, of how the debauchery that Alfonzo had no doubt planned and set into motion was progressing. There might be a few foolish mortals about, easy hunting in the half-ruined, half-rebuilt streets of the city.

Lucita had a lot to consider, after her meeting with Basilio the Elder. The powerful Cainite had been a long way from his own city, and he had walked freely in Adrianople. He could not have done so without the blessings of Licinius, who was prince in that city. It was disconcerting to think that two of such power were colluding so close to Constantinople itself. Even more disconcerting coupled with Basilio's assertion that the crusaders would fall to the Bulgars. If this were true, might Constantinople fall, as well? How far did Basilio's greed reach, and how much was he willing to risk in the face of Mongada's wrath?

It was too early in the game to worry over these things too deeply, but they itched at her mind. Anatole drove in silence, lost in worlds of his own. If it had not been for a soft call from the shadows, one of Anatole's followers, the two might have missed the three shadowed figures, passing to their left and deep in shadow.

Anatole yanked back on the reins and the carriage teetered. The horses shied in their harnesses, backing toward the side of the road as the carriage tilted, then righted itself with a loud crack.

Anatole was in motion before it had settled, and with a shrug, Lucita followed, clearing the seat and landing on the road with knees bent and her hand on the hilt of her sword. She had no idea what the call had indicated, but if it was enough to get this reaction from the monk, it was enough to put her on her guard.

There was a soft rustle down a side street, and they followed. No clatter of sword belts. No pounding of booted feet. The sounds were subtle and hard to make out. Lucita drew herself inward, relying on instinct to guide her, instinct and the back of Anatole's robes as he raced down the side street, leaving their carriage unattended beside the road and vanishing into the shadows.

The pavement was uneven, broken in places and under repair in others. There were carts along the sides that would be filled with the wares of vendors by day, those too poor to rent space in the shops, or who had been run from their homes by the crusaders. It made the going more difficult, and the chase nearly impossible.

Anatole moved like one possessed. Something had angered him, something he intended to catch, and now Lucita's own battle lust was rising. It had been a long time since she'd had the opportunity to use her training in arts other than diplomatic. The blade in her hand felt good, strong, and supple and as much a part of her as the hand that held it. Mongada had made certain she'd studied rhetoric and diplomacy before sending her into the world, but she'd sought out a fencing master in Valencia to provide a more martial education. Lucita of Aragon was a child of the Reconquista and knew well that honeyed words oft-times failed. They turned into a darkened alley, and she saw Anatole's gaze shift upward. The sides of the alley were lined with porticoes, and littered trash in heaps and barrels of dubious content and origin. There was room to move down the center, but not much room, and the stench was awful. Flies buzzed around their heads, and animals scuttled to the darker corners. Something fluttered over the wall to their left, and Anatole lunged.

There was no hesitation. He leaped, gripped the stone sill of a window, and swung himself up. Lucita cursed, sheathed her sword, and took a simpler route upward, having more warning and time to leap to the top of a handy barrel, springing upward from there to a wrought-iron trellis that circled the first level of terraced balconies above. The buildings to either side rose to a height of about four stories, each level a charnel heap of garbage and debris, as if the owners of the shops and homes on the street beyond had been simply tossing the refuse of their lives out the rear windows and doors for decades and allowing it to accumulate.

Anatole had reached the top of the wall, where he was joined by two shadowy figures melting from the darkness on either side. Judging by Anatole's not killing them on the spot, she knew they were his own, and she leaped to the final balcony below the roof, swinging outward from the iron railing, feeling it shake and quiver, as if it might wrench free of the wall and drop her to the alley below, then she was flying, soaring up and over the lip of the roof and landing a few feet to Anatole's left.

"What is it?" she grated, moving quickly to his side.

Anatole scanned the rooftops, and listened. He held up a hand for her to wait, to remain silent, and she froze. Her irritation was growing, but she knew better than to cross Anatole at such a moment. There was no telling how he was about to react, or to what, and it was always best to gauge that reaction from a distance, rather than finding one's self in the center of it.

Something clattered, very lightly, across the next alley atop a long, flat building, and Anatole was in motion once again. Lucita and the others followed, and as they hit the gap, leaping into the darkness and passing easily over the alley to the rooftop beyond, she caught a glimpse of furtive motion on the far side of that roof. Three figures, one taller than the others and all three retreating at a dead run.

Anatole caught site of them at the same instant as Lucita, or possibly seconds before, and he was suddenly gone. Not gone, exactly, but ahead. Moving so swiftly, so suddenly, and with such a show of intensity and power that it nearly caused Lucita to stumble. He hit the edge of the roof and leaped, flying through the air with such velocity that he didn't bother to gather his legs beneath him, but stretched out his arms and let the momentum bear him forward.

Sensing his approach, the three spun. The taller figure handed something to one of the others and that figure dropped over the side of the building, out of site. The two remaining fugitives stood their ground, watching Anatole as he struck the surface of the roof at last, rolled a single time into a fluid run, and charged. Lucita and the others had leapt the gap, in the meantime, seconds behind.

Though they pursued closely, the difference in their speed made the gap between them seem greater. They closed on the three figures facing off on the rooftop.

Anatole did not stop for speech. He had pulled free the blade he carried beneath his robes and leapt at the taller of the two remaining figures, who circled to the side, his own weapon in hand, watching Anatole cautiously.

The other hesitated. He glanced over the wall, where the

third had retreated, but for some reason thought better of following. He closed in behind Anatole, putting the monk in a pincer between two adversaries. Anatole's followers, with no concern at all for their leader's fate, hit the wall at a run and swung over and down toward the street below, intent on pursuit.

With a cry, Lucita lunged, drawing the attention of the one closing in on Anatole's back. He turned, caught the glint of her blade in the moonlight, and dodged nimbly aside, slicing down and back with a long, rapier-thin blade that teased it's pointed tip through the silk of Lucita's gown.

She ignored this, twisting her blade instinctively to press against the sword, speeding its momentum and slapping it far to the side. Before her opponent could recover, she'd reversed the twist of her wrist and her own blade sliced cleanly back through the air. She felt it bite in the muscled flesh of his shoulder, and there was a grunt, then a wrench as he pulled free and danced back a few feet.

Now Lucita could see what she faced, and she regarded him analytically. He had shifted his sword to his free hand. Not the hand to which he was accustomed. The tip of the blade wavered slightly, and she knew in that instant that he did not possess the same control with his left arm.

He was dressed in dark robes, tightly bound about him to prevent dragging. The soles of his leather shoes were soft, and would make little sound as he passed. He was dressed in the manner of a thief, or an assassin, but something in the wild glitter of his eye and his stance as he adjusted to the use of his uninjured arm spoke of a different upbringing.

Lucita slashed upward, going for the throat, and he parried easily enough, though the twist backward seemed to confuse him for a moment. It was his last.

Without hesitation, Lucita brought her leg up and planted a booted foot in her opponent's abdomen. He doubled from the blow, trying to bring the sword around to slice at her, but she beat it back with a hard slap of steel and then, putting every ounce of strength and concentration she possessed into the thrust, she drew the blade in a brilliant arc over his shoulders. His head hung for a moment, balanced on his shoulders and twitching, and his eyes widened. Then she lashed out again, this time with her fist, and struck to the left side of his head, which rolled free, bouncing once and coming to rest against the rail at the side of the roof. Lucita kicked out once more with every ounce of her blood-richened strength, and the body teetered toward its head, arms outstretched and fingers groping, as if searching for what it had lost.

The body stumbled, falling toward the edge, and Lucita watched, fascinated, as it hit the side, leaned out over the brink, and toppled, end over end. She stepped forward, gripped the head by the hair and lifted it, studying the features she had faced off against. He appeared young, but already he was falling to ash, and his age was indeterminate. She didn't know him, of that she was certain, and Lucita knew most of the damned who were part of the night society of the city.

With a shrug, she swung her arm back and tossed the head in the opposite direction that the body had fallen, watching it bounce once, then skitter over the edge of the building and back into the last alley they'd passed.

Turning, she watched from a short distance as Anatole continued his own battle. The taller of the strange Cainites was much more adept than his companion had been. His movements were fluid and careful, no wasted motion. He avoided Anatole's first few attacks with ease, rolling to the side with one thrust and executing a sort of spinning flip in the air that landed him closer to the monk, where he swung his own blade in a swift arc.

Anatole was not there when the blade passed. Simply not there. He moved so quickly that when the sword's blade sliced the air his own motion made it seem a slow- motion parody of a sword thrust. With a cry, Anatole swung his blade up and then down, intending to cleave the other's arm from his body. Anatole was not the only one faster than thought, however. The blade struck nothing and a long leg snaked out, snaring Anatole's ankle and whipping forward. The monk leaped into the fall, rather than letting it topple him, and whipped in a tight circle, but his opponent was already moving, heading for yet another wall and leaping into the darkness. This was no short alley, but a large, wide street. Anatole ran to the side of the building, Lucita close behind, and they stared at the street below. The stranger disappeared into another alley, moving so quickly it was difficult to mark his passing.

Lucita wasn't certain, but she heard a sound that might have been Anatole cursing under his breath. She had never seen him so upset. She had never heard him curse. She heard a soft scrape behind her and turned.

The two that had accompanied Anatole and herself to the rooftop had returned. They were alone, and they did not look pleased. Anatole turned to them, gauged their expressions, and scowled. He whirled from them without a word, gestured in the direction that the taller of the fugitives had disappeared, and the two were gone, over the side and down the wall. Lucita didn't think they had much chance of catching up, but there was no way to tell what resources Anatole could command. He continually surprised her.

"Who were they?" she asked at last, breaking the silence. "Anatole, who in all the hells were they, and"—she hesitated before adding her last thought—"why do you hate them?"

He shrugged, and rather than answer, paced along the ledge that formed a small rail along the roof's edge. Lucita followed, ready to renew her inquiries. Anatole stopped. He grew very still, then he leaned and grabbed something from the rooftop, staring at it for a long time. Lucita saw him brushing the surface of his thumb back and forth across the object, and then, very suddenly, he turned. He tossed what he had retrieved from the roof in a glittering arc, and Lucita caught it deftly.

It was a medallion. It had been on a leather thong hanging from the neck of the man she'd slain. When her blade loosed his neck, the medallion had tumbled to the roof, forgotten. On it was the face of a woman, her features in the Greek iconic style. The medallion was banded in concentric circles of symbols. Very few of them were familiar to Lucita, who glanced up at Anatole curiously.

"Who is she?" she asked.

"Calomena." Anatole spat the word as if it were another curse, and Lucita nearly recoiled at the venom in his voice. "She is Calomena, and they," he swept his arm in a vague arc that indicated the three he had been chasing, "are her children. They are an abomination."

Lucita held the monk in a frank, curious stare. "You answered only half of my question," she observed. "I have heard of them, naturally, though I had thought they had either passed with the fall of the city, or were merely legend."

"They are insane," Anatole answered cryptically, and Lucita barely kept the mirth from flooding her own features. To hear Anatole refer to another as mad was something she'd never expected.

"Like some of the dualist Bogomils," he continued, "they believe that Caine had a sister, Calomena. She will bring salvation to us all, they say, but only at the cost of the children of Caine himself. Caine," Anatole intoned, turning at last to face her and meeting her gaze, "they believe to be the creation of Lucifer himself. His teachings? Lies. The belief in his glory? Misled, and blasphemous."

"How did you know?" she asked.

He glanced at her quizzically, and she realized the question was cryptic.

"How did you know? How did those who followed us and watched us know, who these were?"

He didn't answer at first. Turning away, Anatole stared off across the city, clasping his hands behind his back. The silence grew thicker, and Lucita was about to press her point, when he spoke at last.

"There are vibrations," he said softly, "and then, there are vibrations. There are tones within tones and worlds within worlds, and always there are signs. I did not know they were in the city, but when I was summoned at the road, the others knew, and they passed this knowledge on to me. Did you see what the first of them to flee was carrying?"

He turned back, catching her gaze very suddenly. "No," she admitted, shaking her head and finally sheathing her sword. "I was too busy trying to keep up with you to pay any attention."

"I was much closer," Anatole said softly. "It was a head. That of Isadora Genevieve Parantio."

"Isadora?" Lucita asked, rolling the name over her tongue and thinking. "Not the Isadora that has been so close to Alfonzo."

Anatole nodded. "Yes, her head."

Glancing out over the city toward Alfonzo's mansion, where even from where they stood the lights could be seen, dancing in the night, Lucita said, "I wonder if he knows? I would guess that Alfonzo's feast is not going as he had planned."

Anatole did not answer. He turned away, making his way slowly across the roof and back the way they'd come. They needed to get to the carriage, to return it safely, and to get off the streets. They'd spent too much time on the rooftops, and there were others on the streets who might he less than honest about another's property.

Lucita was hungry, and she silently wished for bandits to be raiding the carriage when they arrived. They'd fed thinly these past two weeks, spent on the road and in the camps, and the action of the night had drained her more than was entirely cautious. There were willing vessels at her Latin Quarter home, but she was in the mood for something less tame.

She followed Anatole off the roof and into the night, still clutching the talisman of Calomena tightly in one hand.

Chapter Six

The manse's ground floor had been sealed without any of the guests being aware. Matteo had sent his people throughout the halls and stairways, blocking off all human avenues of escape. It would he obvious to those of the night that the barriers had not been meant to impede them. This was important. Alfonzo was preparing an entertainment, not a war. He didn't want to excite the enmity of any particular guest, he wanted to impress them with his magnanimity and generosity, as well as the depth of his resources.

Most of those present had attended one of his functions in the past, and knew Alfonzo's taste. They would be excited, not put off, by the closed doors. His entertainments were extravagant and he was trying to make an impression. No matter the political ramifications of the night, this was a party not to be missed.

Matteo was careful to be thorough. There were not so many to be hunted that they could afford to lose any, and things had shifted drastically. The bishop's mood was volcanic and unpredictable. Isadora had not been with them long, but she had risen swiftly in Alfonzo's favor. She had been intended to sit, and then to hunt, at his side this night. Now Alfonzo would hunt alone. Matteo shivered.

Once he was satisfied that all was in order on the lower level, he returned to the hall that led to the kitchen and signaled to Leonid, who leaned against the wall just beyond the kitchens. He was watchful, and not quick to move when signaled by a thrall, but a moment later he slipped down the passage to Matteo's side.

"It is ready," Matteo said, not giving the other a chance to intimidate. There was no time for it. Arturo and Leonid knew their parts in the upcoming hunt well enough, and they knew Matteo's own position. They didn't respect it, but they knew it. Either of them would cheerfully have fed on Matteo and dropped him forgotten to the floor if it had not been for the knowledge of what the bishop would do when he found out. It wasn't that Alfonzo had a soft spot for Matteo—he wasn't foolish enough to believe this. It was merely that Matteo was very efficient at running the household, and such help was difficult to find.

Leonid nodded indifferently and turned his back, disappearing down the corridor in the direction of the kitchens with deceptive speed. Matteo watched him go, then turned toward the ballroom. It was time to slip in among the guests and find his master. Soon, it would begin.

Alfonzo moved through the ballroom slowly. He stopped at each group of guests, his features masked in false cheer and infused with his famous charm. It was obvious he was walking a tight string of tension, and those he spoke with—for the most part—stepped lightly. The memory of his earlier display would not leave any of them soon, and no one wanted to test his strength against their skull in the way they'd seen the crystal flask test it—and fail.

Though he masked his feelings well, Alfonzo was seething. It was an unheard-of breach that any would dare such an attack on a night when his own peace was guaranteed on the party. If the word of what had actually happened were to circulate among those present, there might be a panic. At the very least, his own authority would be in question. How could he offer them a safe haven, even for an evening, if he couldn't protect those of his own house?

And who could it have been? There was a very long list of those who might have wished him ill, but Alfonzo could not attribute the style or timing of such an attack to any of them. And the head. Why had they taken her head?

There was too much to think of and if he was to make it

through the night, he was going to have to push it to the back of his mind. The damage to his party had been done, but the most memorable part of the evening was still to come. He could salvage much from the evening if things went well, and as long as he was able to keep the silence among his own people about Isadora's death, he might find a way to turn the entire business to his advantage. That was later.

Gabriella of Genoa stood alone, to one side, surrounded by her fawning followers, and Alfonzo watched her for a moment before approaching. She had been deep in conversation with a short, bent Nosferatu, one whom Alfonzo knew by sight, but not by name. Feeling the weight of his gaze, she glanced up to meet his eyes.

Alfonzo approached.

"It is quite the party," Gabriella said as he approached. "My congratulations." She paused. "Or should I say, my condolences."

Inwardly, Alfonzo cursed, wondering how much she knew, and how she had come by the knowledge.

"The party is young," Alfonzo replied, sipping the blood-laced wine in his goblet and stepping closer. He noted that her followers closed in slightly, framing her against the wall as if she were one of the works of art she'd taken to collecting. "Who is to say," he continued, "what the sentiment will be by the time it ends."

"Who indeed," Gabriella commented dryly. "Will Isadora not be joining us this night?"

Alfonzo's smile widened. She suspected something was wrong, but she did not know. It was obvious in the twist of her smile. Gabriella did not hold Bishop Alfonzo in high esteem, and it would please her greatly to think he and Isadora were merely quarrelling. Briefly he wondered what sort of relationships she herself might have suffered if she could believe his earlier loss of reason might he attributable to a lovers' spat.

Before he could form a properly cryptic response, he spotted Matteo pushing his way gently through the crowd, and he turned. The boy stepped close, bowed his head, and waited.

"What is it?" Alfonzo asked, knowing the answer, but wanting to divert his conversation before he gave away too much, or sent the wrong signals to Gabriella. She was powerful, and she had her own interests. Genoa would love a larger piece of Constantinople, and she bore watching. She was, after all, Lasombra, and in the clan, intrigue was as important as blood. Sometimes more so.

"We are ready, Lord," Matteo replied. His voice was low, and Alfonzo detected the tremor behind it. He wondered if Gabriella would hear it, as well, and if so, what she would make of it. It wasn't odd for a servant to fear his master, but under the circumstances, he knew he would have to watch every word and gesture.

"It is well. Let it begin."

With a quick nod to Gabriella, the bishop turned and strode slowly back to the center of the room and the raised table and chairs. Matteo had dissolved back into the crowd, and moments later had sent his troop of servers scurrying about the room. Alfonzo turned to face his gathered guests, and gestured to the players, who slowed, then grew silent. Anticipation was palpable in the air, and Alfonzo smiled.

As he raised his arms, torches and lamps were slowly extinguished, one by one, in a pattern, giving the impression of dominoes falling, each lamp snuffing the next in turn. It was an effect that Matteo had practiced again and again, seeking the rhythm that would give the moment an eerie power.

Of course, the light made little difference to those gathered. It was theatrics, smoke and mirrors to add to the entertainment.

"Such a party," Alfonzo called out, still holding his arms over his head, hands flat and reaching toward the ceiling, "has many things to offer. The music"—he gestured to the musicians, who nodded in silence—"the drink"—he downed his blood wine in a single gulp, this time spilling nothing. He set the goblet on the table absently and raised his hands again.

"But there is one thing that every good party brings with it," he continued. "One thing that itches at the mind and grasps the strings of the heart. That thing is hunger. Everything centers on that one, basic need. The music can soothe." Matteo leaned in close to the lead musician and nodded a cue. A rhythmic, pulsing heat arose. Around the room, five small alcoves were suddenly lit by flaming torches, and within each, a drummer sat, staring stoically into the shadowy ballroom. The beat circled the room as the extinguishing of the torches had done, growing in speed, then dropping off again, then growing more rapid still.

Alfonzo stood in the center of it all, feeling the pulse of the drums like the heartbeat he had not known since his mortal life, feeling the call of the blood. His eyes blazed.

"The hunger has but one answer," he intoned. "Let the hunt begin."

At this, the band joined in with the drums, the flute deep and rich, notes blending and sliding off the walls, the strings of twin fiddles rising to play with the haunting silvered tones. It was sultry and dark, the drums coming from all sides of the room resonated the very stone beneath the assemblage's feet. The guests began to mill about in expectation, wondering what would come next, and from which direction.

It was then that another set of torches were lit. These moved from the greater hall, leading up from the kitchens. They were held by Arturo and Leonid, warped reflections one of the other, prancing in almost mincing dance steps at the head of a long procession.

A murmur rose as the chain of girls came into view—each now joined to the next by tiny silvered links that circled each throat, collar-like, and stretched back to the next in line. They were naked, their skin pale and glowing in the torchlight. Each reacted to the moment differently—exquisitely. Some tried to pull back, away from those moving ahead. Others reached out to those they passed, as if they might provide escape. These turned quickly, shuddering and screaming at the faces and touches they met to either side.

At the head of the line, Arturo and Leonid held the ends of the chains that bound the girls, each with a chain in one hand and a torch in the other. They placed the torches to either side of Bishop Alfonzo, where he stood by the raised table, and leaped up to stand beside him. They turned, bowing low to the assembled crowd.

All was silent. All concentration was now focused on the women, the heady scent of their blood, the life pouring through their veins, the fear sweating through their pores and leaking from the depths of their eyes. Alfonzo took the offered ends of the chains and gazed down at his captives. They didn't seem to notice him. None of their eyes were directed too far from the floor. Some had collapsed in small heaps, dragging at those before and behind them, tightening the chains at their throats and causing more cries, more torment. They were exquisite.

Turning back to his guests, Alfonzo continued.

"The hunger, alone," he said, smiling wide, "is powerful. Few can ignore it, and none completely. It is the force that drives us, the one need we cannot overcome. Not by force of will, by ritual or prayer, not by the grace of any other being that walks the earth, but only by the final death can we escape it. The hunger is the one thing we all share, regardless of clan, politics, or religion.

"And there is one thing," he shook the chain for emphasis, "that can ease the burden of that hunger. All good things come to those who wait, and you have waited with me this night, patiently, as we moved toward this moment.

"While we share the hunger, there is one other thing I would like to share. A particular love of my own. Some among you have given this over, preferring the more refined methods of satiation. I dedicate this night to those who have come before. To those who hunted alone in the shadows, wild and free, seeking their prey by the heat and the blood, and feeding as they wished. This is their night. This is *our* night."

The drums were pounding, deep, resonant, and only the force of his will brought his voice above them. All were on edge now. The air was thick with barely controlled need.

Arturo and Leonid moved down the line, gripping each woman in turn, holding her still, presenting her to the crowd and removing the chains. To each they whispered warnings, to be still, to stand as they had been left, or to suffer, long and slow. The twins were thorough in the teasing of both hunters and prey. The atrocities they hinted at as they moved among the girls and women drew gasps, cries, and one piercing scream. Their long-nailed fingers trailed over soft, naked flesh as they progressed.

After what must have been no more than a couple of minutes, and stretched into an eternity, the women were gathered, free of their bindings, into a small circle, just below Alfonzo's table.

He raised his eyes to the room. "We will give them the count of one hundred. One hundred seconds to decide their path. One hundred seconds to define the tiny portion of eternity that represents their remaining lives. We will count to one hundred, and then... Let the hunt begin."

The drums took up where his voice had left off. The beat slowed, once again a heartbeat, and with each pulse, somewhere a voice cried out through the room.

"One."

"Two."

Other voices chimed in. None cried out. Not exactly. The words, the numbers, were spoken with soft intensity. The women seemed confused at first, but Leonid leaned in among them, running the tip of one fingernail up the throat of a girl of no more than 16, holding her gaze and whispering. "Run."

They were gone. All of them moved together, at first, but as they passed through the crowd, Matteo and some of the other servants diverted them, stepping between running bodies and feeling them peel off to either side. The crowd got into it then, their voices joining, one after another, as the numbers rose, and the pale, stricken features of the women passed among them. A hand would reach out to brush across a soft cheek, and that woman would skitter to the side, fleeing through a different doorway than the girl to her right or left. They were broken into groups and fleeing for their lives.

There was no screaming. They were not going to outrun their pursuit. They knew they would have to hide. Instinctively, they were silent. Only the heaviness of their breath, the scent of their sweat, and the blood that pounded through their veins would give them away. The only illumination now was by the drummers. The guests were circling, moving easily through the darkness, and the women stumbled and tripped through them, desperately pressing off of any body they touched, screaming when they came too close to a pale, leering face.

The count reached eighty, and Alfonzo slowly descended to the floor. He could sense the growing tension, the energy crackling through the room. He had them. This was what they'd wanted, what they'd come for. Many of his peers would raise their noses in public and claim such things beneath them, but when the blood called, they answered. It would always he so. Alfonzo's own hunger clutched him tightly. He had expended a lot of energy, repressed his rage, and continued with the night, but he was shaking now with the effort. The scent of hot blood was heady, strong, and intoxicating.

The prey had been driven from the room. They wound their way through the passageways of the mansion, but they would find no escape. They could not enter any of the stairwells, nor would they be able to find their way out through any door, or back down the way they had come. The basements and kitchens were closed off. Alfonzo had stationed his people on the stairs, and the doors would be sealed.

"Ninety-eight."

The air crackled with excitement, and before the echo of the words "one hundred" had faded, the room was a whirl of motion. The darkness that so confused their prey launched the hunters into their own element. Within moments the first screams arose, and Alfonzo was barely able to contain himself. He moved slowly across the room, fighting his instinct to streak to the halls and to scream after those who had been released. They had been beautiful, and the hot scents of fresh blood and fresher fear were staggering, far beyond any blood wine ever bottled.

His senses reeled, and he steadied himself against one wall. He had his own pleasures planned, bittersweet as the moment would be with Isadora gone. At that thought, his rage boiled up again, and he nearly caved in to the desire to hunt with the others, alongside his guests and their followers. He heard screams and moans of fear, and once, as he passed one of the small, dark gardens, he heard the distinct sounds of feeding.

Matteo stood to one side of the door leading back toward the dungeons, and as his master passed, he pulled a lever that slid back a panel in that wall. Moments later, the panel slid shut, and

Alfonzo was gone from the party. No one noticed his passing, and those engaged in the hunt, and the feeding, would never notice his absence. They would disappear, one by one, to seek their shelter as the night grew pale and the brightness of morning threatened to seep through the windows. There would be no more meetings among elders, no more quiet talking or sipping of thin blood wine. The servants had disappeared beyond the doors and walls that would protect them, for the most part, from what went on in the halls and gardens beyond.

Alfonzo walked down a corridor that was narrower than most. He was between the outside wall of the mansion and the inner hall, a passage few knew existed, and fewer still were allowed to walk. He heard movement beyond the stone, an occasional cry. The women were young, and they would he clever, but nothing could save them. There was nowhere to run, nowhere to hide.

Alfonzo knew that the twins would join the hunt. They had barely contained their hunger when leading their charges through the midst of the ballroom, teasing and stroking soft flesh and feeling the pulsing life beneath it. They would now have to be kept on a short leash. They had fawned over Isadora like puppies, idolizing her. Without that additional control, he would have to find ways to divert their energies. Neither twin was quick in thought or keen in judgment, and the potential for embarrassment or outright harm to his affairs was too great.

Alfonzo rounded a corner, pressed on a stone to his right, and pushed open the concealed door which unlatched at his touch. The darkened stairway spun upwards, narrow and steep, spiraling around the main hall inside the walls. Alfonzo took the steps quickly, often flying up several in a single bound. It was time for release. It was time to let the hunger and the tension and the anger boil over, and for this he had prepared a singular entertainment of his own.

He reached the third story, and he slid around the stone silently, careful not to make a sound that might carry through to the other side. The rooms on this floor were private chambers. Alfonzo had spent a lot of time on them, creating a decadent sanctum where he could escape the worries of the lower levels.

Few were allowed access to this floor. Fewer still ever departed. Alfonzo circled slowly. He had such a guest now. He had two, as a matter of fact. A man, twenty years to his credit, son of one of the merchants of the Latin quarter. He was staying in one room of Alfonzo's mansion, and in another, a young woman. Her name was Katrina, and she was the daughter of one of the royal families of Adrianople. The two had met, years before, near the merchant's tents in the market place, and against all rules and logic, they had fallen in love.

Katrina was a beauty, and headstrong, refusing to marry at an early age to fulfill her father's wish of an alliance with a stronger house. In the ensuing years, no less than three suitors had been rejected, the last violently and publicly, and her father's patience had ended. Katrina was to be shipped to a nunnery. Her family would no longer acknowledge her, and she would never be granted the freedom she sought.

Had her father known about Eduardo, he would have had the young man publicly whipped and castrated. The blame would have been set upon his shoulders for the insubordination of the daughter, and both would have been punished. So, the boy had gone to his father, who in turn had approached his secretive bishop, late one night, with the problem. There was a difference between the boy's wishes, and those of his father. Eduardo's father knew enough to fear the wrath of royalty. He wished to do business with the Bulgars and Greeks and knew he could not be in the business of stealing daughters. Alfonzo had listened to the problem from start to finish, and, smiling, he had promised relief.

The girl had been taken easily. The twins had slipped into Adrianople one night, finding her alone in a garden where Eduardo was to have met her. One moment she had stood alone in the shadows, expecting her lover's approach, the next she had been bound, gagged, and whisked away.

Chapter Seven

The morning following the party, a messenger arrived at Bishop Alfonzo's door. He was young, barely into his teens, and ill-dressed. His face was the face of a thousand others, and he bore no identification. Only the message.

The boy was set free, and the message was carried up the stairs to the bishop himself. Matteo bore it. None had seen their master since the night before. None had been willing to break a silence he had imposed. Isadora's rooms had been cleaned, scoured until the stone gleamed, the bed made and everything just as she had left it. Again—none wanted to be the one to disturb something that might make a difference to their master.

The party had not passed without leaving its marks. Matteo had been up with the dawn, and since then he'd had servants working around the clock, cleaning away the evidence of what had transpired, wiping away the blood, and setting the great ovens in the kitchens to incinerate the remains.

The carnage had been incredible. In the darkness, with only the drummer's torches leaking their luminescence into the shadowy halls, it had been a surreal, amazing dream. The beauty of those who'd hunted was undeniable, their strength beyond question—but by day the stark reality of what had passed as entertainment was all too clear.

Matteo had been in this position before. Cleaning up the remnant of what he wished he were part of. It was his place to return the mansion to the daylight world, pristine and bright, the envy of the living, breathing gentry, the facade obscuring the reality of the bishop's world. The living had many stories about this place: it was the home of a wealthy and reclusive Venetian merchant, or the home of a heretical church, or cursed ground left to Latins by devious Greeks. All hints of the truth, none complete. There had to be perfect attention to detail. If Matteo had failed in his task, his usefulness would be at an end, and the twins might get to play the games with him they had always hinted at.

Now, with the sun just setting, holding the message tightly, he made the long slow climb to the upper levels. The lamps were lit, once more, and the barriers between levels had been removed. None were moving yet, except in the kitchens and servant's quarters below.

It felt wrong. Something had changed, something more than just the death of Isadora, and the completion of the party. If it had not been for the message he clutched in his hand, and the possibility that it would prove as important as the messenger had claimed, Matteo would not have mounted that stairway for any price. Alfonzo would come to them—or call to them—when he was ready. The bishop did not enjoy being disturbed

Matteo squared his shoulders and did his best to steady his breathing. He reached the landing that led into Alfonzo's personal quarters, and he stopped. The massive wooden doors were closed tightly. There were no torches lit, and there was no sound. Matteo knew that the outer wooden doors led to an antechamber, where dark and heavy curtains hung from the ceiling to the floor. Beyond the curtains were a second set of doors, wrought of iron and ornamented with the Euagetaematikon, the Holy Scripture of the Cainite Heresy. The blood communion given of Maundy Thursday—the Last Supper when Christ-Caine gave of his blood to the Apostles. One night, Bishop Alfonzo preached, all humanity would share in that holy gift.

Matteo pressed a panel near the outer doors and they swung open. No light. There was no lamp, no torch. The interior of the antechamber was as dark as a tomb, and as he stepped inside, Matteo felt the rush of air as the doors closed behind him.

He had the sudden, irrational urge to turn and bolt. He could open those outer doors, return to the lower levels, and wait for his master to come to him. He could apologize for any sound he might have made, beg forgiveness for not delivering the message immediately. All of these possibilities, and more rushed through his mind, but his body betrayed him. He stepped forward, parting the dark curtains near their center and stepping through. He was not completely confused by the darkness. He had tasted his master's blood, and his sight was more than it had once been—but less than it could be.

He could see the base, fleshy Apostles, praising the unfeeling, spiritual image of the Christ-Caine floating above them. He could see the Hell-faced demons, creatures of the Demiurge, leering in from the sides. He could feel the beating of his heart, erratic and hurried. His skin was clammy, and though every ounce of his being wanted to step inward to his master, his body protested. Before he could shy away, he reached out and grasped the iron knocker near the center of the inner doors and drew it back. With an exhalation of breath, he let it fall forward. The sound echoed, deep and loud.

At first there was no indication that any had heard him. The doors remained closed. There was no light, and no sound. He might have been locked in a giant casket, or the dungeon of a castle. Matteo's hand trembled, and he clutched the message more tightly. He was tensed to flee, already leaning away from the metal doors and the possibility of pain and death that lay beyond them when a soft squeal of metal broke the silence, and a deeper crack of darkness slid down the center of the metal doors.

There was no greeting. There was no indication that any stood within that doorway, or that he was welcome. Neither, he told himself, was there any indication he was unwelcome. He couldn't get control of his racing thoughts, and breathing was more and more difficult as the seconds mounted.

Finally, realizing that there was no other possible action to be taken, he stepped forward, plunging into the darkness beyond the doorway and closing his eyes. It did not matter if they were open, or closed, in that instant. If he died, he preferred to do so with the mental image of the bishop's face smiling at him. He did not want to see any weakness, or deceptive shadow that would haunt his mind. He wanted to be ten minutes in the past and deciding to wait for his master's presence to deliver the message.

"What is it, Matteo?" The bishop spoke softly. "Why are you here?"

Matteo tried to speak. He opened his mouth, and his eyes, though he could see little in the darkness. He sensed another presence, but he concentrated on his master. He wanted to apologize. He wanted to explain the arrival of the messenger, and the insistence that the message be delivered immediately. He wanted to fall to his knees, lower his eyes and beg forgiveness, and at the same time he cursed himself as weak and unworthy. He didn't even know if he had displeased his master, and already he was offering himself as sacrifice.

Unable to speak, he held out the note.

Alfonzo stepped forward and took the paper from Matteo's hand. No words were spoken. Matteo saw his master's head tilt. There was no light. None. Still, Alfonzo read and Matteo could just note the features he adored and see the shoulders grow tense. Alfonzo read, then raised his head, lowered it, and read again.

"When did this arrive?" he asked sharply. "And how?" Matteo found his tongue.

"Not half an hour ago, milord," he stammered. "It arrived by messenger, a boy from the streets. He knew nothing."

"Did you read this?" Alfonzo asked.

"No, Your Excellency. It was addressed to you alone."

Alfonzo's eyes bored into Matteo's, searching—digging. Finally, he turned back to the note. "It is about Isadora," he said at last. "There is information. Something I should know." Alfonzo crushed the paper in his hand so quickly and completely that Matteo half-expected it to fall to dust.

"You must send a response for me," Alfonzo said at last. "You will carry this yourself. No other is to touch or read it. No one is to be trusted."

Matteo gulped in a breath, shivering with relief. He was trusted. He nodded.

"You will carry this to Lucita of Aragon," Alfonzo stated flatly. "You will request that the lady join me this evening for counsel. You will thank her for me, for this message. Is this understood?"

Matteo nodded again. He knew of the Aragonese woman, certainly, though she was not one that his master had often spoken well of. She had moved into quarters near the edge of the Latin Quarter soon after the Crusaders broke the city's back. She was of similar blood to the bishop, but hardly an ally. Alfonzo often muttered questions and accusations with her name prominent, and this change of attitude was startling.

Then there was a scuffling noise deeper in the shadows, and Matteo's thoughts of Lucita and the message slipped away. He drew back toward the doors. Alfonzo seemed not to notice the approaching sounds at first, then he turned. Matteo saw the muscles that had tightened in his master's shoulders loosen.

Katrina stepped slowly from the shadows. She was pale, very pale—and her steps were not steady. Her eyes roved incessantly. Hungrily. Her gaze latched onto Matteo and she moved. One second she was still, the next in motion and Matteo was flung back against the wood frame of the iron doors with bruising force.

"No!" he cried out as she struck, quick as a snake, at the soft skin of his throat.

There was no bite. He felt the scrapes where her nails had dug into his flesh, and his back throbbed. His head had cracked painfully against the door, but his throat was intact. There were two scrapes, barely breaking the surface, when Matteo reached his fingers up to brush over his skin.

He looked up, dumbstruck. Bishop Alfonzo held her tightly, one hand in her hair, the other arm wrapped around her waist. Still she fought. Her eyes were deep and red and she saw no more of Matteo than a wineskin that was denied her. Alfonzo's eyes darkened.

"Go," the bishop commanded. "Go, and send me the twins. I will need them to hunt this night."

Matteo nodded, backing away—forgetting the closed doors and hanging his head a final time before turning, pressing through the doorway, and slamming it behind himself. He tangled in the curtains as he passed, but they did not slow him. He tripped through the antechamber, lunged for the outer doors, and was suddenly free. With deep shuddering breaths that wracked his frame, he leaned his back to the door, trying to stop the whirling of thoughts, and the deep-digging bite of the fear.

Matteo desired nothing more than to be embraced by his master, but this had been so different. He'd never seen madness in another's eyes like what he'd seen in the girl's. Even the twins, young in the blood, were guilty of only a sort of controlled madness. They hunted, but it was the hunt of a pair of cats, toying with their prey. They enjoyed what they did, and the girl that had nearly ended Matteo's life moments before had shown no sign that she could enjoy anything. She had needed him. She had hungered. That was the totality of what he'd sensed in her. It was not what he wanted.

Bishop Alfonzo was a beautiful man. He was tall, strong, and cultured. He could be wicked and hurtful, devious and purely evil, but he was recognizable as himself at all times. He was rational, intelligent, and powerful. That was the dream. That was what kept Matteo striving day after day to find ways to be more pleasing, things he could do to ease every waking moment of his master's existence.

And the blood. Alfonzo's blood called to him strongly. He had tasted it only once. Reluctantly, at first, then greedily. The thick, rust-flavored blood had threatened to gag him when he first thought of what he was doing. He'd tried to pull away, though that was impossible. Alfonzo held him easily, and it was only moments before his struggles to free himself had become frantic struggles to continue. To have more.

Alfonzo denied him as effortlessly as he'd forced him. Now nothing could seep in to the shadowy crevasses of his mind but the thought of that holy communion. Matteo longed to walk among such as the twins without fear. There were hints and unspoken promises, but that one taste was all he'd been allowed, and it wasn't enough. Not nearly.

Before leaving with the message, Matteo stopped on the first floor, where the bishop kept his offices. There were others who managed these affairs, meetings that could not be avoided with clergymen were held in these rooms, complaints and pleas were heard from others in the city, soldiers, merchants, even minor royalty. It was well known that, though there was a certain danger to dealing with the bishop on any matter, there were definitely benefits, as well.

Matteo found one of the clerks, a young man named Eldon, with studious, gray eyes and a nervous twitch at one side of his mouth, seated behind the desk just inside the chamber.

"I will be going out," Matteo said quickly. "I have an urgent message to deliver for the bishop. If any should call for him tonight—and I mean any—they must be turned away with apologies and scheduled at another time."

"But," Eldon asked, half-rising from his seat, "what shall we tell them? They line the streets every night to see him, and we are expecting several local merchants who have been waiting months for an audience."

"Tell them that it is a matter of faith," Matteo replied solemnly. "Tell them that the bishop is fasting, and in meditation over the problems of our city. Tell them that he will meet with them soon. If they are important, slide others down the list to accommodate them. Regardless, do not disturb our lord."

Eldon looked as if he might speak again, and Matteo held up a hand. He caught the slightly younger clerk's gaze, and he held it. He was still disheveled from his narrow escape on the floors above.

"You have not been with us long enough to understand fully," Matteo said softly, "but hear this well. There are times when our lord is not to be disturbed. There are times when you could find yourself in a deeper hell than any you could imagine without taking leave of this city, and this could be one such time. He is not to be disturbed for any reason."

Eldon swallowed hard, and sat down, making a performance of sliding ink wells about on the desk and checking the tips of the many quills arrayed before him. "It will take time to speak with them all," he said at last. "I will do all that I can."

"See that you do," Matteo said, turning without further discussion and going in search of the twins. He found them near the rear gardens. They were searching among the trees, noses close to the ground as if they could sniff the air. It was the garden directly beneath Isadora's balcony.

Matteo watched them for a moment, standing in the shadows and gathering his courage. He knew that they would not give him trouble, considering the message he was bringing, but he hated to disturb them. They seemed intent on something that he could not see, or sense, and if they were on the trail of Isadora's killer or killers, then he was loathe to come between them and success.

Suddenly, Arturo stiffened and turned. The thin, blonde hair hung limply over his shoulders, and he turned his hawk's nose slowly. His gaze rose from the ground, and locked onto Matteo. Matteo froze. For the second time in one night, he was unable to move. This time there was no attack, but the sensation was much the same. He stared into those dead, soulless eyes, and he never even noticed the movement as Leonid appeared suddenly at his elbow, very close.

"What do you want, boy," he hissed. The words were whispered, but so loud in his ears that Matteo feared his head would explode from the pressure. He felt a bone-thin hand gripping his shoulder painfully. The scent of Leonid's breath was fetid and dark with death.

Matteo turned to speak and in that second, Arturo was at his other elbow. The two sandwiched him so tightly that even had he been physically able to move, it would have been impossible without dislodging one of the two. Matteo had no illusions about his ability to make that a reality.

"I..." He choked on the word, hated himself for the fear that robbed his voice, and shuddered. Arturo ran a long, yellowed fingernail up his throat, and the words spilled free.

"I have a message for you."

The finger withdrew, and he was granted a hair's breadth more space to breathe. With all the strength of will he possessed, Matteo concentrated on not closing his eyes, not allowing a tear, and not soiling himself. Silently, deep inside, he made a promise to himself. If his master fulfilled his promise. If he became such as they, he would have his revenge. They were powerful, but not intelligent. Matteo would be stronger, and he would see them fall to ash and kick those ashes to the night wind personally.

The vow gave him strength.

"His Excellency needs you," he said, speaking quickly. "You are needed to hunt. He has embraced a girl."

The twins exchanged a glance.

Matteo continued. "She is very hungry."

Arturo broke away, turning back to where he'd been rooting through the brush and gardens. It was obvious that, though the prospect of a hunt appealed to him, and he knew he would answer the bishop's summons, something was drawing him toward the night. Something he did not want to let go of.

Matteo took a deep breath, and braved a question. "What is it? Did you find something—the killers?" Leonid glanced in the direction his twin had turned, then turned Matteo's face with one finger under his chin. Those dark eyes held no emotion but hatred, yet Matteo sensed, for the moment, that the hatred was not directed toward him.

"We have found little," Leonid breathed, "but we need little. Some are born to talk, others to lead the church in song and prayer. We were born to hunt. They have killed one of our own, and we will find them. They will not die well."

It was the most that Matteo had ever heard either of the two say. He'd heard long, whispered strings of filth, though he'd caught little of it, when they teased or tortured a captive. He'd heard them curse, sometimes at servants, most times at one another. He had never heard one of them utter coherent, focused speech, and the words forced him to reevaluate the dangers they presented. He felt another shiver building, but at that moment, Arturo turned back.

"Where do you go?"

He did not waste words.

"I am to take a message," Matteo breathed. "I am to tell no one."

Arturo held his gaze in silence. It was obvious that he was considering whether to accept this, or to face the consequences of forcing a response. Alfonzo would not be likely to kill either of them if they did so, though he would certainly punish them.

"It is important," Matteo whispered. "It is not because he does not trust you."

Arturo turned away abruptly. He made a last, doubled-over pass through the trees, and then, with a sudden burst of speed that sent him flying past Matteo so quickly that a wind rose, he was gone, back to the mansion, back to their master. As before, the second twin moved in response so quickly that Matteo did not register the movement until he stood alone in the garden, trembling, surrounded by the silence and the dark.

He turned and walked toward the street, and the city beyond. It was not far to where Lucita of Aragon had taken her residence, but at night it was best to move slowly and with caution, and already he'd been delayed longer than he was comfortable with. The twins were a problem for another night.

He passed through the small garden and hesitated very briefly, scanning the shadows. If there was something there, he could not see it, but he very desperately wanted to. He wanted to be the one to bring something important—anything important—to His Excellency. He wanted to ingratiate himself with his master, and, truth be told, he would miss Isadora. She had been devious and cruel, but she had also been beautiful, and she had never been stale or boring. Such as she were rare in the world, both night and day, and eventually he would take time to mourn her passing.

Lucita stood on her balcony once more, watching the city breathe. They were rasping, painful breaths, but there was life in her yet. The activities of the night before were still vividly etched in her mind. In a fold of her robe she carried the small pendant.

She had questioned Anatole at length, but learned little. The Chosen of Calomena were not well known. No clan. No ties of blood or family. They were tied by their belief, the way mortals were tied by theirs, and it grated on Lucita's nerves. There were certain ways that things were meant to be. There were those who hunted, and those who were hunted. There were those who ruled, and those who followed.

The Chosen were born of the malignant wisdom of a fanatic named Stanislav, who had preached on the Latin Quarter and supposedly met his end during the sacking of the city. They believed Caine to be the font of all evil, and his twin sister Calomena to be the savior who would return to cleanse the world. In preparation for this, they had raised a brood—including both vampires and mortals—and begun a hunt of epic proportion. The clanless united was a horror unto itself. The clanless united against the clans was much worse.

And this incident was not without precedent. Alfonzo had lost two of his children to the Chosen. His hatred of them was bitter, and deep. The news she had for him would open doors, but some questions remained: Just what would exit from those doors, and who would step back through?

Anatole had remained silent on his own hatred of the Chosen. He did not know who led them at present. He did not know why they would attack Alfonzo, other than the obvious history they had with his family. He knew none of these things, and yet, he had known who they were, and he had killed their leader-without hesitation.

They would have to be found and watched. If possible, they would have to be eradicated. You could not march soldiers with a madman in their midst, and you could not properly rule a city where the leaders' lives were forfeit at a moment's notice. It would require thought.

She saw Matteo moving down the street toward her long before he was aware of her watching. He moved skillfully, and Lucita saw immediately that he had been touched by the blood. Alfonzo, most likely. No other messenger would have been trusted with this.

What she had sent to Alfonzo was a simple charcoal rubbing of the pendant she now carried, and a short note.

"I know who has taken her," it said. "One of them is dead."

She had known that this would not satisfy Alfonzo. Far from it, the words had been chosen to inflame him, to raise the long-smoldering hatred he held for the Chosen, and to force a meeting where Lucita would initially hold the upper hand. She would have the opportunity to steer their conversation, having something that he wanted. She knew that Alfonzo was Narses' puppet. He might appear powerful here, on his own ground, but in the grand scheme of things, he did as he was bid—for now.

Matteo drew closer, glancing furtively into the shadows to either side of the road. He seemed particularly nervous for one in the bishop's service, but Lucita withheld judgment. Things would be in turmoil after Isadora's death, and there was no way to know what might have transpired in the wake of the party. Only vague rumors had circulated. Most had been of the final hunt, individual tales that reminded Lucita of young boys she'd known before her embrace, bragging over their prowess at some inane game, or how they'd beaten other boys into submission. Alfonzo had planned well. The hunt had erased most of the memory of his party, and the memories he'd left with his guests had ended pleasantly. Grudgingly, Lucita approved.

As Matteo pulled up in front of the large wooden doors below her, Lucita turned and stepped into the hall. With a clap she brought a young girl, Maura, running lightly down the hallway, eyes lowered.

"We have a visitor," Lucita called out sharply. "See him in. Have him wait for me below. Bring him wine and light candles. Make him feel at home. I will be down shortly." Maura nodded, turned, and fled back down the hall. Her cheeks were flushed, and Lucita smiled. Maura was often unable to disguise her feelings, and her love for Lucita herself was intense. Sometimes, the smaller pleasures brought the deepest entertainment.

Lucita returned to the balcony. She heard the doors opening, and she knew her young visitor had been escorted inside. She was not in a hurry. The longer she waited, the more on edge he would be, and the more firmly she would control the moment. Alfonzo was not the only one who knew how to plan.

The girl led Matteo down a dark hallway. Near the far end, a doorway opened to the left, and a soft light glowed from within. They made the turn, and he found himself in a drawing room, centered by a massive carved wood table, polished to an almost liquid shine. Upon its surface sat candles, lined up in holders of various size and shape, artfully placed. There were two chairs drawn up before the table, and the girl ushered him toward one.

"What is your name?" he asked her softly. "Do you serve Lady Lucita?"

The girl nodded, but did not offer a name. At the mention of her mistress, she had flushed bright crimson, and Matteo smiled. She had, he believed, tasted the blood. It wasn't knowledge in any normal sense of the word, but an aura she gave off. He felt it prickle along his skin. She was a pretty girl, and attentive, but he could sense nothing beyond this. After he had taken the offered seat, she turned to the table. There was a carafe of wine waiting, and a single crystal goblet.

Matteo hesitated. He did not want to presume. Perhaps his appearance had given some sort of misconception. His Excellency would certainly have never offered him wine, or sat him among such finery. He remained seated, but his nerves were on edge.

He waited for what seemed an eternity. He crossed his legs, then uncrossed them. Sat forward anxiously, hands on his knees. His wine sat, untouched, as he was not yet certain if he should cry off from the offer and beg her forgiveness for not doing so immediately. A thousand thoughts caromed about inside his head, and none of them would light long enough to be held and set straight.

Just as he thought he would lose his mind, there was the sound of soft steps, and a dark-complexioned, beautiful young woman entered the room. He had expected her to appear older, somehow. She smiled at him, and his heart melted into his legs, giving him the sensation of being made of lead, unable to move properly. Her eyes were deep, and her gaze locked onto his immediately, not quite mirroring the brilliance of her smile.

With an effort, Matteo rose, dropping immediately into a deep bow.

"Milady," he said suddenly, speaking too quickly, unable to stem the flow of words once it had been unleashed, "I am sorry. I presume too much. His Excellency, Bishop Alfonzo, has sent me to you, to bring a message in return. I am only a servant. I..."

She stilled him with a gentle gesture and moved closer, stepping around him and indicating the goblet.

"Drink," she said simply. "We do not get many guests here, servants or masters, and it would please me to speak with you."

There was nothing Matteo could say in response to this. The proximity of her was overwhelming his senses. Her features had softened since she'd entered, the young curves of her body seeming to blur. Matteo's heart pounded. When, he wondered, had her eyes gotten so wide? So deep?

"What is the message you have brought me?" The words were soft, floating to him from some distance he couldn't even imagine.

"His... His Excellency has requested that you join him this evening for counsel," Matteo answered dreamily. "He seemed very eager to speak with you."

Lucita smiled, and Matteo tumbled into that smile.

"Does he treat you well?" she asked.

Matteo was startled by the question. He was too befuddled to work out what the implications of her words might he. How did one answer a question like this one, when the person asking, and the person being asked about were able to read you like an open book, and both could kill you and toss you aside without a moment's thought? "I am happy," he said at last.

She watched him for a moment, took a step, and watched a little longer. "I don't believe that is true. What is your name?"

"Matteo, milady. My name is Matteo."

"Matteo," she repeated. "An old name, old and noble." Matteo blushed. She was moving, slowly pacing back and forth before him, circling closer and closer. "I traveled here with His Excellency as a young boy," he added. "I am from Venice."

"Drink, Matteo of Venice," Lucita said, stopping suddenly. "You will soon have to depart to tell the bishop of your success. I will see him tomorrow night, for I have important things to tell him. You can tell him, as well," she added, as Matteo brought the cool crystal goblet to his lips and took a first, tentative drink, "that I will be accompanied by the monk Anatole. It was he who first unearthed the information I bear, and it is he who is best able to present it."

Matteo nodded. The wine was old. He had never tasted finer. He took a second, longer drink. He could think of nothing to say. He knew that he should not be sitting as he was, watching her move and talk, and sipping wine. His Excellency would be furious, and it was likely that the bishop would read the guilt of the stolen moment in Matteo's eyes. There was little that he did that his master did not intuit.

"Your time will come," she said finally. "He has gifted you with his blood, Matteo. You will not always be his servant."

His heart raced. Had she, too, read his eyes?

"I have waited a very long time, milady," he replied, draining his wine in sudden thirst. "A very, very long time. I have hauled the corpses from his quarters and stood at his side as leaders of church, state and guild marched in and out for counsel or for war. It seems, already, that I have lived an eternity."

Her eyes, if it was possible, grew deeper still. "There are many levels to eternity, Matteo of Venice. Go. Tell your master what I've said, and be swift. I will come when the daylight fails tomorrow. Do as I bid and there will be rewards aplenty, I'm sure."

He rose, stumbling a little. She watched him, and very suddenly, she smiled.

"Matteo?" she asked, as he turned away.

"Yes, milady?" he spun back, ready to kneel, or to bow, to offer himself to her, anything.

"You should wipe the wine from your lips before you return. The bishop is sure to notice."

His face flushed and he licked his lip quickly, bringing up one hand.

Her laughter followed him down the corridor and out the door, into the night. He could still hear it ringing in his heart, and in his thoughts, far down the road.

Chapter Eight

Gabriella rode alone. It was late, and she rode fast, only the moon lighting her way, and a sky littered with stars like tiny sentinels, standing by to guard her. She had always loved these moments to herself, but this night it was a transitory moment at best. She had to reach the inn and make inquiries.

Hadrian's Rest was one of the important inns along the Constantinople to Adrianople road and it was firmly under Gabriella's sway. Trade was the lifeblood of any Genoese worth his (or her) salt, and unlife did not change this. Gabriella used taverns and inns to gather information and seed spies, both under Alfonzo's nose in the Latin Quarter and in key places between the capital and the makeshift camps several nights ride a way. Hadrian's Rest was a day's cart-ride from the Gate of Polyandrion, considerably less by fast horse. It was known to not look too carefully at cargo and to have a complement of rooms in the basement where a Cainite could rest away the day undisturbed. Thanks to it, Gabriella had good information about who was traveling to and from the camps. Information was very valuable, indeed.

What she had learned outside Alfonzo's mansion, however, would prove of use only if she found a way to take advantage of it. It wasn't all that strange that the bishop should embrace a new childe, and he had lost so many in and around the fall of the city. The fact that his new progeny came from Adrianople, and the influence of another, made a difference.

Licinius might not care a whit about the girl. He might, in fact, consider her well gone from the city, since she had been on the verge of being sent away at the time she was taken. On the

other hand, Licinius might well count the girl's father as a supporter, and be stalking his chambers and cursing, wondering
where she had been spirited away to. Such a willful girl might
also have been on the prince's own list of planned acquisitions.

There were many things weighing upon the heart of the
prince. The Latin Empire—the crusaders' parody of ancient
Byzantium—may have been pushed back from Adrianople's
gates, but only at the cost of coming under Bulgarian suzer-
ainty. Things were different among the undead, but that surely
still stuck in Licinius' craw. If rumors were to be believed, then
Basilio the Elder, the undead prince of Sofia, had arrived as a
guest—more than enough to raise eyebrows.

The loss of a single mortal girl, then, of noble birth or otherwise, might be overlooked. It was up to Gabriella to make it into
something more. Something useful. Then there was the matter
of fair Isadora. Something had happened at the beginning of
Alfonzo's party, something important, but despite his outburst
of fury, and the display with the crystal decanter, he had not
revealed it.

Gabriella had intended to send her own servants among
the bishop's own to ferret out the truth, but Alfonzo's sudden
recovery and the onslaught of the hunt had robbed her of the
opportunity. All she had was speculation, and that bothered
her a great deal. Gabriella did not deal in probabilities, but in
realities. She needed information.

She also needed support. Constantinople remained a city
in flux. There were crumbled remnants of power—pockets of
Greek vampires and old fanatics squirreled away in the depths
of the city—and a panoply of Latin and Frankish vampires trying to build a new domain here, like Alfonzo. Like herself. As
the buildings were rebuilt, and the streets cleared, and as the
mortals struggled to reclaim what she knew was forever lost,
another rebirth was happening. The city was without a true
leader. The three ancient Cainites who had built, and then ruled
in the city of Constantinople were gone, and none of their own
progeny seemed able to step up and patch the Dream together,
let alone collaborate in ruling over it. The last of those hoary
elders, the Dracon, was lost to them, perhaps forever—perhaps

for the best. There was no way to reclaim what once had been. The city would never be the dream of the ancients, but it could become another's dream. Gabriella had many dreams.

Bishop Alfonzo was a problem. He had been entrenched in his Latin Quarter when the crusaders hit, and it was there that they had done the least damage, where there was the least to destroy, the least loyalty to the city, the least to be gained by conquest. Few of the invading knights had found it worth their while to ransack stores and warehouses run by fellow Roman Christians, when they had a grand city filled with the riches and wonders of schismatic Greeks near at hand.

So, Alfonzo remained. Both the mortals and their church, as well as the low, obsequious clans he had gathered in the Latin Quarter supported him because, of all the things they remembered, of all the powers that had walked the streets and spun their webs in the shadows, Alfonzo was still strong, and everything else had toppled. He'd had his talons around the throat of Venetian trade in the city before the crusade, and that only made him stronger now. Archbishop Narses watched over him.

Gabriella rode into the inn's courtyard without slowing, still leaning in close to her mount and easily drifting with the rhythm of his flashing hooves. She knew where she was going, and the faster she got into the stables, the less chance there was that any would attempt to waylay her, or waste her time. She had many things, but for once in her long existence, time wasn't foremost on the list.

She dismounted and led her mount into an empty stall. The stable hand appeared soon enough, but he was well trained and knew not to question wealthy visitors of a certain cut. She made for the inn's private rooms where the meeting had been set. These men would hopefully bring word from the camps, where she had a clutch of spies. She'd always cultivated better relations with the Greeks than Alfonzo, and there were now many old acquaintances willing to report what they saw for her continued patronage. Gabriella would have no surprises from that quarter.

She descended the stone steps leading to the inn's cellars. The interior of the stairwell was dark, but she saw the faint glow of light from beneath a second set of curtains at the bottom. She pressed through this second entrance and into the room beyond. There were two seated at a rough table directly to her right. On the table between them sat a chess board with a game in progress. The chamber was dimly lit by candles placed about the room. The furnishings were rough and barely functional.

The two rose as she entered, but Gabriella motioned for them to remain as they were. She stepped closer, examining the board, and then glancing to the player on her left, who appeared to be in his early fifties, gray-streaks flecking dark hair, eyes even darker. His attire was simple, a dark cloak and boots. He met her gaze evenly.

"You are playing well, Ian," she said softly. "You appear to have him on the run."

Ian nodded and smiled thinly, but his attention was only half-focused on her. His opponent, a thin, bright-eyed man whom Gabriella knew had been embraced centuries in the past, though his appearance belied it in almost every aspect, was staring at the board in deep concentration. Then, snake-like, he slid a pawn up one square, far to the left of the main battle on the board.

Ian stared at the move. Gabriella stared as well. It seemed wholly unrelated to the game at hand. A nonsensical move that did nothing to advance the play, and only sped the inevitable victory of his opponent. This was the surface of it. Gabriella, however, knew this other. His name was Pasqual, and he had come to Constantinople many years before, having lived first in France and then in Rome. He was never frivolous. He rarely spoke, even when expected to, unless his words would matter.

It would be the same, Gabriella knew, with this game. Ian did not sense it. The two of them had not been together long, and Pasqual was not one to be known well after a short time. She had known him a hundred years, and still she did not really understand him. She watched in silence.

Ian moved his queen into attack position. The glint in his eye had grown more predatory, and he made the move decisively, focused on the pattern he saw before him. There was no hesitation in Pasqual's return move. He slid his bishop into a diagonal line, one space more advanced than the pawn he'd just moved.

Ian hesitated only a second. He glanced at the pieces, saw no danger in the new position, and moved his queen into line with Pasqual's king.

"Check," he said, his voice tense.

Pasqual advanced a pawn to block the check. It was a seemingly pointless prolonging of the inevitable. Almost contemptuously, Ian slashed the queen across the board and removed the pawn.

Pasqual looked up, just for a second, meeting Ian's triumphant gaze. Then he struck. The moving of the queen had freed the line for Pasqual's bishop. He moved it in line between his king, and Ian's queen. The queen could not take the bishop without being taken herself, but this did not matter in Ian's strategy. With slightly less confidence, Ian advanced his bishop in line with the queen. If Pasqual took the queen with his own bishop, there would be an exchange, and the check would be enforced once again, with the same inevitable outcome.

Pasqual did not take the queen. Instead, he slid his knight, which had lain forgotten along the side of the board, into position and, in a voice barely more than a rasp of wind, whispered, "Check."

Ian stared at the board. He was angry. It shone in his eyes. He was unable to sit back and reassess a situation he felt he already controlled. Gabriella could see the tide shifting, and she watched with interest as, almost belligerently, Ian moved his king one space to his left, out of the line of the knight.

It was over that simply. The bishop that had been moved to be protected by the lone pawn struck, now protected by the knight, which still covered the original square where check had been called. There was nowhere for Ian's king to run. The game had ended, and he was sitting, staring open-mouthed at the board, unable to comprehend how it had happened.

"There is a lesson in this game, I think," Gabriella said softly.

Ian snapped his gaze up to hers, ready to retort, but something in her eyes reminded him of his place. He fumed in silence.

"It is never wise to concentrate all your forces on a single point. There are many directions from which an attack may come, and there are as many forms of attack as there are directions. You have to be willing to adapt when circumstances shift."

Ian tipped his king irritably and slid away from the table. "This is his game," he snapped, pointing a figure accusingly at Pasqual. "It is never enough to win at chess. It is only enough if you can humiliate your opponent. His game," Ian nearly spat, "is to always allow his opponent to believe he is winning."

Gabriella did not share Ian's rage. Her lips twisted into a smile of amusement.

"Then," she added, "I would say there is a further lesson."

Ian turned and strode through a dark hole in the back wall that led to an inner chamber. Pasqual was still studying the chess board. He glanced up at her.

"He could have beaten you, still, if he'd been willing to admit the danger."

Pasqual nodded. "I know. He has not beaten me—yet—but he shows promise."

Gabriella shook her head and turned away. There was a larger table at the far end of the chamber, and she moved to this, taking a seat and turning impatiently to the entrance by which she'd come.

"Where are the others?" she asked. "I don't believe that I'm early."

Pasqual did not answer, he merely shrugged. Already he was replacing the pieces on the board, contemplating an opening.

There was a sound from above, then booted feet on the stairs, and Gabriella watched as two cloaked figures entered. One was small and hunched, leaning near to the ground, almost dragging his knuckles. Seeing Gabriella, the figure straightened somewhat, but his stance was uneven. He had the appearance of an animal, poised to spring or to flee, and uncertain which direction the next moment would take him. His eyes were so dark they appeared black, and his hair, wild and uncombed, waved about his grizzled, hairy face like a stubbled forest.

"You are late," Gabriella observed.

The second new arrival tossed his cloak back to reveal a

pale, boyish face, haloed in wavy gold hair. His eyes sparkled between blue and silver, and there was a sardonic grin planted on his lips that rode his features well.

"And you," he said with a bow, "are beautiful as ever." Gabriella tossed her head and avoided a smile. Barely. "Sit down," she said. "There is little time, and I have things I need to tell you."

The two made their way to the table, and finally completing his careful placement of the chessmen, Pasqual joined them. A few moments later, Ian strode from the back chamber, still scowling, and took the final remaining seat. When all were seated and watching her, Gabriella told them of Alfonzo's gathering. She told them what she'd learned of the girl, Katrina, and she told them of her mysterious ally within Alfonzo's house who had sent the message.

"You say he went to bring Isadora to the party, and came back in a rage?" Pasqual asked.

When Gabriella nodded, he continued.

"It is much like chess. Do you remember when my knight placed you in check, Ian?"

Ian grew livid and half-rose from his seat. The young blonde newcomer held him back with a hand on Ian's arm.

Pasqual paid no attention whatsoever to Ian's reaction, other than to comment. "Yes," he said. "Exactly. This, it sounds to me, is the same reaction that the bishop brought with him when he returned to the festivities. Then, rather than countering the move that infuriated him," this time Pasqual turned to gaze directly into Ian's eyes, "he chose to create a new queen and sacrifice the move."

Gabriella was silent for a moment, considering this. "You think she left him?" she asked at last.

"I think," Pasqual countered, "that one way or another she is gone. I would not be too quick to gift the Lady Isadora with that sort of independence. She is new to the blood, and at present, her position with the bishop is a favorable one. I believe we have to consider that there is a third party involved."

"Destroyed, then," Ian said, regaining his composure with an effort, "or kidnapped. That becomes the question.

Or a lover's spat?" This from the blonde, the twinkle back in his eye.

"Raphael, you are the only one in this entire group who might believe that," Gabriella laughed. "I'm afraid I have a hard time picturing Alfonzo allowing Isadora to disrupt such an important gathering over personal differences. They might have had their problems, but she knew where her interests lay."

"Did he hunt?" The gruff, half-garbled words would have been startling if Gabriella wasn't so familiar with the voice, and its source.

"Who," she replied, questioning, "Alfonzo? No. He left as soon as the hunt began. Why?"

"Then I think she is ash."

Gabriella measured her next response carefully. Gradin was not like Ian, who could be ruffled and patted and put to bed. Nor was he like Pasqual, coldly calculating and infuriatingly right. Gradin was primal. In ways Gabriella only sensed, she knew the old Gangrel had insights she could only guess at, and others that she would not wish upon her worst enemy.

"Why do you say so?" she asked at last.

"He is too angry to hunt, except in private. He is angry, and there is only one thing to make him so angry. She is truly dead. If not, he would have hunted. Maybe not long, maybe only a show, but he would have hunted." Pasqual nodded, and Ian watched Gradin with interest. It seemed that there were lessons coming from all sides this night.

"I agree that this is the most likely scenario," Gabriella conceded. "But we have to be careful not to be caught off guard, if we are wrong. We must get someone in among his people, and we must, at the same time, look into the matter of Katrina. If he has created this childe, it is possible he is replacing Isadora, and if that is the case, we may be able to bend this to our own use. It would be a sign of weakness, this need for a companion. It is a sign of scorn that he would steal her out from under Licinius' nose without so much as an acknowledgement."

"What is the end result you desire, Gabriella?" Raphael asked. "Alfonzo is obviously courting the favor of many houses. What do you think he has in mind?"

"I don't know, exactly," Gabriella admitted. "It is possible he intends to make a bid to be prince, though it would be premature to assume this. At the very least, he is strengthening his position against whatever is to come next."

"I do not think I would enjoy a Constantinople where Alfonzo ruled," Pasqual observed. "There are others more worthy."

He turned then, gazing at Gabriella soberly. "Don't you agree?"

Gabriella didn't answer, but her thoughts were betrayed by the intensity of her gaze. She had played a large part in the history of the city, and it was obvious that she did not want her involvement in those affairs to end.

"There will be time to discuss such things soon," she said at last. "For now, we need to be certain we understand what we are up against."

They all nodded. Then Gradin spoke again.

"There is another thing." He swept his gaze once around the table, then fixing it on his hands. They were gnarled, clawed, and gave the impression of incredible strength. "The camps are no longer stable. There is talk of moving—nothing set in stone, no destination—just the sensation that it is time for this place to dissolve. The city is not coming back, and the lunatics are coming out of the wilds, claiming to have seen every impossible savior, telling all that they should pull up stakes and move on.

"Others want to build on this place, take root and begin to grow a new place. Licinius will never allow that." Ian nodded. "When I was there last, I heard talk of a new city, rebuilding in some far-off place that would not haunt the builders with dreams of former glory, or remind them of the three. The problem seems to be very much the same as that in Constantinople herself. Who will lead? This place is so full of crackpots and dangerous sects that to get a consensus is all but impossible."

Gabriella listened to them with half her mind, the rest focused back toward the city. What they spoke of was no secret to her. She had, in fact, considered taking a hand in trying to direct this migration—making it a pilgrimage to build a new dream. The problem, as stated, was that it was impossible to lead a mob of those who hated one another, or who had absolute opposite beliefs. Much easier to slip into a seat of prominence in a city as it renewed its strength, guiding that growth and extending power from a stable base.

She rose at last, her hands resting on the table. They all regarded her in silence.

"Enough talk, for now," she said. "I must return to the city before daylight, and we all have plans to make. I will return in two days."

They all rose then, though only Gradin and Raphael followed her out through the doorway. They climbed the stairs quickly and stepped into the last hours of darkness together. The stables were empty save for the horses and mules sleeping there, and they guided her mount out to the road. Gabriella nodded at the two, and swung back into the saddle.

"Until we meet again," Raphael said, waving one hand grandly and performing a bow that would have looked silly on the form of most men, but that seemed to fit. Gradin returned her gaze for a moment, but he did not speak.

Without a word, Gabriella turned and galloped into the darkness.

Across the courtyard, in the shadows of the inn's main building, a dark figure stood, watching Gabriella and the others in silence. He did not move from the shadows until long after they had departed. He stood very still, staring into the distance as if he were looking for something—or remembering.

Most others would have been seen by Gabriella's watchers and agents, but this was no regular eavesdropper. Malachite, elder of the Nosferatu of fallen Constantinople could mold the night into a shroud that would hide him in plain sight or give him the face of another with unparalleled ease.

As the first hint of the dawn blossomed along the skyline, Malachite turned, and slipped into the inn proper, wearing the face of a simple traveler named Adam, and sought out the Venetian clanmate he'd been traveling with under that identity. He had been away for some time, his quest leading him long, lonely, disappointing miles. It seemed, perhaps, that he had returned at the proper moment, if he wanted to be a part of the rebuilding of the dream. There was none other more qualified to see that it was done properly. There was none other as pure in vision.

He'd traveled to the camps to await a message from the oracle who'd set him on his course, but he also needed companions and helpers, those he could sway to his cause. Gabriella's agents were skilled but they could not hide from him and he had followed them here to see what the woman had in mind.

It fit well into his plan. As he pulled the doors closed behind him, he almost smiled.

Chapter Nine

When Lucita and Anatole set out for Bishop Alfonzo's mansion, the dark was incomplete. There was still a light scattering of those who walked the streets by day, but for the moment, Lucita ignored them. She was dressed in a dark cloak that she had pulled up to hide all but her face. Beside her, Anatole was dressed similarly, but in pale wool, moving easily with his hands clasped before his chest.

Lucita knew that they were not alone. Anatole's followers walked the rooftops and the alleys, mirroring their route and watching shadows that were beyond their sight. Lucita was growing used to their presence. She had her own people, but Anatole would never trust them. He was a good companion, but his ways were his own. She could accept that or take a separate path.

They moved slowly, taking in their surroundings. The city was not as bad as it had been in the months directly after the fall, but it was hardly healed. The old Latin Quarter remained important because it was near the ports, but with the old housing restrictions lifted, most of the wealthier merchants had taken over the homes of displaced or murdered Greeks. Here, rubble was still strewn across the floor of every alley, and refuse piled against walls, sometimes stretching into the street itself. There was something in the air that made Lucita wish her feet did not have to make contact with the street to pass. The general cast of the buildings became lower and more debased. The grime and dirt here were worn in from years of neglect, not smashed in by falling walls and marching feet. Windows were dark where elsewhere they would be aglow with candlelight, and balconies were hung with rags.

There were a few places that had not shut down with the daylight, dingy taverns and gambling houses. The scents of sweet mulled wine and smoked meat wafted to the street. The hotter scent of blood, pulsing beyond its cage of skin, was intoxicating. This part of the city was more alive by night than it was by day.

Alfonzo's mansion rose above the rooftops it surrounded, at once incongruous and majestic. The rest of the Latin Quarter leaked out from the roots of the building. Lucita hurried her steps.

"You are too eager," Anatole chided. "We should have waited. Alfonzo must believe that we hold something he wants, but he must also know that the control of what we hold is our own. Too much haste, and he may sense that he has the upper hand."

Lucita slowed her steps slightly. "I'm not concerned with the timeliness of our arrival," she replied. "I'm concerned with how he will react. He may not be pleased that we didn't send the information we had in the first message. You are correct that we don't want to appear too eager, but neither should we be hesitant. Confidence is strength."

Anatole didn't answer. He walked at her side, scanning each side street carefully. There was a sense of—something—in the air. It was the odd feeling of a presence, as if they were watched, or trailed. The city itself seemed aware of their passing, and Lucita felt as if their words, and the patterns of their footsteps, were being transmitted through the very stone. She just couldn't figure out to whom.

They reached the walls of Alfonzo's mansion and moved along the side, glancing into the gardens and alcoves as they passed. Lucita made a mental note to give Alfonzo counsel on the apparent lack of security. She sensed no guards, though it was possible that she was not penetrating the gloom deeply enough to do so. The lack of light would lend strength to the bishop's childer, but would hinder any mortals employed. "He should have more guards," she said, frowning into the last of the small gardens.

"Until the night of his party," Anatole observed, "he had no reason. It has been a long time since any has had the temerity to cross wits or swords with the bishop. Perhaps he has grown too complacent in the aftermath of the Crusade."

"That may be the truth of it," Lucita admitted, "but it does not change the underlying logic. There are always enemies. Some are patient, some are not. If you leave your guard down long enough, one of them will take his opportunity and remove you from the world."

"Always the cynic," Alfonzo laughed softly. "Nothing is ever removed. Things change, shift, warp and recombine." Lucita would have snorted at this, but she knew better than to risk casting Anatole into one of his rants. They were nearing the front entrance, and she threw back the hood of her cloak. Her long hair fell back over the soft material, blending with the deep rich color as if it were part of the fabric.

There was a movement to their left. Anatole turned, dropping into a crouch. A cry rose from the shadows and Lucita slid toward the wall, turning her back to the stone surface and scanning the street. Nothing. There was nothing to be seen, but the sounds of a struggle rose. It was coming from back the way they'd come, off to the left of the road. There was a clang of metal, another quick cry that cut off before it could really begin, followed by a dull thump.

Anatole had moved to her side, and keeping close to the wall, they started back toward the sounds at a run. Lucita had drawn her blade without thinking, the weight in her hand familiar and comforting. Anatole held nothing, but she knew he was as dangerous without a weapon as with one. He was unpredictable. She likened him to a strike of lightning. Absolutely devastating, and impossible to predict or plan against.

They did not have far to go. A sound issued from the darkness, and Anatole stopped. He put a hand on her shoulder to draw her up beside him.

"Wait," he hissed.

He answered the soft cry with one of his own, and moments later, two figures melted from the deep shadows. Between them, they dragged something that trailed in the dirt. As they approached, Lucita saw that it was a body. Both gripped the man by his hair, and one of the two carried him under his free arm.

They did not speak. They stopped a few feet from Anatole, nodded and dropped their burden face down in the street. It was a mortal. He was near death, but not fully gone. One of the two handed over a box, apparently taken from their captive, without a sound. The two stepped back then, awaiting instructions.

"Did he follow us?" Anatole asked sharply.

Lucita recognized the two from the adventure on the rooftop. One was tall and thin, his flesh closer to desiccated leather than skin. He stooped slightly, and she knew he was Nosferatu. No other creature on earth could move so well and look so diseased. His companion was slightly shorter, very broad and sported a mane of hair that sprung out from the sides of his head in wild tangles. Lucita met this one's gaze, only for a second, and she whispered two words to herself.

"Another madman."

"No," was the simple answer. The Nosferatu spoke calmly. "This one was trying to find a way inside. He was in one of the gardens, scratching at a doorway behind a copse of trees."

Anatole nodded. He glanced at the box in his hands, then turned, holding it out to Lucita.

Without hesitation she reached up and flipped the lid open. She stepped back a half-step, then grimaced. Inside was what had once been a skull. The bottom of the box was littered with ash, but there was enough bone left that she could make out the forehead, and long strands of hair wisped from the collapsing bone.

"Isadora." she said, unable to hide the distaste in her voice. "My God."

Anatole shook the box, and the lid fell closed once more. He turned back the way they had been headed, and nodded toward the main entrance.

"We will be late," he said softly.

Lucita nodded and turned, returning to her original course. She didn't look back, but the scuffling sound she heard behind her was enough to tell her that the two were dragging their captive behind. It wasn't the gift she'd intended to offer to Alfonzo, but it would serve. This, along with the information they already possessed, should sway the bishop to the opinion that, at the least, she could prove a strong ally.

"Can't they carry him?" she asked Anatole testily. "If he dies, he will serve no purpose at all, and it will take days for his blood to wear off of the street."

Anatole smiled. He made a simple gesture with his right hand, not looking back, and the scuffling sound ceased. They continued to the main entrance.

The doors opened as they approached. They had been expected, and Lucita was pleased to see that—at least on the surface—they were welcome. The young man, Matteo, stepped clear of the doorway and bowed low. He did not meet her eyes, and his face was flushed. None of this was lost on Anatole, and Lucita grinned.

"Hello, Matteo," she said softly. "Tell Bishop Alfonzo that we have brought him an unexpected gift."

Matteo's gaze swung up, and, managing to tear his eyes from Lucita and glance over her shoulder, he saw the two who followed and what they carried. He eyed the box in Anatole's hands warily, then turned back to Lucita. He nodded.

"He awaits you in the main hall, milady," Matteo said, backing away quickly and leading the way inside. He was moving so quickly that Lucita couldn't quite make out his features, and she didn't want to push. She sensed his heartbeat speeding, and her smile widened. It seemed she had made quite the impression.

As they passed inside, Anatole glanced at her speculatively, but she ignored him. Anatole was wise, but he didn't need to know everything. That would make him boring.

They passed through the foyer and down a dark passage. Lucita could sense the blood that had spilled recently, and realized what she was sensing was the remnant of the hunt. She imagined the bodies piling into this hall, scurrying in every direction and seeking misguided solace in the shadows and alcoves. She could almost hear the voices of the women as they fled for lives long lost, and she shivered. Alfonzo was a showman, but the show was not without its merits.

They entered the large hall and immediately Lucita felt smaller. The room was huge, with a vaulted ceiling stretching toward the sky and walls so remote they faded into the shadows that lined them, giving the impression of the infinite. Across the room, there was a single light. It was a candle, its flame flickering and dancing above the surface of a long table. At the head of that table, leaning against an ornate, carved wooden throne, stood Alfonzo. He watched their approach in silence, but Lucita could feel him taking in every motion, every detail. This was not one to be trifled with. His strength permeated the room. He had made it his own, and they had entered. No matter what came next, he had that advantage. Lucita had no doubt there were others in the shadows, silent and watching.

Ignoring Matteo now that their host was in sight, Lucita and Anatole strode forward with confidence. Despite the situation, they knew that what they carried, and what followed behind them, would grant them a degree of control that they would otherwise not have possessed.

Without a word, Anatole, motioned the two behind to step between himself and Lucita. They did so, dropping their burden to the floor heavily at the foot of the table where Alfonzo stood at the head.

"Who is that?" the bishop asked. If he was more than idly curious, it was impossible to tell it from his voice. If he was upset that their meeting was starting on such a note, he gave no indication. He leaned on the huge chair, watching them carefully, and waiting.

"A good evening to you, as well, Bishop," Lucita said, unable to hide the hint of a smile in her voice.

Alfonzo frowned, just for a second, then his mask fell back into place with an almost audible snap, and he waited.

"We are not sure," Anatole said at last. "We found him crawling about the walls of your home. He was carrying this."

The monk proffered the wooden box, holding it out so that Alfonzo would have to step nearer, giving up his position of assumed control, to open the lid. Alfonzo stared for a long moment, as if considering options, then he stood upright and stepped around the table, approaching his guests.

"I apologize," he said, offering his hand, palm up, to Lucita. "I am not usually such a poor host. This has not been an easy time for me."

Lucita placed her small hand across his, meeting his gaze. "It is a hard time for many," she countered. Without further ceremony, she reached over and flipped up the lid of the box Anatole carried. She watched in silence as Alfonzo looked inside, just for a second, then back. It was not a movement of disgust, or fear, but of pure anger. Lucita saw a wash of emotion cross the bishop's face, very quickly, but filled with a rage that thrilled her, and at the same time put her on her guard.

Anatole flipped the lid closed on the box and placed it gently on the table.

"Where...?" Alfonzo said softly. "Where did you get that?" Lucita kicked the inanimate form at their feet roughly. "He carried it," she said simply. "We only chanced upon him as we came for our appointed talk." She hesitated, trying to gauge Alfonzo's emotions, the continued. "I am sorry for your loss. I wish that I could have been here for the party, but it seems that—perhaps—it was not such an ill fate to be absent."

Alfonzo stared down at the man on the floor. There was still the faint murmur of a heartbeat. They could all sense it. The bishop fought for control. The urge to rip the sack of flesh at his feet into strips and preserve them to feed to whomever had masterminded the attack was nearly overwhelming. They hadn't even come back themselves—they'd sent a *mortal*—and it had taken guests, wandering in off the streets, to catch him.

Alfonzo stepped forward and, using the toe of his boot, flipped the man to his back. He was middle-aged, dark skinned with a Saracen cast to his features. His eyes were closed, and his mouth gaped. His lungs labored for breath, and Alfonzo struggled against the urge to flatten them with a single crushing blow.

"Who is he?" he asked at last. "Do you know?"

"If you mean do we know his name, or where he has come from," Lucita answered, "the answer is no. If you mean do we know who is behind his actions...perhaps." Alfonzo stared at her. He was obviously warring with himself, itching to explode with anger, or self-righteousness. The loss of Isadora had had a greater effect on him than he would let on, but there were emotions that could not be contained.

"I assume," he said at last, "that you have come to share this information with me?"

"Of course," Lucita answered quickly. "I would have sent what I knew with your messenger, but I feared he might be intercepted. Also, truth be told, I'm unhappy that I had to miss your gathering. I have wanted to speak with you for some time, but circumstances have denied us."

Alfonzo still watched her, but the antagonistic glint in his eye had faded to a dull gleam. He stepped back to the table, reached for a large silver carafe, and poured three goblets full of its content. Lucita smelled the blood wine, knew its quality, and she smiled as Alfonzo stepped back to offer two of the goblets to his guests.

"I am sorry for my lack of hospitality," he said. "I have begun to suspect that things are shifting in the city. Those I thought to be allies have shown their true colors, and others I thought to be enemies...."

He let this die and released the goblets as Lucita and Anatole took them gratefully. Lucita watched the bishop's face as he backed away. She could not discern an emotion. He was a master of control.

"Have you made any progress seeking Isadora's killer?" she asked pointedly. She glanced at the box on the table. Alfonzo followed her glance, cursed softly, and turned away. He met her gaze, his expression noticeably colder.

"None." He admitted. "I have hunters out, but so far nothing has been uncovered. They came, and they left, and their passing seems to have been as unnoticed as the wind."

Lucita sipped her wine.

"We have caught the wind," she commented, flashing a short smile. "Sometimes it is only necessary to be in the right place at the right time and in the right company."

Alfonzo fell silent, waiting.

Anatole took a half-step forward. "What have you heard lately, milord, of the Chosen of Calomena?"

Alfonzo stiffened. His countenance darkened, and he drew up and away. He had gathered strength and appeared taller—more imposing. Shadows slid from the floor at his feet to writhe about his ankles, twining upward. Lucita paid him no heed, and Anatole continued.

"You will forgive my question," the monk said matter-of-factly. "I know that you have had your problems with the Chosen in the past. I loathe them, as well. It is an old grudge, deep and binding."

"Are you telling me," Alfonzo asked, "that the Chosen are here? That they have taken Isadora from me and sent this..." He fell silent, but he lashed out with one booted foot, lifting the man at their feet from the ground and drawing forth a loud groan. He gathered his strength. "That they have sent me this messenger to taunt me? I thought that they were gone from the city, possibly gone for good."

"They are not gone," Anatole said softly. "They are as well and as warped as they ever were."

Alfonzo took a long draught of the blood wine. He stared at Anatole, and his stare irritated Lucita into speaking up. She had to hold his attention.

"We were out of the city the night of your feast," she said. "As we returned, we were spotted ne'er-do-wells or intruders crossing the rooftops at high speed, and we pursued. They were leaving your manse, and they were carrying this." She stepped forward and opened the box again for emphasis.

Alfonzo did not look at the box. The stiffening of his frame showed his desire to take a final glance, the morbid curiosity her action had brought forward, but he held himself steady. Lucita continued.

"While Anatole killed their leader," she said, "one of the others escaped over the wall with the remains." She pulled the pendant free of her robes, holding it out to Alfonzo. "I killed a third, and we took this from his body." The bishop was no stranger to Calomena. Her followers had cost him two valued childer in prior nights. Now they had cost him a valued companion and partner, something he might be called upon to explain both to Prince Licinius and to his own sire, Archbishop Narses. The

Venetian prelate would surely receive reports with the first fast ship arriving from Constantinople. Very little escaped Narses' eye.

Alfonzo took the pendant and held it in his hand. He obviously recognized it for what it was. The cold, emotionless face of Calomena stared up at him from his palm, and Lucita sensed the effort it cost him not to crush it between his fingers.

"You found this wretch at my walls?" he asked at last, indicating the prisoner.

Lucita nodded. "He was in one of the small gardens that line your lower story. I would suggest that you place a series of guards around the periphery of your manse. Whatever the rules have been since the Greeks fell, they are shifting."

She waited as Alfonzo stared at the pendant a moment longer then nodded, stuffing it into his pocket without asking if it were acceptable to keep it. Lucita's smile deepened. A debt, however slight, was always an advantage.

The bishop's countenance had darkened another shade, and his eyes grew far away. "I do not know if you have heard the story of my troubles with these...vermin," he said at last. "It seems I am prone to reliving my own failures. When I first heard of the Chosen, of their belief that Caine was a child of the Devil himself, and that they—the clanless and filthy—were to become the instruments of a holy sibling, this Calomena, I laughed. I laughed, and I spoke of them as so much dust to be blown into the night."

He spoke at Lucita rather than to her, unable or unwilling to make eye contact while reliving his troubles. "They are a varied lot. They employ mortals, wild ones with no sense or sanity. They kill those of the blood indiscriminately. They kill suddenly, and without warning. Though many of them—including their leader at the time, Stanislav—are of the blood, they hunt in teams, their belief a bond spanning even mortality.

"At another party much like that just passed, I lost two of my closest progenies. Juliano, and Adrianna. They were not young, but among the first I embraced, and they looked to me for both wisdom and security. I failed. I hunted drunkenly that night, staggered to my own safety before the light, and in that time, the

Calomenan whoresons struck. They came at dawn, slipping in and barring the route to safety. With the sun at their backs, they slew my own as I slept, unaware that those I'd laughed at would laugh last. They were killed, of course, and slowly. Drained and left in the streets, but that cannot bring back what is gone."

Lucita snapped back from the images cast by Alfonzo's story as the bishop turned, raised a hand, and summoned two dark figures from the shadows. Lucita had not sensed their presence, but Anatole did not seem surprised when they appeared. The two were both blonde, very similar in size and appearance, though one was slightly taller than the other.

"Take this away," Alfonzo said, gesturing at the box on the table. "And this." He pointed to the body at his feet, nudging the man with one booted foot. "See to it that he does not die before we have a chance to chat."

The twins, for it was Leonid and Arturo who had melted from the shadows, did not speak. Lucita met their gaze as they moved closer, eying Anatole and her with distrust. Arturo reached for the box on the table, and Leonid squatted, gripped the dying man on the floor by his ankles and dragged him forward.

"Carefully," Alfonzo said, frowning. "I said that I wanted him alive. You may have him when I have finished speaking to him, but I want him alive when I am done here. Am I clear?"

Leonid glanced at Alfonzo for a long moment then back down at the body he held by the feet. With a shrug, he bent lower, gripped his captive's waist in both hands, and lifted him as if he were a feather. With the body carefully held over one shoulder, he moved into the shadows after his brother, leaving the three to their counsel.

"They are not much for conversation," Alfonzo said apologetically, "but they are among my most loyal followers."

Anatole said nothing. He had not reacted to the twins in any way. Lucita had turned, watching the two disappear into the shadows, and she turned back to face Alfonzo, one eyebrow raised.

"Twins?" she asked. "You took them both at once?"

Alfonzo shook his head. "I took one. Isadora took the other. They are bound, a strange bond, one that I cannot explain. I have found them to be both a source of comfort and of strength. They were hunting Isadora's killers themselves, but I have held them back. Had I released them to the night, they might have dragged that one in themselves."

"I believe they were supposed to," Anatole said softly. "I believe a mortal was sent so that there would be no chance that your guards would not discover him before he was successful. If he *was* successful, they would have told the world how you were outwitted by a mortal. If he died—which they expected—he would serve the dual purpose of bringing you the evidence of what they had done, and providing you with the information of who they are. We have done that for you, releasing our mortal friend to his fate. The question remains—what will you do with the information?"

Lucita held her silence. Anatole had voiced her own thoughts, possibly more eloquently than she could have done herself. Alfonzo watched them both then he asked a question of his own.

"I know that Lady Lucita and I have much to speak of," he said at last, addressing Anatole. "I am certain she is here, at least in part, at the insistence of her sire, Mongada. I have expected the visit, and I have planned for it. None of my plans took into account what has come to pass.

"What I do not understand," he continued, "is your own involvement. You've turned up at the last minute in some of the worst moments of our history. Now you have stepped into my world, dragging behind you evidence that an enemy I thought I had vanquished is stalking me on my very doorstep. Why should I trust you, monk? Why should I believe there is any sanity behind those gray eyes and that ashen cloak? Do you read your prayers from the Euagetaematikon?"

Anatole held his tongue for a full minute. "They have hurt me, as well," he said at last. "They do not play favorites, the Chosen. They believe all the children of Caine should die, and that they themselves are exempt. They do not seem to understand that we spring from the same source. I have had my problems with them in the past."

"What problems?" Alfonzo was not accepting the generalities of Anatole's statement.

"Let me end this by saying," Anatole replied, his eyes flashing and his body tensing, setting Lucita near panic, "that we have both lost a childe to them."

Alfonzo stared at Anatole in silence. He did not, at first, seem to be satisfied with the answer, but as it became obvious that it was the only one he would receive, he relented. Draining his cup, he turned to the table and reached for the carafe. Lucita smiled, just for a second.

She drained her glass and when Alfonzo turned back to them, she held it out.

He filled it without comment, as well as Anatole's. "We must put an end to them," Alfonzo said at last. "It is enough that we fight among ourselves over points of shared belief. We don't need insane murderers invading our homes."

Lucita smiled again, this time letting the expression leak free as Alfonzo watched. She raised her goblet, waiting for him to meet it with his own. The bishop stood for a moment, staring at the crystal as it caught the dim candlelight, then reached out and tapped the side of his own goblet against hers.

"We are well met, Lucita of Aragon," he said with a smile. "I had thought we might come together under other circumstances, perhaps even under less than cordial ones, but it seems the fates have planned differently."

Lucita nodded slightly and sipped, watching the candle flame dance. She had to be very careful now. They were in the door, and they were in the bishop's good graces, but she hadn't even begun to walk her intended trail, and she had no way to judge which twists it might take once she did.

"The Chosen are but one of many problems we face," she said at last. "The city is coming back to life, but there is a difference. When the Dream was born, it was controlled. It was carefully crafted and managed. The hands that held those puppet strings are lost to us, and wolves prowl the streets, singly and in packs. It is a shame."

"A shame?" Alfonzo said, watching her as she walked slowly around the table and came to a stop on the far side, raising her eyes to meet his gaze. "How so?"

"It is a shame," she said without looking away, "that there

is no one to take up those strings before it is too late. Once an arm, or a leg breaks loose of its string, even the most talented puppet master will fail to make a good show of it. This city is on the brink of chaos, and with all that has gone before, I find it to be a shame."

"There are many," the bishop countered, "who would say that the so-called Dream was never more than that, a vaporous image conjured by three doddering old fools, and that the collapse was the inevitable outcome of placing too much faith in fantasy and paying too little attention to the realities of the world."

"The realities of this world," Anatole cut in, "tend to lean in the direction of control. A city, a family, even a childe—uncontrolled—is a menace. Nothing powerful can he built on a foundation without focus."

Alfonzo sipped the blood wine and contemplated Anatole's words, seeking the proper response. He was intrigued, Lucita could see it in the intensity of his gaze and the tension in his shoulders, but he was wary. There was no love lost between Venice and Madrid, and Anatole was a rogue in any pack. There was reason to step lightly, and Alfonzo walked the moment like a tightrope.

"There are many realities of this world," he said. "One reality is that three of our most powerful leaders, three who were respected and revered as gods, built something beautiful. For this, eventually, we destroyed two of them. The third, I am told, walks free—somewhere, still dreaming of his perfect city. What do you suppose would happen if he returned? Do you think he could pull together the childer of his lovers and recreate what has died? Or would we destroy him too?

"I ask this, because the question becomes very relevant. Will we always destroy those who lead us? And if so, why would any wish to lead?"

"Leadership has its price," Lucita acknowledged, "but for myself, I will never believe that it is better to leave the leadership to others and share only in their dreams. The past is not the future, though at times it seems to run in cycles. All things can change. There was a time when this might not have seemed true, but all one needs to do is to step to any window in Constantinople and glance outside to know the truth of it."

"There is no new thing under sun or moon," Alfonso intoned. "No, not one."

"Say instead," Anatole commented dryly, "that there is no eternal thing. If a thing is new to you, what does it matter if it is new to the world?"

Alfonzo laughed at that, and it was a full-throated laugh. Some of his caution had slipped away. "Perhaps you are right, monk," he said. "And perhaps there is something to be said for being one who shapes those new things, rather than being shaped by them. I have lived here in the darkest part of this city for a long time. I know the heartbeat, the veins, and the extremities of the lowest levels. I know who knows who, who knows what, and how to bend all of it to my whim.

"The mortals who come to me do so because they believe I am the embodiment of the wrath of God. If they do not believe this, they believe I will make them rich, or powerful. The thieves and the whores cross themselves and bless me when my name crosses their lips. The taverns remain open and the market thrives because I have engineered it. The dream has become the nightmare, and in that transition, those who lived on the fringes of nightmare have come into their own. These are my people.

"Do you know that there are Gangrel in the alleys? Do you know that, though they have crawled all the way from Austria on their four feet, hair sprouting like mangy hyenas and eyes dog-yellow, they answer only to me? Do you know that there are Toreador walking the streets, Michael lost to them and the dream fading, who have shifted their music to other tunes, and their minds to darker pleasures—pleasures I control?

"This city was once so grand. So proper and full of itself. Now, brought to her knees, Constantinople has been brought down to another level. My level, and if she is to get up again, I believe she will do so with my collar at her throat."

Alfonzo's eyes were gleaming, and Lucita held her silence.

"I cannot do this alone," Alfonzo said at last. "As painful as that is to admit, I am what I am. I have strengths, and

I have a great deal of power in this twilight city, but I am not the only one that will be listened to. I am not the only one with influence, and there are those as far away as Rome and as close as Adrianople who would walk to the throne of the new Constantinople, whatever it might resemble, by placing their boots firmly on the back of my head."

He turned to Lucita, staring pointedly. "I would have placed your sire on that list, and you as a likely candidate to take those steps."

The moment had arrived. Lucita took a final sip, then met the bishop's gaze steadily. "I am not cut of the proper cloth to rule," she said simply. "I would wither and die at such a task, and my sire is well aware of this. I am his, but I am also my own. Do you not have the support of Narses himself to fall back on? Surely this is enough..."

"Narses covets Constantinople," Alfonzo admitted, "but whether he does so through me or another—I am uncertain that this matters to him. There are times when his convictions," Alfonzo stopped, sipped his blood wine, and thought for a moment, glancing away into the shadows, "are stronger than any ties of blood. I am not certain, were I to present him with dominion over the city, that he would not draw me away and place another in that seat of power. One he could more easily control."

"You need not present it to him," Lucita suggested carefully, "or to anyone. You might find support in places you had not expected. You might find that those convictions—the ones that Narses would put before blood—are less of a draw than they once appeared."

She hesitated, then continued. "I hear they have sighted Caine near the camps."

Alfonzo snorted, nearly spitting wine. "Yes," he laughed. "They have spotted Caine, and I'm certain the Chosen you chased across the rooftops would speak of how Calomena herself walks atop the city by night. They say that Michael has come and spoken to those who still believe, and that the three will reunite beyond final death to make a more perfect union than they did at the founding of the city. Next, they will say that

Jesus has come among us, offering his blood in return for a roll in a hay barn."

"They are a people without a purpose," Lucita said softly. "The camps were a temporary haven that would house them until the city regained its feet. Those feet were cut out from under her. The Constantinople they are awaiting will never return. They should move on."

Alfonzo stared at her. "Move on? To where? Shouldn't they come back to the city, to their homes?"

"Their old existence is gone," Lucita said with certainty. "They must follow whatever dream has replaced the one that has fallen. They must he *given* that dream, that purpose, and set upon the road away from here. The Frenchman Hugh of Clairvaux tried to give them a new crusade, but left them adrift. Before the future of the city can begin, the past must be put to rest. They are a danger, fermenting like barrels of bad wine, so close to Adrianople that they leak beneath her walls. They will remain a danger, growing wilder and less stable as time passes. They must leave, and soon."

Anatole had listened in silence, but he spoke now. "They were cast out by a crusade and left stranded by another. They should move on in a pilgrimage. Their faith in this city is shattered. The leaders they trusted are gone—some destroyed, the rest dispersed or lost forever. What they have now is a fanatic desire to believe in something, in someone—and they will not turn this direction for that belief. Whatever becomes of Constantinople, in their minds it will ever fall short of the dream." He looked directly at Alfonzo. "And who are we to assume all their visions are empty? Is it wise for the progeny of Caine to deny the possibility that he might speak to any of us? That might be a dangerous oversight. Better to say that it would be in our interest if those he spoke to were located further from our own doorstep."

Alfonzo remained silent. It was obvious from the tilt of his head and the glint in his eye that he was deep in thought, and Lucita thought it wise to leave him with those thoughts, before anything could happen to tilt the scales in some other direction.

"I have enjoyed this talk," she said, "and I am sorry that it took a loss such the one you have suffered to bring us together."

Alfonzo regarded her openly, attempting to see through the layers of her words and her masked emotions to the plot beneath. Lucita allowed the appraisal, standing calmly. Anatole appeared to be lost in thought—or bored. Perhaps he was still thinking about the camps.

"I thank you," Alfonzo said at last, "for what you have brought me, and for your words. I will think on what you have said. Perhaps there is more merit in your counsel than I would previously have believed. We must speak again, and soon."

"And the Chosen?" Anatole cut in. "Whether you hunt them or not, I will not let this rest."

Alfonzo's face darkened. "If they are hidden within this city," he said, "I will find them and I will destroy them. They have to answer to me twice, and I will not let it pass. If you would allow it, I will send Arturo and Leonid to hunt with whatever party you organize."

"Can they be trusted?" Anatole's words were icy, and Lucita feared he had gone too far, just on the verge of success. Alfonzo stiffened, then smiled.

"In as far as they fear me, they can he trusted. They were absolutely devoted to Isadora. You can count on them in any hunt for her killers."

Anatole nodded. "Tomorrow night," he said. "If you can gather intelligence before that, all the better."

Alfonzo nodded, dismissing the subject, and turned to Lucita. "What of Mongada? You have said little of your sire."

"Archbishop Mongada would see a Lasombra on the throne of this city," she replied flatly. "He would not support Narses, because he is not a fool. He does not fear Genoa, but neither is he going to trust. There is the possibility, however, that he might trust one working in his own interests. It is hard to mistrust that brand of honesty."

Alfonzo laughed again. "Indeed," he agreed. "Indeed it is. Go in peace, Lucita of Aragon." He raised his arm again, and this time it was Matteo who emerged from the shadows. He came to stand directly at his master's side.

"See them to the door," Alfonzo said with a wave of his

hand. He turned then, disappearing into the same shadows from which Matteo had appeared.

Matteo was staring openly at Lucita, something dancing just beyond his eyes, a question he would not ask, but that begged to be plucked from his mind and answered. She smiled, and turned toward the door, striding off without looking back. Anatole was at her side, and Matteo scurried to catch up, flushed with embarrassment and something deeper, cutting through his being.

Deep in the shadows, Alfonzo paused and watched the exchange in his hall. He frowned slightly, as Matteo staggered after their guests. Then, thinking of Katrina waiting in the rooms above and of the hunt they would share before the dawn, he dismissed the matter from his thoughts. He could hardly blame Matteo—Lucita was beautiful. Beautiful and full of unexpected surprises.

Lucita could not quite restrain her frustration. "You almost snapped, Anatole. You could have ruined it all." They had returned to Lucita's haven on the edge of the old Latin Quarter, away from prying ears—she hoped.

"Do not worry," he answered. "Alfonzo is well suited for your games."

"Malleable," she said with a smile.

"Faithless, rather."

"He wears the robes of a bishop," she pointed out. "Although a heretic, I'm not so sure—"

"A heretic at least has the courage of his convictions," Anatole answered, "but he is no heretic. Have you ever read the Cainite Heresy's supposed holy texts?"

Lucita thought uncomfortably of the religious instruction she'd suffered at her sire's hands. That had been more than enough guidance for her. "No."

"It is dangerous and demented, simultaneously denying the physical aspects of Caine and lauding the embrace as not only sacred, but a universal good. A transformation to be imposed on all the world."

"I had thought you saw God's work in our condition?"

"Yes, certainly, but that the Curse of Caine can be channeled toward serving God does not prevent it from being a curse. The Heretics preach the embrace erases sin and foresee a world when all the living share in its sacrament."

"Alfonzo's taste in entertainments would certainly fit with a belief in which he were immune from sin," she said.

"True, but the heretics preach other matters, as well. This grand spread of the blood of Caine will come with the reappearance of the Dark Father himself. Their scholars have even called a date for His rebirth into flesh. They calculate it to be one thousand two hundred and six years after his last incarnation, as the Christ."

"But then...."

"Yes, *this* year. The stories of Caine in the camps are drawing heretics like flies and the refugees to the Heresy. But Alfonzo—"

"Dismisses the stories out of hand," Lucita completed. "Indeed."

Chapter Ten

Alfonzo stood on the highest walls of his mansion, staring out over the streets, hovels, secrets and refuse of the Latin Quarter. It had not been so long since he'd thought of Juliano and Adrianna, childer lost to the Chosen of Calomena before the fall of the city. It had not been so long, and yet it seemed an eternity. So much had come and gone in the interim. So many things had fallen or gone away. Stanislav was certainly gone, slain and gone to final death. It seemed that his legacy lingered.

The killing of Isadora had been a symbolic slap in the face. Returning the head in a box was nothing more than a way of showing contempt, taunting the bishop into—what? An attack? A war? The Chosen had been ordered from the Latin Quarter years ago, but in the chaos of the fall of the Greek Empire and the rise of the Latin, they could easily have returned. What was an order to one who believed he moved with divine right? What would Alfonzo's orders be against the promise that dark Calomena would slip in one night from the wilderness and rise to take her rightful throne, deposing those who followed her brother Caine, and smiting vampire and mortal alike in her fury?

Neither his orders, nor the fear of his wrath had been enough to stay their hands in the past. He had learned that lesson on the hard road, twice now. He had no intention of walking it a third time. If Calomena existed, and she was sending her dogs into his world, that was fine with him. Let them come. This time he would show them what Caine's legacy truly meant in a way even the Dark One's sibling might understand.

Still, there was something not quite right. The gesture of

Isadora's death—for that is what it was, in the end, no more than a gesture to them—was very calculated, and calculation had not been Stanislav's weapon, or that of his followers. It was odd, as well, that Mongada's childe would be the one to point out the focus behind the attack. And Anatole. Where did the mad one play into all of it? Too many riddles, and at a time when Alfonzo had other matters on his mind.

He had been rash to take Katrina as his childe. If he had merely killed her, as intended, and discarded her remains along with those of her foolish lover, then no ripple would have been made in society. No one would begin to question his motives, his plan behind the plan. No one would wonder if he had brought this girl—this highborn of Adrianople—into his house with the intent to slight the prince of that city, or to spirit her from beneath his nose. He'd yet to send word to Licinius, but caution urged Alfonzo not to delay much longer. He had acted rashly, but the solution was not to follow up with inaction or hesitation.

Still, there was the chance that Licinius would not even take note of it. He had not spoken for the girl, and in fact, she had been on her way out of the city within days to be raised by nuns, away from the temptations and machinations of court. Latins and Bulgars still threatened Licinius' domains. For Alfonzo to throw himself in amidst all of that might simply complicate a matter already in control.

It had been nearly twenty-four hours since he watched Lucita and the monk depart. He'd sent the twins to the streets, then, noses to the ground like a couple of hunting hounds. News of the Chosen. News of Lucita herself. News of any sort involving the bishop, but first, and foremost, news of the cowardly vermin who'd taken Isadora from him.

Katrina was growing in strength, and rapidly. She was perhaps even more beautiful than Isadora had been, but she was young in both blood and years, impatient and immature. She would take time to mold into a companion of any sort, were that her fate. She had much to learn, and still a bit of what she had been to leave behind. Alfonzo was uncertain of his own patience in the matter. He was growing restless, tiring of the

simple games of the Latin Quarter, and wary of the powers raising their heads about him.

That Lucita remained in Constantinople after Tommaso
Brexiano's departure spoke volumes on the concerns of Madrid.
That Lady Gabriella continued to hang at the outskirts of all
that was happening, keeping quietly to herself at her villa on
the Golden Horn, but extending her claws into the camps near
Adrianople, was another sign. Alfonzo was well aware of her
machinations in that quarter, not that she'd made any particular
secret of it.

And the camps themselves were becoming a problem. They
were taking on too much of the aspect of a lasting settlement.
They were attracting every mindless cult and wandering madman the land had to offer. It was only a matter of time before
they all sought more permanent settlement, and Constantinople
was still too unorganized to resist them. It was only the five-
nights' travel that had kept the refugees from flooding back
over the last year, and the zealots seemed less intimidated by
that distance. Their words already carried weight in the night
streets of the capital. The past had shown, time and again, that
not all madmen were mad. The longer those camps remained,
the greater the chance some real threat would rise from their
midst.

Alfonzo didn't know if the camps were the hole that the
Chosen had crawled from, but his own spies had told him of
mortals walking the streets of the city, claiming to have been
in the camps by night and to have seen Calomena stalking the
children of Caine and drawing her followers to her side. He had
heard rumors of others, as well: Michael the Patriarch returned
from beyond to rebuild his city; Caine appearing in dreams
worrying to lead a final crusade of his own children against
the powers of the land. None of it was anything to Alfonzo but
cabin-fevered madness, but there, again, was the complacency
that had cost him so dearly. It mattered less whether Caine spoke
to those in the camps than whether they believed he did. It mattered less whether Caine's sister would slay every damned soul
in the city than it did what the thought of that wrought in the
minds of the mindless.

It was time for those outside the cities to decide. They must return to rebuild on the crumbled ruins of what had once been, or they must move on. There were ways, he knew, to stir them. He could play into their very superstitions, start rumors of his own. The Red Pentecost, a key ceremony in the Cainite Heresy, had already been celebrated in the camps more than once. He could harness those mad preachers with his own heretical authority. It was so easy to convince the faithful that you believed.

It didn't matter to Alfonzo where they went, only that they left. He had his own worries. Narses, for one, grew impatient with the progress of the new Byzantium. If Constantinople was to be rebuilt, then Narses intended to figure prominently, and he expected that influence to come to him through Alfonzo. Always through another now, never by direct intervention. Alfonzo was beginning to suspect that his sire saw nothing in his childer but pieces on some grand game board, moving them here and there but never risking anything more than a few of those same pieces—nothing personal. Never sharing what was won, only the losses.

Alfonzo glared out at the city. Behind him, he heard soft steps and felt the soft breeze of Katrina's approach. She moved slowly, tentatively. Alfonzo stiffened, then relaxed. Whatever the problems of Constantinople, he could not hope to solve them all in a single night. Better to solve more immediate needs, and leave some of what was to come to those he trusted. Taking Katrina by the hand, he slipped into the interior of his chambers, through the outer doors and into the halls beyond.

The twins moved as one, their long, loping strides in perfect sync, their bodies low to the ground like animals on a scent. There was no scent, of course, not at this late date, and in any case, they were not Gangrel. Still, it was their nature to slink, to move in opposite directions toward a common center, hunting in tandem. They were a product of the bond that had grown between Alfonzo and Isadora, but they were much more than that, as well. They had been born twins, and they had been reborn as darker twins.

Now they had a single purpose. They carried two things. Arturo held the small pendant of Calomena tightly in one hand, and Leonid held a sliver of carved wood from the box that had held what remained of Isadora's skull. By now, it would have held only dust—if Alfonzo hadn't smashed it into the back of one of the mansion's huge fireplaces the moment they'd left.

The bishop's instructions had been clear. Find those responsible, and destroy them. No questions were to be asked, no prisoners taken. Anything that was found would be reported, of course, but by the twins alone. No others would hunt with them—not that they would have allowed it—and no others were to hear what they found before Bishop Alfonzo himself.

They had moved through the streets quickly and viciously, dragging mortal and Cainite alike into the alleys to show them the tokens they carried. The story was the same everywhere they went. No matter how much pressure the two exerted—and more than once they exerted enough that they were forced to move to a new source of information—either no one knew the whereabouts of the Chosen, or no one would tell.

The twins had begun searching near the center of the Latin Quarter, choosing first the darkest side streets and the least-traveled roads, and worked their way outward in a slow spiral. More than once they'd been forced to secret themselves in a dark alcove or on a rooftop to await the passing of some other, grander predator. These were all familiar dangers, not enemies exactly, but not any the twins would have cared to trouble over this search.

They were waiting above the streets, watching from a dark balcony leading into an empty, decrepit room when two voices rose from below, and the twins slid to the edge of the balcony, crouched and ready, listening. The voices were not familiar, but they were calm. Whoever it was, they were not frightened by the prospect of traveling the Latin Quarter by night, thus they were to be respected. For the moment.

"I'm telling you," a gruff voice nearly spat, "Alfonzo is no fool. He will remember these Chosen, and he will not sit still for this. What could they possibly hope to gain?"

"You are no doubt correct," a lighter voice replied, "but still

I'd like to know who is behind it, Gradin. I, for one, don't believe that the Chosen exist anymore. Or," he hesitated a second, "if they do, I don't believe they have changed from the fanatical hatred of all the childer of Caine to a personal vendetta against the bishop."

"Raphael, you are too quick to dispose of revenge as a motive. Their own leader is dead, this Stanislav. Alfonzo is reputed to have had a hand in that."

"I discount nothing," Raphael responded. "It just doesn't ring true this time. Too much planning, too much care. I have heard stories of the Chosen, how they train mortals in their ways and send them raving into crowds before the temples and synagogues, slaying at random, crying out to their dark savior to deliver them. Dying like dogs."

At that moment, at a quick nod from Arturo, Leonid dropped over the edge of the balcony to light on the ground a few feet ahead of the pair. His twin dropped to their rear, sliding into the shadows. Both moved silently, but Gradin had dropped to a crouch with the first whistle of flesh through the air, and Raphael had drawn up against the wall on the far side of the street, shoulders pressed to stone, fist wrapped tightly about the hilt of his sword.

"Who are you?" he asked, watching Leonid carefully. "Who is that with you? Have him show himself."

Arturo made no move to do so, at first, taking a moment for effect. The effect was nearly lost, as Gradin trembled, ready to launch to his left, where he sensed Arturo hovering in a porticoed entrance.

Leonid stepped into the center of the street. "Just who you are is the question," he said, his voice low and whispered, though it carried down the deserted street powerfully. "Who are you to speak so of His Excellency, and what do you know of Calomena?"

Raphael pushed free of the wall, but he did not release his blade.

"Who are you to ask?" he replied, though he knew full well. Such as the twins would be nearly impossible to hide, even in the Latin Quarter, and rumor of their hungers, and their oddities had spread to the camps, and very likely beyond. No reason to let them know they'd been recognized too soon, so Raphael repeated his question.

"Who are you to ask?"

"We seek those who have done harm to our bishop," Arturo cut in from the side. "We seek news of their location, or their movements."

"And you have found nothing?" Gradin asked, stepping closer to Raphael, so they both stood with their backs protected by the same wall. Neither was especially concerned by the pair they faced, but they were cautious. There were the stories, after all.

"We have found what we have found," Arturo said, strutting closer. "We have found the two of you skulking about the streets and talking of our Lord as if it were your business. That is more than nothing, I think."

"Oh, much more," Leonid agreed, slipping up to his twin's side. "Far more. Maybe you know more than you pretend? Maybe you knew we were hunting and thought you'd toss a few words to the wind and draw us down?"

"If that had been our plan," Raphael laughed suddenly, "We would certainly seem a success in our endeavors."

Arturo scowled. "Perhaps you underestimate what you do not know," he said softly. "We have our orders."

"You would be equally well counseled to know your enemies," Gradin growled, growing impatient. "You have no quarrel with us, nor we with you. Nor do we care a whit about the Chosen, other than that they are on the lips of all we pass. Where are they? Why are they here? Are they here? Why do they target the bishop?"

"The same questions," Raphael added hastily, "that you seem to be attempting to answer. You say you have been hunting? May I ask, how far? How long? None know these back streets as the two of you, or so I am told. What news do you bring?"

"If we had news," Leonid stood a bit straighter, "We would share it only with our Lord Alfonzo. As it happens, we have none. Only the further reaches of the Quarter remain, and if we find nothing—then they lay beyond. The city itself, some other den—the camps."

"We have word from the camps," Raphael spoke up quickly. Gradin glared at him, but he continued without hesitation. "There is talk there of the Chosen, of course. It is much as here, though. Talk. As far as I've seen, or heard, there is no stronghold of the Chosen in the camps, and if there were, it would not be easy to hide. For one thing, their mortal followers are not given to caution or silence. So I'm told. All we hear are rumors, and most of those are of the city, and the Quarter."

The four stood, facing off uncertainly. It was obvious that the twins were itching for a reason to start trouble. Gradin himself seemed unopposed to the idea, but Raphael was the very vision of stability and reason. He knew Gabriella would never forgive them the wasting of such an opportunity to delve more deeply into Alfonzo's affairs, and she would be furious if they angered the bishop by killing his favorite pair of hunting dogs for no more reason than that they were irritating. Besides, they were not on an idle stroll, and the night was passing.

If things went sour, the two would be but a moment's entertainment for Gradin—another fact they needn't give away too easily, even to Gabriella herself. She knew them only as travelers seeking a cause. No reason she should know their heritage, and a thousand she should not.

"How do we know you do not lie?" Arturo said at last. "How do we know you haven't come from the Chosen themselves on a second mission to our lord? How do we know you don't bring another death to Alfonzo's house?"

"Death?" Gradin said, his word half a question, half an exclamation of surprise. "Whose death? We knew of no death, only that you sought the Chosen, and that they had disrupted Alfonzo's party."

Leonid looked uneasy, but Arturo continued. "The Lady Isadora," he said softly. "My sire, Isadora. She was destroyed by the vermin who bore this." He held forth the pendant, an icon of Calomena, and Raphael committed the design to memory. "They came in a group, stole in like rats over the walls, and they killed. For this, they will be destroyed."

Raphael blinked and said, "I did not know that she was your sire," he said softly, "nor did I know, until this moment, that she had met her final death. We had heard rumors this was possible, but there were other rumors, as well. No one is certain what took place that night, only that the bishop was very upset by it."

"You would do well," Leonid said, gripping his brother by the arm and pulling him away gently, "to forget that you know it now. It does us no harm that they are unaware. His Excellency is not without enemies, and it is perhaps better that he not appear to have suffered too great a loss."

As he spoke, Leonid gazed deep into Raphael's eyes. He seemed to be waging an inner struggle, and for just a second, an expression of confusion crossed Raphael's features. Then this cleared, and he smiled, nodding to the twin, and winking. "We never met," Gradin said roughly, pushing away from the wall and eyeing Leonid and Raphael curiously. He hadn't missed their silent exchange. "We never spoke, and we two have no further interest in yourselves, or the Chosen." He hesitated, waiting to see how his words would be received.

Raphael bowed low, though his gaze never left the two faced off against him, and he spoke a final time.

"Good hunting," he said.

The twins stood uncertainly, wanting more from the chance meeting, but sensing that they had gained all there was to gain. It seemed that Arturo suddenly became as aware of the passing darkness as Raphael himself, and he took a step back.

"We have no more time for questions," he said, as though it had been Raphael and Gradin who had detained them, and not the reverse. "There is not long before the dawn."

Without a further word he turned and leaped at the nearest wall, sending tendrils of shadow before him like the tentacles of some ancient kraken. His twin leaped scant seconds after, and in perfect time. A second set of shadows reached the walls, sliding up like vines grown rampant, weaving with those of his brother until the shadows were so completely meshed that the wall was obscured. One moment they had stood, haughty and distrustful, the next they were gone, leaving only a small trail of dust to trickle down from the rooftop in their passing.

"So," Raphael, said, turning slowly to his companion, "Isadora is indeed murdered."

Gradin was silent. He turned and continued the way they'd been traveling, lost in thought. After a few short blocks, they turned left into an alley, skirted around a pile of refuse, and came to a halt beside what appeared to be a solid wooden wall. Rats scurried from beneath their feet, and the stench of rotting food was horrible.

Gradin reached up and smacked the palm of one hand into the wall three times. He paused, then knocked once more. A louder thump that echoed through the darkness.

A panel slid open in the wall, and the two slipped inside, letting the wall snap back into place behind them as if it had never opened. The rats returned to feasting on the piles of garbage, and the moon passed overhead, on her way to dawn.

The club's interior was dim. Smoke wafted from the main room, where meat was being roasted and served to an unsavory mortal clientele. In the corners and at the ends of the bars, small groups of patrons met. Gradin shouldered his way to the bar between two burly men and planted his elbows on the bar. Raphael slipped up beside him, taking advantage of the hole his partner had brought about, but shaking his head at the lack of subtlety.

Gradin growled at the rat-like bartender, who only glanced up long enough to pin the voice to a face before moving through the curtains behind the bar and into a back room. This was an establishment that catered to all the needs of the Quarter, and the two were well known. There was no need to place an order.

A moment later, the man returned. He held a large iron key in one hand, but he did not offer it immediately.

"Who's paying?" he said, glancing up at Raphael, past Gradin's groping hand. "Last time I saw the two of you, I ended up with an empty purse and a cuff to the side of the head for my trouble. I'm not falling for your game twice."

"And well you should not," Raphael replied, smiling widely. "Of course, you realize that was a terrible misunderstanding.

I thought my friend here," he gestured at Gradin, who rolled his eyes in exasperation, "had paid you upon our arrival, or I certainly would not have given you the trouble that I did on our departure."

"Who's paying?" the man repeated, taking a step back toward the curtains. "No gold, no key."

This time Gradin did growl, and started over the counter after the impertinent barkeep. Raphael restrained him carefully. It was a long-practiced dance, and Gradin allowed himself to be held back, barely. His eyes were red flecks of fire, and his lips were parted, as if he were panting with hunger.

"I understand your concern," Raphael said again, "but there is no need to be rude. My friend, as you can see, is very hungry. If we don't do something about this soon, and I assure you, I mean very soon, then I can't be held responsible for the outcome."

The man stared at him, unflinching.

"It has been a *very* long time," Raphael added. Gradin, meanwhile, was trying again to climb over the bar and grasp the key. The man backed slowly again, glancing uncertainly over his shoulder. Raphael knew that, while the bar was tended by mortals, they would not be the only force to reckon with. Their actions were staged, intended to create the diversion that they were creating, and no more. Judging that they'd gone far enough, Raphael reached into a pouch at his side, widening his smile.

"Here, here," he said, tossing a small handful of gold coins to the man almost carelessly. "I really don't see what you are going on about. It isn't as though we were trying to steal from you, now is it?"

The man didn't respond, but he caught the coins deftly from the air, and they disappeared into the folds in his clothing in an amazing display of dexterity. Without another word, he stepped forward, not quite close enough for Gradin to reach him, and tossed the key. Gradin, who'd been waiting for just such a move, stepped back and caught it, straightened himself and nodded to the bartender.

Raphael watched as his shorter, stouter companion turned

away from the bar and made his way toward the back of the building. Gradin was holding the key where anyone watching would see, twirling it around one finger and licking his lips. There were murmurs, grunts, and a few short bursts of laughter at his passing. Raphael watched until Gradin had disappeared into the shadowed nether-regions of the bar, where a heavy satin curtain covered a doorway leading to the rooms in back. Each room was equipped for the particular needs of the customer. The room Gradin would open with his key would have chains on the walls, a young, very alive meal dangling, and privacy for the meal.

Gradin's room would have something more. The bartender, while he knew every nook and cranny of this pit, and most of the faces that slid in and out of it, did not know everything. He didn't know, for instance, that Gabriella was the money behind the place. He didn't know that the very capable bouncers in the next room reported as often to Raphael himself as to anyone, and he didn't know that the annoying, cocky, and far-too-clever Cainite he served so often was checking up on his operation, the darker sides of other patrons, and checking for messages from Genoa, which would arrive in the form of the snack-of-the-day hanging in a certain room, at a certain hour. It was better this way, and certainly best that Alfonzo know little or nothing of the place.

The bishop's people frequented the club as often as any, but they assumed it to be just another part of the Quarter under their master's sway. Alfonzo exacted tribute for his protection, and made it very clear that without his protection, he was the thing they must fear the most. Gabriella made certain that the fees were paid on time, and proper obeisance was shown. Even the bartender believed he was Alfonzo's man.

The other regulars thought they knew Raphael and Gradin well. They knew the two would steal the beard from a blind beggar given the chance, that they were hungry, bloodthirsty, and fought dirty, and that they enjoyed a good time. They could be counted on to bilk the bartender out of the payment for whatever form of late-night entertainment they favored in a given moment, to start at least one fight and to entertain everyone.

Already wagers were hitting tables all over the room on how long before Gradin returned, and in what kind of humor.

Raphael's smile widened, just for a moment, and he called to the bartender for a glass of the house's special wine. The man eyed him with equal parts distrust, and distaste, and Raphael barely contained a laugh. Of all the checkpoints he and Gradin would hit in the period of a week, this was one of his favorites. The two had worked their act to perfection over a period of years, but it never ceased to amaze him how much simple fun could be found in making fools of others.

Raphael turned his back to the bar and scanned the crowd, looking for any new, interesting, or important faces. The usual crowd was tossing a set of bone dice on the corner table, and a small group of dark-cloaked soldiers leaned back heavily in solid wood chairs circling a wooden table near the center of the room. They were getting louder, calling for drinks almost as often as they bellowed in laughter at one another's increasingly slurred commentaries on life, love, and the other patrons of the tavern. Spoiling for a fight.

Raphael glanced toward the back of the room, but there was no sign of Gradin. With a sigh that barely dipped the tips of his smile, he pushed off the bar, raised his goblet in a mock-salute to the bartender who'd yet to quit watching him warily. He took a gulp and moved closer to the table where he could hear the soldiers more clearly.

They were mortal mercenaries, either come here with the Crusade or to fight the Bulgars and Greeks, but they had fallen into the service of the night-born prelate who lived near here. The conversation of the moment was centered on certain of the serving women who served in the bishop's kitchens, and the lack of social graces and morality among the same. Raphael listened intently, wondering if they'd slip into any details more intriguing than rubbing their hairy flesh against that of the willing or not-so-willing women of Alfonzo's house. One of the men glanced up and caught sight of Raphael standing nearby.

"What are you looking at?" the man grunted. "Go back to the bar, little man, and bring me beer. You do that for me, maybe I won't use you to show my men here what young Helena and I were about last night."

Raphael's smile widened perceptibly. He took another gulp of his wine.

"As tempting as that offer is," he said with a half bow, "I will have to beg off. I rarely involve myself in bending over tables with so fresh an acquaintance, and in any case, I have a preference for the young, slender, and athletic." Raphael stepped closer again, and he watched the man carefully, intrigued by the way the blood rushed to fill the ruddy features, and the way those features contorted into a very presentable likeness of a gargoyle in a very short amount of time.

"Really, chough," Raphael continued, "you do have the advantage here. It seems you have liberated and carted away with you at least one barrel of beer already," he nodded at the man's prodigious gut, "so you'll not go thirsty if I decide not to be your waiter this night."

The soldier's friends pushed back a bit from the table, making no move to help their friend, but leering at Raphael with expressions that clearly said they did not believe he would be with them much longer. Raphael set his goblet carefully on the table.

"You talk like a girl, or a pretty boy," the soldier growled, wiping a ham-sized fist across his filthy lips. "I don't know which I hate more."

"My, you are having a bad night." Raphael brought his hand to his chin, tilting his head to one side, as if in deep thought. "Do you think maybe your belt is too tight? Your boots the wrong size? I really don't know what I can do to help."

The man roared, lurching from his seat and reaching for Raphael, or where Raphael had stood. The man stumbled into the next table, his belly striking wood and whipping his chin down to crash into the table's surface directly beside a wine goblet belonging to a tall man Raphael recognized as a Lasombra trader.

Raphael moved in quick as a cat. He caught the spinning goblet, stopped it, and replaced it on the table with a glance that said "I'm sorry, but what can I do?" to the Cainite, and grabbed the soldier by his dark, filthy hair. He lifted the man carefully from the neighboring table, not spilling any further drinks, and turned him easily, holding him at arm's length as he watched the blood that had been so eager to suffuse those porcine features draining back toward his feet.

"You slipped," Raphael observed, tossing the man back toward his chair, where he hit with a *thump*, crashed into the back of the chair, and tipped over backward, boots flipping into the air. As he did so, he kicked the table, sending it crashing over toward his friends, beer and wine flying. Raphael nimbly plucked his goblet from the air as it flew up, turned, winked at the Lasombra whose wine he'd already saved, and took another drink.

Now there was pandemonium. The rest of the mercenaries had decided at once that Raphael was more than they had bargained for, and someone they needed to kill to save face. They rose as a unit, barely avoiding the crashing table. Now, with their companion flat on his back and groaning, there were four, blades drawn.

"Hey now," Raphael said, saluting them with his goblet, draining it in a single gulp, and tossing it over his shoulder. He heard a short laugh and knew that the Lasombra had caught it and placed it on the table. Raphael stood, watching the wavering, drunken group before him with interest.

"It seems," he said finally, "that your friend doesn't walk as well as he talks. And these chairs," Raphael kicked one of the other chairs for emphasis, "well, they certainly *look* balanced, but...."

Two of the mercenaries lunged. For all their drunken appearance, they moved quickly and in unison. They had fought together before, many times, and they fully expected their blades to bisect Raphael's center and leave him in much the same position as their fallen comrade, only more permanently.

Raphael leaped. The blades passed beneath him as he seemed almost to hover at the top of his jump, bringing his legs up in the air. Then he was coming down, as the blades shot back, their shocked owners still not certain what had happened. Raphael caught the edge of the toppled table with his boots and pistoned his legs downward. It flew up, legs beneath it once again, and Raphael flipped back, landing a few feet away, beside the table where his goblet had been left. He glanced down and saw with a smile that his new friend had refilled it from a flask in the center of the table.

The mercenaries were staring at him, blades at their sides, hesitating between anger, confusion, and terror.

The first of them was finally getting to his feet, looking groggily about the room, belligerent as a charging bull. It was then that a door in the back of the tavern slammed open. Gradin came barreling in, wide-eyed and growling.

"What in all the hells is going on out here?" he bellowed. "Can't a man have the peace and quiet his gold can buy? Eh?"

"There is a problem," Raphael called out with a laugh. "The furniture keeps leaping on people, and the beer seems unsatisfied to linger in the glasses."

Gradin stared at his partner as he might have stared at some large and very odd bug. He stalked from the back to the center of the room, banging chairs and tables aside, jostling the few customers not quick enough to move out of his way. There were flecks of fresh blood on his lips, and his collar, and his wild hair shot out to the sides of his head and face at crazy angles. He resembled a wild animal more than a man at that moment, and everyone in the room with the exception of Raphael himself, and the smooth, dark-haired vampire seated behind him, had begun to back away.

"I was hungry," Gradin rasped. "I was...feeding."

"And a fine, messy job you've made of it," Raphael laughed, noting the blood stains on Gradin's cloak. "Still, you seem not much merrier for a fine repast that—I might add—I did not share."

Gradin spat.

The first mercenary spun, hearing the approaching footsteps, and he lunged for Gradin as he had for Raphael, the rap of floorboards on his skull having done his sense of strategic action no good whatsoever. Gradin did not sidestep. He didn't move at all. He stood, watching the maniacal figures rushing

David Niall Wilson

at him across the room, and he reached up absently, brushing at the droplets of blood.

It took only a moment. The huge, drunken mercenary slammed into Gradin's smaller, stooped form. There was a sickening crunch as the two met, and then, oddly, the soldier continued on. He was running in the air, several feet off of the floor, and Gradin was stalking straight toward Raphael, as if nothing had happened.

Raphael, unruffled, motioned to the bartender, and grudgingly, the man produced another goblet, bringing it warily around the bar and holding it out to Raphael, who winked, took the goblet, and passed it to Gradin who drained it in a gulp.

Moments later, the tavern erupted in cheers. The mercenaries, those remaining on their feet, stumbled to the back, dragged their bruised and bleeding companion to his feet and out the door, muttering under their breath about demons and threatening to tell some unknown power of what had befallen them. They were washed from the room on gales of laughter, and Raphael, sensing his moment, turned and extended a hand to the Lasombra at the table.

"I am Raphael," he said with a smile, "and my hairy friend is Gradin. May we join you?"

The young-seeming Cainite glanced up with a grin and motioned to the chairs to either side of him. "It would be my pleasure," he said. "I am Francesco de Valente, and I must say," he added, "that this was the finest entertainment I've had since leaving Rome."

Chapter Eleven

The three shared blood wine, swapped stories, and watched as the patrons who had witnessed Raphael and Gradin's antics came, went, and were replaced by others. At some point, Francesco rose, stepped to the bar for a few hasty words with the bartender, who continued to watch their table warily. There was some shuffling, and the bartender eventually made yet another trip back behind the bar for instructions. In the end, the three were escorted to a private room in the building's upper floor, where they could converse more easily and freely.

"It is a long way from Rome," Gradin said as they seated themselves. "There must be many stories you could tell of your journey."

"There are always stories," Francesco replied with a quick smile. "Would you rather hear the famous ones, the ones that all travelers tell of places they claim to have seen, or would you hear the bleak reality? It is not such an interesting road, most of the time. The dangers are overrated, the cities laid waste by the Crusade and the Bulgars are only now on the mend. I've heard of caravans overloaded with the undead adding to the mess in Thrace. It is a poor time to travel, if you are of good spirits and inclined to fun."

"There has been little time for fun," Raphael interjected. "Too much is at stake now. Too many have left, fallen, or been destroyed, and those who remain are less focused. Rather," he added thoughtfully, "they are too self-focused. What was once a dream has become a scattered cluster of nightmares. As much as one might enjoy entertainment, it will be many nights before anything honestly resembling it surfaces."

"You are a dour one," Francesco intoned with a wry grin. "Still, while it may have been a show, and a particularly good one, I saw your expression as you played with those downstairs. Existence is never without its amusements, and you strike me as a pair rich in both experience and amusement. Tell me I am wrong."

Gradin actually chuckled, and Raphael turned to him in amazement, then laughed. "Guilty," he replied, sipping his drink. "But that changes little. What brings one so far from Rome? There is little that goes in or out of that city that has no importance. What can you tell us?"

"I know little of what is happening in Rome," Francesco replied. "I have been on my own for a very long time. I have been sent to check in with one of my own, but I am told I have come to the city too late." He drained his glass, then he met Raphael's gaze. "I was to have met with the Lady Isadora."

All humor left Raphael's face, and Gradin slowly lowered his goblet to the table, his brow furrowed.

"You know, then?" Raphael asked softly.

"That she is destroyed?" Francesco asked. "Yes, I know. I have known for some time, though the reports had her angry, run away from the bishop, or secreted in the camps and plotting to overthrow the city. I have spoken with several who witnessed the scene at the Venetian heretic's party. I know that she is no longer with us, and I know that—despite the things I have heard that lead me to despise him—Bishop Alfonzo was devastated by the loss." Francesco hesitated, then continued. "What I do not know is who, and why. I have no idea what enemies the bishop may have earned after the city fell, or what powers he may have aligned himself with. I have been to the camps near and they are rife with odd rumors. Since they make no sense to me, I have come to see what I can find on my own."

"And what is it that you have found?" Gradin inquired, reaching for his goblet once more and relaxing slightly.

"I have found," Francesco chuckled, "that the inns and taverns of Constantinople are filled with some very interesting characters. I have found that rumors fly faster than eagles when powered by wine, and I have found that no one seems to have any idea why Isadora is dead, or who might have killed her. Not even Alfonzo, as I have spoken with one of his servants this very night, and learned nothing."

"It might be," Raphael said guardedly, "that we have some information you would find interesting. Of course," he winked at the Roman across the table from him, "information demands its own. Nothing is ever free."

Francesco regarded him skeptically. "You know who felled Isadora?" he asked pointedly. "That is, of course, the only information I am currently seeking."

"I don't know a name," Raphael admitted, "but I have information that could lead to one. You aren't the only one who has had a conversation with Alfonzo's minions. Those who we spoke with, however, were a little closer to the top."

Francesco waited, then, seeing that he would have to offer something first, leaned in to the table conspiratorially. "Well, I did hear a few things on the road," he admitted. "One thing in particular I believe you might find interesting. There is one who is headed back to the camps—or already in the camps—that could well be a factor in the future of the city."

Gradin and Raphael shared a quick glance, then returned their attention to their companion.

"Who might that be?" Raphael asked slowly. "Caine himself? I have heard those rumors too many times already.

"Not Caine," Francesco admitted, "but I saw Malachite myself, and if he is not in the camps now, he will be there very soon. He believes, still, that he can find the Dracon, drag him back to Constantinople and revive the dream. He speaks as a madman, but for all of that—others listen."

"And he is in the camps?" Gradin growled. "You know this?"

"I caught word that he was coming when I was there, and saw him on the road between Adrianople and here. If there has been time for me to reach the city at my leisurely pace, I am certain that same time was sufficient for his arrival in Hadrian's city."

Raphael nodded. "If he intended a week ago to be there, he is there. That is indeed news. I had heard, of course, that he was returning, but then, I have also heard that he found the Dracon—that he was headed to France—and that he had been destroyed. My sources said he had headed into Anatolia. If he is now in Thrace, then what does that mean? Why not return here, to the city where some would make him prince?"

"He had not found the Dracon when I spoke with him," Francesco replied. "Unless he found him on the road to the camp, he is still alone, but looking to gather strength."

"To what end?" Gradin asked, leaning forward. "Without the Dracon, he cannot succeed in his quest. Will he take these followers with him on the search?"

"That I do not know," the Roman shook his head. "I know only what I saw, and the few words I heard in passing. He is unpredictable, and I had a mission of my own to pursue. I didn't ask questions."

Raphael thought about this for a few minutes, then, nodding slightly, he leaned forward again. "Have you heard of the Chosen of Calomena?" he asked quietly.

Francesco watched Raphael's face carefully, apparently saw what he was looking for, and nodded.

"Of course. They were broken when their leader, Stanislav, was destroyed. Killers of their own kind. Worse heretics than our fair bishop. Why do you ask?"

"Perhaps not destroyed," Gradin cut in. "Perhaps very active, as a matter of fact. We have heard that those who killed Isadora were just such followers of the dark queen." Francesco shook his head. "To what purpose would this killing be directed, then?" he asked. "They have no argument with Isadora, or Rome, other than the obvious desire to see us all cut down, burned, and destroyed. Why go to such elaborate lengths for one death?"

"The bishop has a long history with the Chosen," Raphael replied. "He lost two childer to them prior to the fall of Constantinople. He played a hand in destroying their leader. While it makes little sense that such a fanatical group would begin to target their victims with precision and planning, in this case there might be an exception. If the Chosen still exist, and they are aware of what the bishop has done to thwart their efforts, they might send a message."

"The bishop's trained dogs are in the streets," Gradin growled, "hunting as we speak for just the ones we speak of. They have been working their way out from the center of the Latin Quarter, and have found nothing. No sign of Calomena, or her followers, either mortal or Cainite."

"It could be a ruse," Francesco said slowly. "If Alfonzo has a known quarrel with the Chosen, who might gain by angering him and sending his forces in different directions by such a distraction? Surely, if they were holed up in this Caine-forsaken slum, these followers of Alfonzo would have flushed them out? Unless we are talking a group only one or two strong, where would you hide them? Fanatics are not the silent type, and they would hardly be confining their work to the bishop's house alone. Have there been other deaths attributed to them?"

Raphael shook his head. "I have heard nothing else about them, but Constantinople is hardly the city it was. There could be room for them to hide in the ruined homes of Greeks. And you know the stories that circulate in the camps."

"In any case," Francesco said at last, draining his goblet and rising slowly, "there is little more to be gained this night. The dawn is not far off, and I have a ways to travel before I reach safety."

Raphael and Gradin rose as well, and Raphael extended his hand once again. "It has been a pleasure," he said with a grin. "I don't get to say that often enough, so I thank you."

"The pleasure was mine," Francesco laughed. "I had expected a night with no more interest than those of the past few, questioning idiots who insist on being plied with beer and then confide the wondrous secret that they can find me a good time, if I only have a few more drinks' worth of gold and the time. Gathering information in this city can be like picking one's teeth. Bits and pieces fly all around, if you are rough, but only the careful pluck will leave the morsel stuck on the pick."

Gradin laughed again, clapped the Roman on his back soundly, and turned toward the door. "We'd better be off ourselves," he said. "And I don't think we'll be leaving the Quarter this night."

"Too late," Raphael agreed. "We'll have to visit your friend the bartender one final time and arrange for quarters. I swear, if he goes into that back room one more time and is ordered to serve us, he may snap and go for your throat with a carving knife."

"It would be a shame," Gradin laughed. "I am fond of that one. I would hate to have to kill him."

The three exited the room, Francesco turning toward the street, and the others toward the bar, where their friend the bartender waited, scowling at their approach. Before they could reach him, he turned, and entered the back room with a resigned slump to his shoulders.

Gradin laughed. "It seems," he said softly, "our friend will last yet another night."

Beyond the walls of the tavern, the last of the night was scurrying into corners and crevasses, pulling everything that did not belong to the daylight in behind it. Windows were closed, as others began to open. Doors were barred, and with a *thud* of finality, the tavern door joined the others. Gradin and Raphael walked to the stairway in the back of the tavern and started down, a heavy key ring dangling a single iron key in Raphael's hand. He moved slowly, the sluggishness of dawn in his limbs, but there was still time. The bartender watched them go toward their room, his eyes narrow and dark. He polished the same goblet for so long that he noticed, suddenly, that his fingers had grown hot from the action, and the knuckles of the hand holding the stem of the goblet had gone white. With a growl, he turned, and exited through the doorway to the back of the tavern a final time, cursing under his breath.

"You'll get yours," he said softly. "One of these days, you hairy bastard."

His words were too soft to echo, but they lingered in the air as he passed into the kitchen and out into the predawn haze, shrugging the cares of tavern and night off with a heavy yawn.

In the distance, a cock crowed, and the bartender rubbed his eyes blearily. When the blow fell, he didn't even see it coming, and there was no struggle as he was dragged quietly back through the doorway and into the tavern, or as the door was closed with quiet finality.

Unconscious, he began to snore.

Lucita and Anatole stood, once again, at her balcony. The darkness was passing swiftly, and there was little left to the night, but they waited. Anatole had many followers, not all of them bound by the darkness, and the two awaited word. Stories had come to them the night before, both from the camps, and from the Latin Quarter, and what they learned this night might well decide the fate of a city.

There were too many forces on the move. In the camps, all were restless. Those gathered there met in public more frequently, crossing boundaries of clan and belief, listening intently to the stories of inspiration and madness. There was an energy crackling through those dark hovels and dingy streets that had little to do with either Adrianople or Constantinople. It was the sort of energy waiting to be directed at something, and Lucita knew that it must be directed *away* from Byzantium. Things were too delicately balanced, as it was.

And someone was out there. That much she had sensed herself, someone old and powerful. Watching and waiting. Dozens of names entered her mind and exited as swiftly. In the end, it did not matter. If a Lasombra was to be prince, and if she were going to ensure that the Bishop Alfonzo would be that prince, she would have to act swiftly and decisively.

On the street below, a shadow melted from an alley and stopped, just for a moment, to glance up at them. Anatole nodded, and the man scaled the wall without further hesitation and slid over the edge of the balcony.

Lucita slid a sidelong glance at Anatole, raising an eyebrow. "Must it always be so dramatic?" she asked. "We do have a doorway and stairs."

Anatole remained silent, and his agent stood quietly to one side, awaiting instruction.

"What have you found?" Anatole asked.

"I spotted two men known in the camps spending their night in the Latin Quarter, in the tavern on Lambas Place. They met there with Francesco de Valente, from Rome, and they did not come out. The Roman left. He is Lasombra, but not of great importance."

"And the others?" Lucita cut in. "They were there as well?"

"No." The answer was quick and certain. "But just as I was turning to leave, two mortals, touched by the blood, but not turned, appeared at the tavern. They took the bartender, and they slipped inside. They were robed, and it was too dark to tell who they might be. I felt it best to make for here before sunrise, to bring you the news." Lucita frowned. Francesco was unexpected. She had no idea what his purpose might he in this, unless he were checking up on Isadora, in which case he was in for a nasty shock. She had no time or concentration to spare him.

"These others," she asked quickly, "the mortals. You are sure they went inside?"

"I watched until the door was closed behind them," the man said, "then ran here." His eyes were deep gray, and though he also was hooded, Lucita caught sharp, aquiline features and a pointed chin.

"I wonder what they are after?" Lucita asked out loud, nodding her respect to Anatole's men for their effort. They might not have returned from such an undertaking.

"Or who," Anatole added. "If I am not mistaken, the tavern of which he speaks is under Gabriella's influence. The two from the camps were likely her men. I would suspect Alfonzo had sent these, except that I am certain he is too arrogant to believe a tavern in his own quarter is not truly under his own influence. To send mercenaries in secret to his own establishment would seem a sign of weakness."

"Then who?" Lucita prodded. "If not Alfonzo and not Gabriella, then who else is involved, and why? The Chosen? Do you think those two entering the bar were more assassins?"

"I think," Anatole replied, turning to stare out at the cresting dawn, "that it is too late for us to find that out this night. I have some who can move by day, and you have your own men."

"Fine," Lucita said, turning quickly from the window. "But I'm not sending them to skulk in the shadows. I'm sending them into that tavern, and I'm going to find out who those two were, whatever the cost. We can't operate safely without knowing our allies—and our enemies."

"Assume that you have no allies, and you will always operate most safely," Anatole said, appearing at her shoulder as she left the room. "Whoever has sent them, we should not take these two lightly."

"I don't intend to take them lightly," Lucita snapped. "I intend to take them fully, completely, and to have them stripped and chained before me when I rise."

Anatole grew silent. It was difficult to read the monk, sometimes impossible. This was one of those times. They went below, each to summon their own people and get them on the move. Beyond the walls and the balcony where they'd stood, dawn was painting the skyline in reds and deep orange fingers they would never see. The other city, the Constantinople of the daylight, was coming to life.

Within the hour, four dark shapes had slipped out the ground floor of Lucita's stronghold. Two wore the simple ashen robes of those who followed Anatole. One was a dark, sultry woman with deep brown eyes and swarthy skin named Viola. She moved easily, despite the robes, which concealed more than just a slender, powerful form. A blade, as long and slender as its owner, hung at her side, fully concealed.

With her went a tall, broad man, Alejandro, who sported a shock of wild black hair that was flecked and streaked with gray, his arms like the gnarled roots of an ancient tree. His eyes were wide and deep, and they shifted hue oddly when the light hit just right. They mirrored the gray of his hair.

At their side were two young men of Lucita's, Jacob and Esau. These two wore dark tunics, dark boots, and their weapons hung openly at their sides. They were mercenaries, but hardly fools. They both had dark, intelligent eyes, Latin features, and moved in such close unison that they might have been twins, like Arturo and Leonid, though they were not. Long days and nights, hard fights, and many years had blended them into the single unit that Lucita valued. They were also more than proficient with their weapons. Most of her followers doubled as teachers in one manner or another.

The four slipped down the street and into the daylight

madness that filled the Latin Quarter. Booths had opened on all the corners, most no more than carts with a tarp drawn back and wheels broken so they could never move again. Others peeked from beneath the porticoes and tattered awnings of broken buildings or dark alleys. The space between was given over to traders checking others' wares, stevedores and sailors moving goods to and from the ports, and a wild assortment of displaced Greeks, erstwhile crusaders, and other ne'er-do-wells. Every corner was a business, and every business had the same purpose, to part one from whatever money he or she carried by all means possible. None bothered with these four.

As they passed, the daylight denizens of the quarter scampered out of their way, slipping into the shadows to watch them pass. Whispered words trailed them and disappeared into many ears, funneling back to those who traded in information, or rumor. Lucita's men were known by reputation, but had seldom ventured into the quarter. The others were not known at all, but the huge, dark-haired madman drew a lot of attention. The story of their passing traveled almost as quickly as they themselves.

When they turned down the alley behind the tavern and moved to the door, there were no less than three sets of eyes watching their every move, but this was as expected. Lucita was not after stealth; she wanted results. Their orders were clear, and none of the four paid any mind to those around them. If they found what they hoped to, then it would matter little who saw, or who that information was passed to.

Alejandro knocked on the tavern door roughly, and they waited. During daylight, the place was a tomb, closed and locked. There would have to be those whose job it was to clean, however, to wash and sweep away the refuse of one night to make way for that of the next. No place of business could ever afford to be truly closed for long.

Nothing happened, so the big man knocked again, louder this time, adding a rough kick of his boot to the solid wood in emphasis. They had been ordered to try every normal means of entrance first, but his patience was short, and they couldn't afford to be in the street for too long. The rumors that flowed so swiftly away from them would return, and they would bring others. Alfonzo's men, possibly others. There was no way to know for certain that those who'd entered earlier were alone, and if they were not, then there could be others watching even as they knocked and waited patiently to be attacked.

When there was no answer to this second knock, Alejandro turned to his companions, shrugged, and drew back a foot or so from the door. With a huge explosion of power, he drove his boot into the wood, directly beneath the latch. There was a shuddering crash, the sound of rending metal and splintering wood, and the latch gave way. The door swung open with a crash, and the four were inside.

Jacob and Esau slipped immediately to the left of the door as they entered, fanning out into the tavern's main floor. Alejandro followed the momentum of his crashing boot straight in. Viola, watching the street behind for a fleeting moment, paused to draw the door closed behind them.

There was no light on the inside. There were no windows in the main room, and there was no light coming from the kitchen beyond the bar, or the hallway to the back. It was as silent as a tomb, and they moved in quickly, scanning the shadows.

Viola nodded to Alejandro to follow, moved toward the kitchen. He stepped forward quickly to hold aside the curtained door, and she was through in a blur of motion, wrapping herself around the wall and slipping to the right. There was no need. Once inside, she smelled an all-too familiar scent, and she stopped. Her eyes had grown quickly accustomed to the darkness, but she didn't trust the silence. The scent of death was too fresh. Nothing moved. She reached into her robe, pulled out a flint and quickly located a candle. The flame danced up, stretching long fingers of yellow light through the dingy room. Alejandro entered behind her.

Sprawled on the floor was the body of the bartender. His throat had been torn from his body, and a very small pool of blood had leaked to the floor. He was pale, drained, and very, very dead. Not far beyond him, wafting in the slight breeze from the curtain over the door, the dust of a Cainite swirled away from a small fragment of bone. An empty cloak lay on the floor surrounding this, and an ornate dagger had fallen useless to the floor. Apparently, the kitchen had not fallen without a fight.

Viola knelt and grasped the dagger by its hilt, glancing at it in curiosity, but already focusing on the tavern beyond the curtained door. Whoever had been here, they were gone now.

A sudden, sharp cry from the back of the building launched her into motion. Alejandro held the door a last second, allowing her to slip through, and he was leaping the bar, diving toward the back, where the clash of blades and a loud curse drew them onward.

The shadows were cut ever so slightly by the slivers of light escaping from the kitchen, where the candle had been lit. Jacob and Esau flanked the entrance to the rear hallway, and they were holding someone, or something, at bay. Deep guttural curses sounded from beyond that doorway, and the flash and clatter of steel was furious, blades slashing and dipping like small lightning strikes.

"How many?" Viola asked, moving up cautiously on the left, behind Jacob.

"There are two in the hall," he grated through heaving breaths, "but there are others beyond."

She nodded to herself as if something had clicked into place. "Let them out."

Some sign must have passed between the two, because Jacob and Esau stepped back a full pace each, allowing a short slip in their guard, and at that moment, two others lurched from the hall. They stumbled, each turning to face an opponent, obviously believing they'd won ground. As they turned, Alejandro stepped from the shadows in the center of the room.

For just a second, all light was blocked, and the fight fell into darkness. In those seconds, he struck. Two massive fists pounded down, and before the two understood what had happened, they were pummeled to the floor, trying vainly to swing blades up and back at the giant and finding that those blades were suddenly pinned under booted feet to either side. Viola paid no heed to any of them. She was watching the hallway, and listening. There was a sound, then another. Stealthy, but still somewhat deeper and further away than she associated with threat. Softly, she called into the shadows.

"We will take them," she said. "Your rest is safe."

She hoped they would believe she was associated with the tavern, that what had happened had been controlled.

She knew there were rooms beneath the tavern, little more than dark pits where the sun was forever barred and the doors sealed from within. How these two had managed to breach such a wall was a question for a later hour. For the moment, it was vital that they take them, and get out. Others would come soon, might already be on the streets and moving.

Nothing happened. No sound or answer from the shadows below. They waited, then Viola spoke. "Bind them quickly. We have very little time."

Lucita's men trussed the two quickly and efficiently, and Alejandro swung one of them up and over his shoulder with no more effort than that of a father lifting his child. Something clattered to the floor, and Viola bent down to retrieve the small medallion fallen from the prisoner. On the face of it, Dark Calomena glared into some forgotten eternity. She slipped it into her cloak.

Jacob and Esau picked up their second prisoner, and, with a quick glance into a street that was, for all they could see, vacant, they moved off down the road quickly. The woman carried her blade openly, as if daring any to bar their path. There was no opposition, and they slipped out of the Quarter with only the glances of merchants, stevedores, and washerwomen to mark their passage. They found the back entrance to Lucita's own kitchens and lower levels without incident.

The streets were alive with the story.

Chapter Twelve

When Lucita arose, she was greeted immediately by three of her followers. There were prisoners, two of them. Anatole was with them. There was a messenger, Matteo once again, sent by the bishop, who was demanding to know what had happened that day. The girl who spoke—no more than fifteen, very pretty, and nervous as a bird—looked ready to burst into tears from the stress. Under Brexiano's watch, Lucita's time in the city had been relatively quiet, marked only by receptions with some of the Cainites circling around Constantinople's empty throne. Such an uproar—prisoners in the house!—was not within the girl's scope of experience.

Lucita brushed past her, telling her to go to Matteo and ask his patience, that she would join them shortly. Then, without hesitation, she made her way to the rooms behind the kitchen, where stairs led to the basements below. The house was built on a slope and there were stables below, with a means of exit at the rear, near the street. The stalls had not housed livestock since years before Constantinople's fall, but they served well enough for a makeshift dungeon.

It was there, in the third stall, that Lucita found Anatole and his two followers. Viola had thrown back her cloak, and stood off to one side, her eyes fixed on Lucita as she entered with an expression caught somewhere between envy and desire. She was lovely, very much mortal, and her blood flowed deliciously, pulsing at her throat. Lucita shook her head and turned away from the woman. It was no time to worry over her own needs, and this one was Anatole's, but still…

"Who are they?" Lucita asked, stepping to Anatole's side. At his feet, trussed like animals ready for the slaughter, two men lay in the dirt and filth. Their clothing had been torn away, and they shivered, naked and bound. Lucita saw that each already bore the mark of Anatole's questions. Bruises had risen on their chests, at their ribs. One breathed in heavy rasps, as if something were broken and causing him pain.

"I have learned little," Anatole replied calmly, "but I have not yet begun to apply any real pressure. The first important thing was this." He held up the medallion that had been brought to him. It was identical to the one they'd found on the rooftop. Calomena's glare was as dark and empty as ever.

"The Chosen?" she said softly, then turned to the two at her feet. She reached out with one boot and lifted a chin off the floor, studying the bruised face. The man glared at her for a moment, then his features broke into a spasm of fear and he turned his gaze away. She let him drop and turned back to Anatole.

"These are fanatics?"

"My thoughts exactly," the monk smiled enigmatically. "They had killed the bartender, a mortal and one of Gabriella's watchers, but that was largely due to surprise and the daylight. Those sleeping below were putting up a good fight of their own when our people arrived."

"I know little of the Chosen," Lucita said, lost in thought and staring down at their captives once again, "but I have heard they are nearly mad with their faith. It is said that they kill mortals and Cainites alike without fear, seeking only the redemption of Calomena. These two do not look prepared to die."

She lashed out then, kicking the closest prisoner hard in the ribs and bringing out a choking cry.

"We have tried beating them," Anatole observed, though his smile belied any chiding she might have heard in his tone. "We have threatened them with every physical abuse one can imagine, but they will say nothing. It seems they fear something, or someone, more than they do our blows."

Lucita laughed then, kneeling beside the first captive and reaching down. She slid one long, sharp nail under the man's chin and raised his head from the floor so that his flesh rested with the full weight of his head, pressing the skin of his throat into that nail. She turned him easily, reaching down to grip his hair with her free hand. She caught and held his gaze, and though he tried to shake his head and look away, he was helpless. She drew her nail to one side, then to the other, digging into his soft flesh and smiling as a thin trickle of blood began to trickle down her fingernail.

She held him by his hair, brought her finger to her lips and licked it clean very slowly. "We have plenty of time to discuss matters," she said softly. She dug her nail in deeper and filled the cup of it with his blood, bringing it to her lips once more. "Our guest will tell us everything we need to know, won't you sweet? Isn't it simply the sensible thing to do?"

She held the man's gaze and he tried again to shake his head and negate her words. Again, he failed. She dropped his head contemptuously to the floor and turned away. Anatole followed. He turned to the woman who had brought the prisoners in. "Find out where they come from, who they speak for, and why they chose Calomena to cover their tracks. We will be in the parlor entertaining our guest."

The woman nodded. There was a low moan from one of the men on the floor, but it was ignored. Lucita and Anatole left the room, mounted the steps to the kitchen, and made ready to meet with Matteo.

"I wish I already knew what information I can offer," she said, softly enough that none could overhear. "I know that we have the key to Alfonzo's questions, but what is the specific answer?"

"I can make a guess," Anatole replied, not meeting her gaze. "I had a few moments to speak with the two below, and while they offered no information of any use, they did speak. They both have a decided accent—Venetian, I would say. They are also very well equipped and trained for fanatics. I would rule out Calomena altogether, and begin to wonder who in Venice might want to rile Alfonzo, and at the same time harm Isadora."

Lucita stopped at the head of the steps, thinking. "Narses?" she said incredulously. "Why...?" then she fell silent. If it were known in Venice that Isadora was figuring prominently in Alfonzo's affairs, it might be assumed, as well, that the influence of Rome would be felt as well, or that—at the least—there would be leaks from the city, and that Alfonzo's operations would be suspect. She frowned. "His own sire?"

Anatole didn't reply. His features were as stoic as always, and he continued on down the hall, not waiting for her to follow. Lucita caught up with him, but she said nothing further. The monk could be infuriating when he chose silence, more infuriating still if he chose to start babbling about things that might or might not be relevant. Better he walk in silence and consider the implications of his words.

While she'd never have considered it herself, now that the thought had been implanted in her mind, it seemed obvious. Narses had always tried to keep his childer on a short leash, not wanting any uprising or mutiny, particularly in those who were far enough from Venice to be problematic.

Alfonzo was strong. He was powerful, arrogant and ambitious. Venice was a long way from Constantinople, and there were any number of powers who might reach out, dangling just the right morsel, and draw the bishop under their sway. Narses was certainly right to worry, though too late, as it turned out, to stop the inevitable. Lucita smiled.

They stepped into the parlor together, Anatole with his long, wispy blonde hair flowing over his shoulders, resting on his darker cowl, had his arms clasped and stood to the side, remaining silent. It was Lucita's home, and it was for Lucita to entertain visitors in whatever manner she chose.

She stepped forward gracefully, extending a hand to Matteo, who colored and nearly backed away at the sudden, almost intimate greeting.

"We meet again," Lucita observed, smiling as the living man fought for control of his voice. She moved deliberately closer, so that their clothing brushed. He could see nothing but her eyes, and seemed willing to stand, just as he was, silent and trapped in those deep pools until she set him free. She didn't wait too long. Better to let it be slow, gradually drawing him in and leaving him with the guilt and fear of betraying Alfonzo by wanting to be near her. Lucita wasn't certain yet what part this young man would play, but she felt it was important to draw him in a bit more at every opportunity.

"I..." he gasped the words, then swallowed, unable to continue immediately. He tried again. "I have been sent with a message, milady." The words poured from him when they finally broke free of his tangled tongue. "The bishop handed it to me, to deliver only to you."

She waited, smiling. When he finally realized she was waiting to be given the message, he tore the paper from his tunic and presented it to her, hands shaking. When she dropped her gaze from his to read the bold script on the envelope, she heard the escape of his breath, and realized he'd been holding it. His blood pulsed faster, and her smile widened. While she read, she ever-so-slowly traced the tip of her tongue back and forth across her deep red lips. She heard his breathing stop again, and almost laughed. She found that she was enjoying herself very much.

The note was short and to the point:

I have reports of what happened last night. I know that you took them, I want to know why. We will meet tonight. Do not keep me waiting.

She almost smiled again. So predictable. Men of the bishop's type, whether living or dead, could be depended upon to react in certain ways. She knew that she should have sent word to Alfonzo herself to let him know of the night's adventure, but she'd seen more advantage in making him wait. Now, Alfonzo had put himself into the position of wanting something she possessed, and letting that desire flash to the surface. He was impatient, and he was angry.

Turning back to Matteo, she said softly, "Your master does not appear to be very pleased with me."

"There has not been much to please him since Isadora's death," Matteo replied. "He is driven. He talks constantly of revenge, of finding these—Chosen—and of destroying them. Even his new childe can't hold his pleasure for long."

"Katrina?" Lucita asked. "She is young, too few years to give her enough wisdom. That may come in time, if she lasts. Regardless, I have news for Alfonzo that may set his mind at ease, or at least, change things. I am not ready, though. I have more to learn before I come."

"He will not be pleased," Matteo said immediately. "My orders were to not return without you, milady."

"Then you shall stay," she laughed. "I would not send you back to face the bishop's wrath alone. You shall stay, as my guest, until I have the information I require. I will make the visit well worth your master's time and patience, but I can't afford for him to interfere at this point. I am very close to answers that may be of importance to us all." Matteo stared at her. Emotions warred across his features. He knew that his instructions had been to come, and to bring her to the bishop immediately. To play games with his master's words was a dangerous thing, but there was nothing he could do to compel her. She would go, or she would stay, and all he could do was what he was bid. Somehow, as he stared into her deep, beautiful eyes, he found that he cared little. To do as she bid was reward enough.

Matteo shook his head. "I will wait," he said at last, "because you know I have no choice. Though it cost me my life, I will wait, and I will accompany you when you are ready to return."

Lucita laughed. "So gallant," she said. "We will not be so long as that, Matteo, and my intention is not to anger your master, but to bring him news that will ease his mind. Whether or not he is angry with you for the delay, he will forget that anger in the face of what we will have to tell him."

"Then it is true?" Matteo asked. "You have captured them? The Chosen?"

"We have captives," Lucita answered slowly, "but I am not convinced that they truly care about Calomena. There is something more complex behind this, and that is why I wish to wait. If we take the captives to Alfonzo, and he destroys them in a rage, we may never know the truth, and those who are guilty may go unpunished. We may, in fact, even further their purpose through our own actions. That is not something I can abide."

Matteo stared at her again. "Why?" he asked at last, backing away a step. "Why do you care whether Alfonzo destroys two who have caused him harm? Why do you care if he knows the truth? I have heard of you, milady. The Archbishop Narses would not approve of your involvement, but this you know as well. So, I ask you, though I have no right," he lowered his eyes, "to question you in any way: Why would you help my master?"

"Because," she said softly, reaching out to lay a cold palm against his cheek, her fingers caressing his chin, "this city has wallowed in its own destruction for too long already. Because there are powers lined up from the Golden Horn to Thrace, ready to step forward, claim her for their own and plunge it back into chaos. I would neither rule myself nor see the undead mimic the shameful dynastic pantomime of both Greek and Latin emperors. Thus, I have a choice to make.

"I have to decide," she said, releasing his chin and feeling the heat of his skin where her palm had pressed against him, sensing the speeding of his heart and the shortness of his breath, "who I will support. I could, I suppose, support Gabriella of Genoa. She is not a stupid leader, and she is Lasombra. Her loyalty, however, is to Genoa, and I am uncertain how she would react if I were to approach her. She might distrust me. She might try to destroy me.

"I could wait for the Greek Nosferatu Malachite to return, but what if he succeeds in his madness? What if the Dracon returns, and they try to drag the dust of the fallen buildings back into a mockery of what has been? This has no appeal for me.

"Alfonzo is in a position of power. He is a half-step from becoming a prince in this city, and I would be there when this happens. I would be there to offer the counsel of Madrid, and whatever wisdom I might possess. And then, there is the matter of what I suspect we will find when our captives break. They will break, you know. We will know who they are, where they have come from, and why. When I have learned this, if I am right, then I will have something that Alfonzo needs even more than he needs to be prince. I will have the key to his greatest enemy, and that is a barter point I have with no other."

"But," Matteo stammered, fighting for control of his tongue against a suddenly very dry mouth, "we already know who the prisoners are—where they come from. I was told before I came here of the Chosen...."

"I do not believe that the followers of Stanislav are behind this," Lucita said, turning away from him and walking to a window. She felt the weight of his gaze on her back, the heat of his desire, both mortal and beyond. He hung on her every word and movement.

"A leader in Alfonzo's position," she continued, tracing her finger along the framework of panes that made up the window's surface, and watching his reflection in the glass, "has many enemies. There are obvious enemies, like the Chosen, and there are those more subtle in their machinations. There are levels to treachery, and bloodthirsty fanatics are at the very surface level. These prisoners do not have the aspect of fanatics. They were sent to perform a particular act. They were sent to destroy two who were in that tavern, and not followers of Alfonzo this time. Though his influence is great, that place is not his. It belongs to Gabriella, and it was two of hers who were inside. I know one by name, the other by reputation. Their presence in that tavern surely boded ill for Alfonzo in some way, and it was not to harm him that they were targeted. They survived, incidentally, and now our Genoese friend will find herself in my debt as well.

"There is someone else. Someone with power, influence, and much cunning, who is behind both of these attacks, and who stands to gain by causing a disruption in both houses. Alfonzo and Gabriella have little in common, so we must seek to find another connection. A reason. Who would gain by the deaths?"

Anatole stepped forward, breaking his silence. "There is a difference," he stated simply. "I do not believe we can simply look to the leader of each house and find a common enemy, but we can look to those who were, and were to be victims, and things shift."

"What do you mean?" Lucita asked, turning slowly. "Both Alfonzo and Gabriella would have lost those close to them. Where is this difference?"

"Simply this," Anatole said softly. "Gabriella would have lost two of her most powerful allies in the city. Lieutenants. Soldiers. She would have had to search long and hard for replacements, and maybe she could not have replaced them at all, though I'm not at all convinced the two below would have succeeded in their mission, even had we not intervened. I also know of the two in that room, and I do not believe they would have gone into eternity easily, or quietly.

"Alfonzo, on the other hand, lost Isadora. She was his companion, a diversion, someone he shared with intimately. She was not essential to any operation of his, nor was she a powerful ally. She was, in fact, a link to Rome—a link that could have proven a liability, had it been granted the opportunity to progress further. Alfonzo would have been pulled between his own ties to Venice and the necessity to assuage any bad blood his relationship with Isadora might have fostered, balancing him on the tip of a blade that might easily swerve to sever one or the other thread.

"So," Anatole concluded, "we now have a different situation to evaluate. Who would gain by removing Isadora, and weakening Gabriella, without anyone the wiser to his involvement in the situation? Who would gain by getting Alfonzo angry, causing him to tighten his hold on the Latin Quarter and on the city?"

Lucita was quiet for a moment, then spun to the window again. It was Matteo, who was still uncomfortable speaking in their presence, who next broke the silence. "Archbishop Narses?" he asked softly.

"Could it be?" Lucita turned back, and now she was smiling. Things were beginning to snap into place like a child's wooden puzzle. The image was clear. Of course, it was Narses. Who else? Who would know the power of Alfonzo's hatred of the Chosen, sparked by the childer they had taken from him before the city fell? Who would benefit most with Alfonzo as prince? She wondered suddenly how quickly she could get a message to Mongada. He would not be pleased, at first, and that was another fight she would have to face, but suddenly it seemed an easier battle than it had moments before.

She turned to Anatole. "Go below. Assist them in getting the information we need. We will leave within the hour. The one I spoke to should have the loosest lips, but he must be managed carefully. I know that your people can be very—persuasive—but these are skills that they have learned from you, and I think we need all the speed that is possible. We have to be the ones to bring this information to the bishop, and he is far from a stupid man. We don't want him to figure it out before we have the chance to present the proof."

Anatole nodded, a glitter in his eye that could have been read many ways. Lucita ignored him, for the moment, and turned back to Matteo.

"Go to Alfonzo," she told him, catching and holding his gaze anew. "Tell him nothing of what you heard here, only that we will be there shortly with the answers to his questions, and more. Tell him that we do, indeed, have the two prisoners, and that we will bring them as well."

"But I cannot lie to him," Matteo had begun to tremble, backing away, but could not look away.

"No one has asked you to," Lucita replied, keeping her voice soft, following as he backed away from her, just quickly enough that she drew nearer at each step. He hadn't taken the time to glance behind him, and was brought up cold by the frame of the door. Lucita continued forward until she pressed tightly against him, holding him to the wall. He was trembling violently, coated in a sheen of slick sweat. His heart hammered furiously. "I have only asked that you deliver a message, Matteo, exactly as I offered it. Surely that is not a problem?" She leaned in so that her lips—then the tips of smooth ivory fangs—brushed his earlobe. She allowed one small prick to the softness of his skin and after waiting for it to bead, licked the single drop of blood from him with a slow curl of her tongue. She pulled back so that he was again fully trapped in her gaze, but her body pinned his to the wall.

"I..." he gasped. Then, unable to speak, he nodded suddenly, and so violently that the shudder the movement brought to his tense form nearly caused him to smack his forehead into her face. The near accident unnerved him further, and if she had not been holding him to the wall, he would have sunk to his knees in that moment.

Slowly, Lucita backed away and allowed him to breathe. He did so, eyes closed, one finger lifting involuntarily to the place she'd pricked his earlobe. Lucita's hunger was rising, and she knew that she had moved away none too soon. He was delicious, and she could detect the faintest taste of something that could only be Alfonzo. She waited, and when he finally opened his eyes, she spoke a single word.

"Go," she said.

Matteo turned and fled, not waiting for servants to lead the way. Lucita watched until he was out of sight, then stood until she heard the thud of the great front doors closing. One of her girls stepped into the doorway to see if she was in need, and Lucita moved.

She grabbed the girl's arm, dragging her into the shadows beside the door with a quick jerk. Before a word could be spoken, she'd thrown the girl's head back, watching the cascade of auburn hair that slid off down her back, baring the pure, white skin of her throat. Lucita leaned in and bit deep, feeling the rich, red flow—drowning in it for a moment, erasing the hunger that had risen. Moments later, she stopped, pulling away hastily. The girl was pale, weak, but alive. Lucita lowered her against the wall, dabbed at the wound on the girl's throat with her tongue to lick it clean, then turned away.

She passed no one in the hall, but she knew someone would find the girl, tend to her, and remove her from the parlor. Her head was clearer and she headed for the stairs, leading down to where Anatole would be busy with the prisoners. She cursed herself silently over the young man, Matteo, and the momentary slip of control she'd allowed. She would have to watch that, particularly with all that would soon come with Alfonzo. It would not do to anger the bishop right on the verge of a partnership that could be valuable to them both.

A scream rose from below, and she suddenly smiled. It would not be long.

Chapter Thirteen

The attack had been loud and crude and that had been enough to alert Raphael and Gradin. They could not emerge from their rooms, but they were not going to be easy to dislodge. The quarters beneath the tavern had been constructed with just such a necessity in mind, and they were well-made. There were any number of day-light creatures, mortals and others, who might find a reason to wake a sleeping Cainite, and it was always in the best interests of the tavern to protect those it served.

What Raphael could not understand, was what had driven the attackers away. They couldn't have gotten as far as they did without keys, so the watcher and any mortal workers who had been left to guard the place were out of the picture. Who had intervened? There was nothing to be done but to wait, and to wonder what would come next.

All sound from above had ended soon after the aborted attack. Eventually, there had been footsteps, the sound of things moving and being dragged. These were signs that someone had come to clean up the mess. These would be Gabriella's men. Someone must have gotten word through. The tavern would open on schedule. There would be a new bartender, a new watcher, and as far as the regulars were concerned, no other changes.

The wait was interminable. Though they rested, Raphael and Gradin forced awareness. They concentrated, listening and taking advantage of sharp senses and attention to every detail. There was nothing. No one came to disturb them, and at last, they felt the sun dropping, the release of the pressure that bound them in the stone-walled sanctuary that might well have proven to be their tomb.

Rising, Gradin cursed and kicked at the door.

"What in the seven hells was *that* all about?" he grated. "This place has always been safe. Always."

"Things are shifting, my friend, that much is certain. Let's get ourselves far away from this place, and see what we can find. I, for one, will be spending the next run of daylight beyond the city walls. Constantinople is beginning to lose its appeal to me."

"You don't suppose the Roman...." Gradin said.

"No, not that one," Raphael answered. "He was honest enough, as far as it goes, and he is far from Rome. I don't see any advantage in his attacking us, even if he knew who we served all along. And I don't believe it was Alfonzo, either. He is certain that he controls this place—there would be no need, as far as he can see, to attack his own people."

Gradin growled low in his throat. He yanked the bolts free on the door and drew it open with a bang. Without a word, he ducked out into the hall and ascended the stairs. He had his blade in one hand, and he crept carefully up along one wall. Raphael fell in one step behind him on the opposite side.

When they reached the top of the stair, they paused, then at a sign from Gradin, they sprang upward, spinning one to each side, backs to the wall and weapons at the ready, staring into the room.

At the bar, facing one another across the polished wood surface, their faces in deep concentration, Ian and Pasqual studied a chessboard that lay between them. Behind the bar, a tall, burly man bustled about, placing bottles and glasses just so, cleaning up where things had been tipped or spilled or broken. Pushing off from the wall with a grunt, Gradin cursed again.

"Now you come," he spat. "Now, when all is quiet and there is nothing for you to do but to play chess, you arrive to save us."

Ian looked up, barely managing not to grin as he replied. "You didn't really expect that we would burst in the door in the middle of the day and rush to your aid, blazing in flames? There are certain restrictions to the help we can provide."

"You control plenty of those who walk by day," Raphael said, the amusement not far from his voice. "You could have sent *someone* to help."

"The truth is more simple," Pasqual said, smiling and moving his bishop in line with that of Ian's, pinning it effectively with the king trapped behind. "We did not know about your predicament until after the damage had been done. You don't appear the worse for wear, in any case. Sleep well?"

Gradin growled again, but Raphael burst into laughter. He was fond of the Frenchman, and of course, Pasqual was right. Nothing could have been done without prior knowledge of the attack.

"The important thing," Raphael said, "is that we find out who was behind it. And for that matter, who stopped it. I must say, that was the easiest I've ever escaped such an attack, and I don't have any idea how."

Ian turned back to the board, frowning at his pinned bishop. He advanced a pawn, obviously trying to buy time for something. Pasqual barely glanced at the board before sending his knight into apparent danger from Ian's queen. "They didn't leave much behind," Pasqual said, as Ian glared at the board, deep in thought. "They killed quickly, and efficiently, but there is evidence that they themselves were taken—and alive. There is blood in the kitchen, and there were the two bodies that provided it, but there was not much blood out here. There were signs of a struggle, a few small blood stains here and there, but no indication that anyone else was killed."

"Alfonzo?" Raphael asked. "You think he might have taken them?"

"It seems not," Pasqual answered, shaking his head. "Our people report that the bishop's household is in a frenzy. He's angry, but he won't speak of just why. He has sent a messenger to Lucita and the monk Anatole, but again, no word as to why."

"She must have them!" Gradin cried. "How in the seven hells did she know they would be here? Who were they?"

"Easy, my friend," Raphael cut in, placing a hand on Gradin's shoulder. "Let's not jump to conclusions. If Lucita took them, we owe her a debt, albeit a grudging one. Let's not waste the gift of our lives ranting and raving. We must get to Gabriella with the news that we have, of Rome, and of this, and then we can formulate a plan for Lucita."

"I don't trust the monk," Gradin growled. "There are already too many preachers over in the camps and prelates here in the quarter. I'm not certain that waiting to deal with his and the Iberian woman is wise. What could they be planning? And what, for that matter, would they be doing here, helping us whether by choice or chance? What would they gain?"

"And why," Ian asked, sliding his queen in line with the bishop that was pinned to free it, "would Alfonzo send a messenger to the two of them? Does he know of this attack, as well? What, if anything, connects those two? Separately, they are not such a danger that we can't face them, but together? I would hate to think of that."

"Thinking is not your strong point," Raphael said, grinning. "You must watch his knight."

Ian glared for a moment at Raphael, then turned his attention back to the chess board, just in time to see Pasqual slide his knight to the center of the board and catch his king, and his queen, in a forked attack that would end in the loss of the queen.

Gradin had stepped up to the bar and was eyeing the board. He grunted again. Ian whirled on him.

"What? You know, too? You can see what I cannot—tell me, what do I do?"

"Attack," Gradin replied without further comment, turning toward the door. "You spend your game worrying over what he is thinking, and what is the third move beyond his last, and why. You must worry about your own moves more, or you do nothing but play a game with time, waiting to be slaughtered."

Ian stared after Gradin, and Raphael performed a slow bow on his way out, following his friend. "He's right, you know," Raphael said. "You really do sit back and wait for the kill."

Ian was still cursing them as they hit the streets. "Did you truly see an attack?" Raphael asked, as they hit the streets and turned toward the gates of the city.

"Of course not," Gradin laughed very suddenly. "I just like to see him pulled in three directions at once. Nothing could keep Pasqual from winning that game."

Raphael nodded. That is what I thought, but then," he

chuckled, "I have learned to trust your instincts, particularly where attacking is involved."

It was a rare thing for Gabriella to be alone, but for the time being she sat in solitude, in her room at Hadrian's Rest for Raphael and Gradin to report. They were late, but that was nothing new. She'd heard of the attack, and had sent in Ian and Pasqual, but she wanted to hear straight from the two what had befallen them, so she'd chosen to wait.

There were so many things to watch, so many things she had to be aware of. She had been neglecting the camps. They had been largely stagnant since Hugh de Clairvaux's destruction, the ravages of the Latins and Bulgars fighting over Thrace only adding to their number and their dismay. Last year, her spies had told her of the departure from the region of Caesar Valerian, the powerful envoy of the Parisian Grand Court who'd meddled in some of her affairs after the Crusade. Andrew of Egypt was ferrying him west, a good riddance that was. Ultimately, she'd thought the camps might either become a small, dirty extension of Adrianople and remain forever, or collapse into bloody bickering and the pursuit of apocryphal legends.

Instead, her men reported that there were more and more places where groups of former rivals and enemies now gathered. Greeks and Turks, lords and serfs now stood together sullenly, grudgingly making an effort to band more tightly together. It was still a fragile union, but just such a union had come very close to setting off to conquer Egypt not two years ago. Something was drawing them together, and she knew that she would have to make herself aware of that thing, study it, and see where the advantages of such knowledge might lie. It could be that they were just growing tired of living like savages. Constantinople had been a city of luxury, of magic and dreams. The powers that had ruled there had faded and grown corrupt, but they were great powers nonetheless, and even their shadows had been filled with a richness that a place like the camps could never offer. Not even to fanatics.

But what could make them act as one? What could bring Nosferatu crawling from their dark corners together with

Toreador tramps? *Maybe,* she thought, *the question isn't answered by a what. Maybe it's a who.*

A scuffing noise on the stairs brought her attention back to the present. She turned toward the door expecting to see her men enter any moment, instead there was a tall, slender, and cloaked man standing inside the room. He had not been there an instant before, she knew, and she braced for an attack.

Instead, he leaned against the wall with a quiet confidence. He shielded his eyes with the hood of his cloak, but a gnarled, claw-like hand, was visible—held close to his side, the nails long and yellowed. The robe, it seemed, concealed more than his face. It was meant to shield those he met and spoke to from his appearance.

"Nosferatu," Gabriella whispered.

He pulled back his hood, and she knew him—had known him. She gasped and took a step back, but he only stood, watching her and twisting his warped, caricature of a face into a rictus that vaguely hinted of a smile.

"It's been a long time, Gabriella," he said softly.

Gathering her wits, she stepped forward again. "It has indeed, Malachite. I had heard that you were…gone away.

I have traveled many miles since the fall," he said, nodding. "I have seen a great many things, but I have been drawn back to this place, as I knew, eventually, I would be."

"And your quest?" she asked warily. "I do not see the Dracon at your side."

"I have not found him," Malachite replied, not dropping his gaze, "but I hold steady in my belief. The Dream must return. It was the focus, the central power of our peoples. Without that focus, we are no better than the mortals, plotting in shadows and fearing each sunrise as if it will bring the final death. In Constantinople, our peoples ruled. Here, we rule only shadows."

"The emptiness becomes you," she said disdainfully. "You seek the dream of a puppet."

He seemed to spread, becoming slightly unfocused and expanding to glare down at her. His features contorted, if possible, into a more ghastly grimace than the smile he'd worn moments before.

"You mock things that you do not understand," he said at last, calming himself. "You seek to steal the truth from my words by diverting them to a joke, but they are no less true. Who rules in Constantinople? Who will draw our people together and hold the peace? Who will prevent the next wave of Crusaders from razing the city? Alfonzo? You?"

"Perhaps," she said without hesitation. "There are other powers than those that ruled in Constantinople. But," she said, as if thinking it over, "your dream is not without merit, except for its one fundamental flaw. The trinity of elders is gone. The Dracon is but one, and the followers of the others will not necessarily gravitate to the one who is left. More likely he would come back to his city and be shredded, torn limb from limb and consumed by his own children."

Malachite did not reply immediately. He studied her, and he waited, then he continued.

"I did not come back to rebuild the city," he said at last. "Not yet. I am here for other purposes, on other errands. I will not stand here and debate what once was, or what could be with you. We do not agree, and it is unlikely that we will he any more in agreement when we part. Still, I believe I can be of help to you."

Gabriella laughed softly. "If you could he of help to me," she said, "why would you? What would you gain? What would I lose? These are not times of generosity and good will, so tell me, why would you help me, and what is it you think I need your help in doing?"

"Alfonzo is only a few nights away from the power to proclaim himself prince," Malachite spat the words, as though he'd sipped bad blood. "His corruption is spilling from the cesspool of the Latin Quarter like a plague, infecting the city as he goes. He has no love for what was beautiful in the old city. He has no patience for what was important. With Narses behind him, he will spread his wealth, draw in those who remain in the city and buy those who are in doubt. You know this. You have been there, and you have seen." Malachite fell silent for a long moment, his head bowed, then he lifted it again suddenly, his eyes blazing. "I would not see one such as Alfonzo ruling in

Michael the Patriarch's place. It is an abomination, blasphemous and tainted. I will be honest, Gabriella, I have no love for you or Genoa, but I would give the city into the hands of Rome or Paris before I would surrender it to one such as Alfonzo, with his decadent disregard for anything but his own pleasure."

Gabriella smiled. "Perhaps you should go to the city instead of lurking here, near its gates, or in the camps," she suggested. "You could draw quite a crowd of supporters if you did. Maybe you could rebuild a corner of your dream without the Dracon."

"I will not set foot within her walls," he stated flatly. "Not yet. I have a thing to do, a road to follow. I am heading back to the camps and from there to France, and I believe a great number of others will leave with me. They are ready to be out of this place."

"To follow Caine?" Gabriella's voice was laced with sarcasm, but Malachite stood very still, as if he hadn't heard her at all.

"I do not seek Caine," he said at last. "If Caine is fated to come among us, we will all meet him together. For myself, I seek one that is real, who can bring us back to something like what we have known. One who cares for the city, for the structure and the order that was Constantinople. What stands on the bones of the city is a travesty, a ruined parody of itself. Those who walk the streets have no notion of what is right, and they make not the slightest pretense at civility among the clans or their own families. There is nothing there, but that can be changed."

Gabriella stood silent, watching. She was thinking, and the thoughts surprised her. She was wondering why this one, so well-thought of by both Greeks and many Latins among the undead, did not step forward and rebuild the dream himself. The Dracon hadn't been seen for centuries, and even if he was still extant and was somehow found, the odds were no better than even that he'd return, whatever the pressure Malachite and his followers applied.

Malachite caught her thoughts with eerie precision. "I have been given signs," he said. "I don't expect everyone to understand. It is enough that I understand, and that I act on the understanding. It will not be long before this place breaks apart, and when it does, I will be leaving."

He hesitated for a moment, then continued, "You could come with me."

She laughed then, but not at him. She laughed at his sincerity, at the ludicrous image of the expressions her followers would present her with if she announced such a departure. Turn her back on the city, on the past and her sire, wander into the desert at the side of a deformed lunatic.

"I did not believe you would go," Malachite said. There was just the hint of amusement in his own voice, and Gabriella fell silent again, then spoke.

"I mean no disrespect," she said, controlling her voice. "It is just that what you suggest is so far from my nature. It was the last thing I expected you to say, knowing who I am."

"It was a thing that needed saying," he said. "Now that it has been said, I will say this. You could go with me, but I know that you will not. There are others who will not. Most of those in the camps will leave with me, whether or not we share a dream. This place has reached the end of what it can offer. It is dying, and the only release is in the wind. We must move with it as we may. That is my road. I understand that you, and many others, will not follow."

He stopped speaking for a moment, turning toward the shadows. Gabriella thought he might turn and just leave her standing alone, but at last he continued.

"I do not wish to see the city left in the hands of bandits, or fools," he said at last. "I cannot go there myself for long enough to make a difference. You can. You have the support of Genoa, and contacts in the city."

She stood silent, listening. Then she spoke. "You are telling me nothing that I do not know, and offering me nothing that is not already within my grasp."

"Not so," he said, stepping a little closer. "I have my own connections. I am not without resources in the city, and not all of those who answer to me will leave with me, despite my wishes. I can help you."

"How," she asked sharply, "and to do what? What is it you think I want?"

"You want to be Prince of Constantinople," he said simply, "It is not your nature to stand by and watch one such as Alfonzo lead."

"You do not have a high opinion of the bishop," she commented. "He wields a great deal of influence in the city. It would not be easy to bring him under control, and it would be harder still to keep him there."

"Everyone has their Achilles' heel," Malachite said, and grinned. The expression fit so imperfectly on his features that Gabriella almost grimaced in distaste. "Alfonzo has made his mistakes, and he has made many of them quite openly. It is a challenge, I think. He is waiting to see if you, or any other like you, will accept the gauntlet and attack him."

"And this is what you think I should do?" she asked. "Not at all. I think you should do what the Lasombra do best. You should let him draw just enough rope over the edge of his own walls that he can hang himself in the sunlight for all to see. Then, while the city returns to a new level of turmoil, you should step in and set things right. A direct attack would surely fail."

Gabriella nodded.

"There is the matter of the Roman girl," Malachite continued. Gabriella showed none of the surprise she felt at his easy knowledge of the situation in the city. "Now there is the matter of this Katrina, and her ties to Adrianople. Perhaps nothing will come of it, but that could change. The right words in the right ears might make a difference.

"Licinius is anxious for the camps to clear," Malachite said. "It is my intention to clear them, but I could make this seem a favor. If he were indebted to me, I believe he might be encouraged to use his influence in Constantinople. Alfonzo is rash, arrogant. He flaunts himself in the face of others' influence, stealing away in the night with that which belongs to another."

"Not exactly truth," she said, fighting the smile.

"And this is a problem?" Malachi asked dryly. "My point is simple. I am leaving, but I would leave things in competent hands. If I can offer my influence to that end, I will do so. I will not stay away forever. I will not claim any love of the Lasombra, or of yourself. I will not even promise that, should I return, I would support you. At this particular point in time, however, it suits my need."

"You would have made a formidable Lasombra," she replied, at last giving in to the laugh. "I am no more anxious to see Alfonzo in control of the city than you are. I've only been biding my time, waiting for the proper moment to make my intentions known. It wouldn't do to move too quickly and lose to superior numbers. Better to rearrange the odds first, then stand in the shadows and collect your winnings."

Malachite nodded. "In return, I ask only that you spread the word among your people. Let it be known that we are leaving Thrace, that the time to put the past behind us has come, and that I have been seen. Don't tell them we have spoken. Don't hint that we are in collusion. Say only that you have seen me, from a distance, and that there is a gathering. I don't expect many of your own people will be interested in following, though they would be welcome. I do believe, however, that they could spread the word, and that it could speed the process of my departure."

Gabriella nodded. "I would like to see an end to this place, as well. It is too difficult to watch both the camps and the city. There are too many warring factions, most of whom have no legitimate conflict, but only a desire to destroy someone or something in payment for the destruction of their homes—their city. Adrianople itself has conflicts in her future, and in the midst of such a battle, this place would be laid to waste in any case. Better that you—they—depart now, while there is a chance to escape and start again in some other place."

"Then we are agreed," Malachite said, turning away. "I will speak to Licinius this very night. I don't know what his reaction will be. I can't promise that the prince will care about the girl being taken, but I will do what I can. My advice to you is to concentrate on the dead one—Isadora. Contact Rome. Let them know what has happened and mention Alfonzo's name often."

"I have been considering this," she replied. "It will be as you say, and I will tell all that I see of your great—pilgrimage."

Malachite stared at her. Then he smiled again, the grimace

sending a chill through her small frame. "That is an apt name for it," he said somberly. "A pilgrimage, indeed. A new beginning—a rebirth."

He turned and walked out the door and up the steps. Gabriella rushed after him, but by the time she was up the short flight of stairs and out of the inn, he was gone. The courtyard between the inn and the stables, the only place to go at the top of the stairs was dark and empty. She cursed the Nosferatu's gift for vanishing.

After a moment, she headed back down to await her spies. She had a great deal to get done tonight.

In the shadows, a second yellowed set of eyes watched Gabriella of Genoa head back into her rooms in the cellars of Hadrian's Rest. Brother Torquato pressed himself back behind the stable and tried to make sense of what he had just heard. The traveling companion he'd known as Adam was revealed as the very creature he'd been asked to find. This was a strange business indeed.

He was a long way from his native Venice and though his mission was to Constantinople, and several local taverns within the city, he'd stopped in the camps of Adrianople to see the truth behind the wild tales there. Adventure was at a premium in the wine cellars of Venice, and Brother Torquato intended to return with a head full of them to weave into tales for the late, quiet nights. Now he found himself in a position he'd not sought, with knowledge he shouldn't have, and still he had a job to do. When the Lasombra had departed, and the streets were silent once more, Brother Torquato made his way to the wagons he'd driven to the inn and slipped up into the driver's seat. He barely had enough time to make Constantinople proper and there make contact with those that he'd been sent to meet.

As he drove away, he wondered at what he'd heard, but for the most part, he dismissed it. It was no real concern of his now. He had told "Adam" of his message for this Malachite, so his boon for the Giovanni family was complete. Now, he had only to unload and sell the wine in his wagon, and to depart. He was expected back in Venice next year, and the journey, with no help, was not an easy one.

Turning down the road, he pulled his cloak up tightly around his shoulders and lowered his head. Any seeing him might have thought him mortal. Unless he smiled, he might even keep up that illusion. For a Nosferatu, he was remarkably clean. Unblemished, in most of the normal expressions of that particular blood, he was often able to wander among those of the daylight without attracting notice. Even others of the blood were not quick to guess his heritage. It was a burden at times, but on the road as he was now, it was a blessing. No one questioned the simply ugly. It took a truly hideous countenance to draw undue attention.

No one noticed the lone wagon slipping into the night.

Chapter Fourteen

Lucita and Anatole reached Alfonzo's door within the hour. They were expected, and a breathless Matteo met them as they were ushered inside. Lucita was calm. Matteo was on edge, as though he were walking a thin rope above a mesh of razor-sharp wire and afraid he'd stumble and be sliced to ribbons.

"He is waiting," Matteo said. "He is not happy to be waiting."

"He will be happy enough," Anatole said calmly, "with what we have to tell him."

Lucita smiled at Matteo and reached out to run one long nail down his cheek. He made a choking sound, tried to pull back, failed, and then she was past him, already moving down the hall toward the room where they'd met with Alfonzo before. She heard Matteo's hurried footsteps as he spun and followed after. She also heard the pounding of the blood in his veins and knew she'd put him in a predicament. Alfonzo would not fail to notice this, and she wondered where such a thing would lead.

They found Alfonzo pacing. He moved from one end of the long table to the other, hands clasped behind him. As they entered, he whirled, and was suddenly at their side, as if there had not been yard between them. As if he'd stood there all along, calmly awaiting their arrival.

"I sent for you many hours ago," he said curtly. "I expected you to answer."

Anatole stirred, and Lucita reached out a hand to settle him. She gazed evenly at the bishop. "I am not your servant, Bishop. Surely you realize this." Her voice was soft, but it had an unmistakable edge. "When I receive an invitation to meet,

I always assume that the choice of whether—and when—to accept is still mine."

Alfonzo started to draw himself up, then stopped. Lucita wasn't sure if he'd won an inner battle to contain himself, or if the short glance he gave Anatole had convinced him. The anger faded.

"I control a great deal of this city," he said at last. "The Latin Quarter has long been mine. Your affairs are, of course, your own, but when they intrude on my territory, I have an interest. You took prisoners from a tavern last night, this much I know. There are rumors that these prisoners have something to do with the Chosen and Isadora's death. I have been able to get scant little from the ones you brought me—it seems Arturo and Leonid could use lessons in subtlety. So, you can see why I might he impatient for news?"

"That is why we have come," Lucita assured him. "I wanted only to have a complete story to tell, rather than short pieces. I'm happy to report that Anatole and his followers have mastered the subtlety your own have not." Alfonzo almost bristled at this, but seemed to realize he'd set himself up for it, and let it pass.

"What did you find?" he asked at last. "Did you take more of them? The Chosen?"

"We took two prisoners," Lucita said. "We took them from the tavern you mentioned, where they had been sent to assassinate two who rested within. The two who were to be targeted belong to Gabriella of Genoa, and as a passing note, you may want to reconsider how you watch that particular tavern. It seems that the place is, and has been for some time, a haven for her agents."

This got Alfonzo's attention. Lucita could see the thoughts whirling: a quick flash of emotions flickered across the bishop's features, then was gone. He contemplated her words a moment longer before speaking.

"There are always some weaknesses," he said at last. "The owners of that establishment have paid their tributes. My men go there frequently, as they do to all other such places within my control, watching and questioning, collecting what is owed.

It does not surprise me to hear that Gabriella was unable to resist sinking her claws into the quarter at some point."

He fell silent again, then continued. "Why would the Chosen attack her people? If they are after me, what would be the purpose in flushing out a potential enemy?"

"Think carefully," Anatole said calmly. "When there appears to be a conflict between two realities, one of your assumptions must be false."

Alfonzo stared at the monk, thinking.

"There is no doubt that they have done me a service," he said. "I might have been years ferreting out Gabriella's people."

Anatole nodded and smiled. Lucita remained silent. "But still," Alfonzo went on, turning away and pacing again as he spoke, "they have certainly dealt me a personal blow, here inside my own walls."

"Have they?" Lucita asked. "Have they really?"

Alfonzo spun on her, ready to argue the point, but his spin lost momentum. He watched her, and remained quiet.

"You have lost a companion," she said. "You feel the hurt and the insult personally, but your position in the city has not been harmed by this, beyond the slight lapse in your security that allowed the attack in the first place. There are those," she added softly, "who might believe that a clean cut from Isadora, and Rome, actually strengthened your position."

Alfonzo started at this. "What?" He said, "But who?" Again, the silence. The possibilities whirled once again, and Lucita decided that she'd kept this going long enough. She opened her mouth to speak, but at that second, she caught a movement to her right, and tightened her lips.

It was Matteo. He carried a tray, three goblets and a flask, held in unsteady hands. He would not meet her gaze, but the skin of his neck was flushed, and he stumbled as he grew nearer, nearly tripping.

Alfonzo snapped at him impatiently. "What is wrong with you? Have you suddenly lost the ability to walk?"

Not trusting himself to speak, Matteo lowered his eyes to the floor and presented the tray. Alfonzo started to dismiss him, then thought better of it and reached for a goblet, already filled with the deep, rich, blood-spiked wine. Anatole did not drink, but Lucita accepted a goblet graciously, stepping closer to Matteo as she did, letting him feel her near to him. The tray shook, and she laughed lightly, stepping back with her drink.

Alfonzo stared first at Lucita, then at Matteo. His eyes darkened, and he clenched his goblet more tightly, then he laughed. Very suddenly, very loudly, he laughed, throwing his head back. "You are a fool," he said to Matteo. "You have no more control of yourself than a boy in a candy store. Tell me, Matteo, does the lady please you?"

Matteo remained silent, trembling. Alfonzo advanced on him slowly. "I have made promises to you," he said softly, moving first to the side, then behind the young man. He was quick, so quick that his form flickered from one spot to the next. There was no sense that he walked, but more that he disappeared from one spot and reappeared in the next. His voice seemed to come from all sides at once, hypnotic and deep. Matteo shook like a leaf in a strong wind, the tray and its contents rattling violently. He held very still, biting his lip and wishing for the pain to take him away from the moment. It failed, though a thin trickle of blood began to wind its way down his cheek. He was aware of this, acutely aware of it, and the dangers it presented.

Alfonzo was suddenly directly behind him, a hand on his shoulder, lips very close to Matteo's ear. The bishop's voice was like the wind, whispering and still strong enough to brush everything within reach, rippling around the room. Alfonzo watched in amused silence. Lucita watched as well, conflicting emotions warring within her. Then, just as Alfonzo began to build his anger, one block upon the next, and to tighten the grip of his hand on Matteo's shoulder, she spoke.

"The Chosen have nothing to do with Isadora's death," she said very softly, so softly that only ears attuned beyond the mortal would have been able to pick her words from between Alfonzo's own. "Isadora was not killed to attack you, but to cut your ties with Rome. Gabriella's followers were attacked in the hope of weakening her influence in a time when the two of you could easily be considered rivals for control of this city. Who would gain, Alfonzo? Who would gain from such steps? Who

would gain if you became stronger? Who would be most satisfied if you had no ties to Rome?"

Alfonzo stopped moving. He stopped speaking. His hand
continued its tight grip on Matteo, who was rigid with terror,
knees weak and arms losing control of the tray he held too
tightly.

Alfonzo moved back.

"Narses," he said softly. It wasn't a question, but a revela-
tion. Lucita saw the totality of the betrayal sweeping across his
features. Matteo stood forgotten, and Alfonzo dismissed him
with a curt wave of one hand. The boy cut and ran, the flask
tilting, falling across the tray, but miraculously not dropping to
the floor.

Alfonzo barely seemed aware the boy was gone.

Lucita pressed her advantage.

"Gabriella was taken in, as well," she said. "Even Anatole,
who has had his own problems with the Chosen, was quick
to believe they might be back. The question now is not what
has happened, or who has gained, but what to do next. You
know that your sire will deny this. You know, as well, that he
will expect you to question nothing, and to continue as if you
believe."

Alfonzo was thinking. Lucita could see that he was considering her words, but at the same time, he was considering other
things. Perhaps he was remembering other times, other places
when he'd placed blame, and ignored the obvious. Manipulation
was an old Lasombra game. Intrigue was a given, without it
there would be nothing to exist for, but this was different. This
was the wrong end of intrigue, the false security of Alfonzo's
own power. It was quite a different matter when one was the
victim of intrigue, particularly when the perpetrator was one
he had trusted.

"I cannot allow this to go unanswered," he said at last. "The
last time we spoke, Lucita, you offered your support. I know
that your sire will not approve. No more than Narses approved
of Isadora. Should I accept your offer, is it only to find a knife at
my own throat when Mongada discovers your deceit?"

Lucita smiled in answer. "There is no deceit," she said.

"Already, I have sent word of what I have offered to Madrid. You are right in assuming that Mongada has no love of Venice. The Heresy had gained too much strength already, and he would not support anyone in a position of power who practiced the Red Pentecost. This is not," she added, "necessarily a problem. He has no hatred of you personally, only of what your sire has stood for. If you are cutting one tie, why not the other? Or are you waiting for the Dark Father to knock at your door and lead you away to a new world of darkness?"

"I should be a pawn of Madrid, then?" Alfonzo answered, pointedly ignoring her last question.

"Cooperation is not fealty," she replied. "A prince should not be a pawn of anyone, but neither can he rule without allies or support. Narses offers you support at the cost of intervention. I offer you reciprocity—support to be earned and favors to be returned."

Alfonzo turned away.

"There is the matter of Gabriella, as well," Anatole cut in. "Let us not forget that, though you now know of the tavern and her machinations there, you do not know the extent of what she might be planning. You also cannot afford to allow this to pass without a lesson, or she will feel free to do the same again and again."

"I do not need lessons in warfare, monk," Alfonzo growled. "That is what this has become. There are casualties, and there have been a few skirmishes. Let's see how Lady Gabriella enjoys a real battle."

"Perhaps," Lucita cut in, "you could start at the tavern? My own sources tell me that, though her two lieutenants have departed, others remain, cleaning up the mess and preparing to reopen. Perhaps there might be something to be learned there, if you are discreet."

Alfonzo appeared ready to argue this. It was obvious that he was feeling the sting of Narses' betrayal, and the anger of being duped by Gabriella, even on such a small scale. He wanted to attack directly, squash the threat beneath his boot and move on quickly. Lucita knew that such tactics rarely won out.

"I will be expected to send my people in," he said grudgingly.

"I can instruct them to act as if all that I know of is the attack. If they appear to be seeking information, and nothing more, concentrating on questions about your people, how you invaded and made off with the prisoners, I may be able to learn more than they are expecting to divulge."

"If you can take one of her people," Lucita said calmly, knowing this would be more to his liking, "that might not be a bad idea. My report has two of her own in the tavern now. If you are careful, you might be able to cut the one out without immediately alerting the other. There would be more to learn from one who is close to her counsel than from the mortals who run the tavern."

Alfonzo nodded. "I will see what I can do. The twins will have to go, but I won't send them into the tavern itself. They would he noticed, and those inside would grow cautious. If I can lure one of the two out of the place, they will take him and bring him to me."

Lucita nodded. "I have my own connections," she said. "I am heading for the camps tonight. There are rumors that those who dwell there have grown restless at last. They might pose a threat if they turned toward the city. I intend to see that they do not. There are other places, other new beginnings they can seek." She smiled again. "If you are to rule here," she said softly, "then I will try to see to it that the ascension to the throne is no more difficult than it needs to be."

"I have heard things myself," Alfonzo admitted. "There is unrest in the camps. There are a lot of strange beliefs in this world, and perhaps their focal point in this world now lies directly against the walls of Adrianople. There is no stability there. They could return here, but most of them follow roads that would find little comfort here. They could try to slip in through their rat tunnels and blend with Adrianople, but they would be forced to bow to Licinius if they chose that road, and I do not believe this to be likely.

"He might have brushed them from the wall of his city long before now if he didn't have problems of his own. The crusaders and the Bulgars haven't finished their warring, I think. It is time for those who dwell there to move on."

Lucita nodded. Anatole had grown silent, but he stepped forward now, and Lucita noted with alarm that there was an uncharacteristic tension in his movements. Before she could reach out to him, he spoke.

"You both speak very easily of the fates of others," he said. "You speak of roads to be walked, and I wonder, do either of you walk any road that serves any but yourself? If there is to be a pilgrimage of those who have fled this city, then there is more at stake than that they not come back here. The question of where they end up, what they believe, and who leads them to that belief is not one to be ignored."

Alfonzo didn't speak, but his eyes darkened. Lucita stepped forward.

"What difference would it make to you?" she asked, her voice sharpening. "Do you see yourself leading them? You showed no such compassion on our last visit to the camps. In fact, you showed no interest in them at all."

"There are other powers at work," Anatole said, his features placid once again, but his eyes belying the calm. "There are things worse than a group of fanatics camping at your doorstep. There are those," he added, "who would look at myself, and those who follow me, in much the same manner."

"You are growing soft," Alfonzo said without inflection. "You see insult where none is intended, and take personally things that have little or nothing to do with you. I have heard that you are mad—I have never heard that you were stupid. I do not believe you are stupid now. So," Alfonzo stared at Anatole with open distrust, "what is it that you hope to gain, for whom, and by what manner? I see no obvious gain to you insulting me. I also see no connection between yourself and those in the camps. By your own instruction," Alfonzo nearly smiled, "this would seem to indicate that one of my assumptions is incorrect. Which is it monk? Do you harbor secrets that I should know, or are you just raving and ready to froth at the mouth at a moment's notice?"

Anatole did not rise to the bait, though Alfonzo had straightened and stepped back half a pace, watching closely. There was a long silence. Lucita chose to wait, watching them both, wondering just what Anatole thought he was doing, whether she'd miscalculated her own trusts, and how Alfonzo would react.

Anatole spoke first.

"I have been accused of madness on many occasions," he said softly. "On as many occasions, my madness has proven more than it appeared. I have been accused, as well, of fanaticism. I prefer to think of it as strong belief. Principle. I see more in the evacuation of the camps than you seem to, and so, I have voiced this concern. Perhaps I have been too long in the city myself."

Alfonzo didn't reply, but neither did he seem to be angry. Lucita waited.

"You might not be so far off, at that," he said at last. "Constantinople, before the fall, held many powers. Most of those have dispersed, or been destroyed, but not all. I have contacts in the camps, but they can only report what they can see and learn openly, without risking detection. If Gabriella can have such influence as you have revealed to me so close to my own doorstep, then who knows who—or what—might exert such influence in that camp, or which direction that power might turn next. You have counsel?"

The question was reluctant, but sincere. Anatole, still calm, replied easily.

"I have no counsel for you, Alfonzo. You have counselors aplenty, and power of your own. It may be, however, that I have counsel for those in the camps. It may be that I can suggest roads they have yet to consider, or present the truth behind those already chosen. I am not made for long periods of inactivity, nor for the role of counselor to the destiny of others. Perhaps, though I see many things, I am only just now grasping my own situation."

Alfonzo nodded. "Perhaps. You do not strike me as a follower, for all your quiet ways and advice."

Lucita was bewildered, but relieved that the situation had not grown more volatile. It was obvious that there was something in what she planned that Anatole did not approve of, but she was not certain what, or why. He had given no indication prior to this moment that there was a problem, and she was angry that he would wait until they were in the midst of such a crucial meeting to speak.

"You are certainly under no constraint to remain," she said pointedly.

Anatole met her gaze evenly and without emotion. He did not speak.

Lucita turned back to Alfonzo.

"There is little time," she said. "If you are to catch Gabriella at her games, you must act swiftly. She will know that time is short, and I doubt she'll leave any of her people at the tavern longer than she must. Now is the time to act."

Alfonzo nodded. "I will send my people in, and the two of you will take your own counsel on the camps." He stared at her for a moment longer, holding her gaze. "Two things," he said before turning away. "This time, when you have information for me, I do not expect to be kept waiting for it. If we are to trust one another, then you must give me reasons to offer that trust. If you hesitate when I ask for information, I have to assume you have other things on your mind, and that they may not all bode well for me. I find myself a bit short on trust just now. Don't give me a reason to withdraw it."

"The second thing?" Lucita asked, not committing to an answer.

Alfonzo grew thoughtful, then smiled. "The second is of little significance, in reality, but something that must be addressed. Matteo has been with me a long time. He runs my affairs during the daylight hours, and he knows more than most of my affairs. I could not miss the longing he feels for you—nor," the bishop appraised her openly, "can I blame him, in truth. I suspect, however, that he is not entirely at fault in this, and that you have encouraged him. I have need of him, still, at least until another can be found for his duties. I would not be pleased at his embrace at this time."

Lucita returned Alfonzo's smile. "Understood." Anatole was paying no attention to the two of them. He stared off toward the doorway, and the night beyond. She wondered what was happening behind those deep, deep eyes, but it was not the time to ask.

"I will send someone to report when I have returned from
the camps," she said, striding toward the door. Anatole fell into
step at her side as if nothing odd had taken place, and inwardly,
she shrugged. The two passed from the large chamber, leaving
Alfonzo staring at their backs. They made their way down the
long hall and out into the darkness of the city silently, each lost
in their own thoughts.

At the tavern, deep inside the Latin Quarter, Brother Torquato's
wagon had turned the last corner and pulled up to the head of
the alley that backed the building. He glanced up and down the
street, not completely comfortable with leaving the wagon unattended and in full view. He saw no one, however, and finally
he slipped from the driver's seat and into the alley, walking
quickly to the back door of the tavern and rapping sharply on
the door, as he'd been instructed.

He was certain it was the right place. There were symbols,
not easily visible in the shadows, but clear enough to any who
sought them. They were etched lightly into the stone beside
the door. His instructions had been clear. He was to deliver
the wine, take any parcels or messages that awaited delivery to
Venice, and be on his way. No stopping to enjoy the local cul-
ture. No side trips, though his sire, Jacobo, had requested that
he keep his ears open. People felt at ease around Torquato. He
was quiet and unassuming, and he could be counted on to pay
attention and to follow instructions. Of course, he was a long
way from Venice, and he had not made many such journeys. If
Jacobo himself had not insisted he do so, he would not have left
his cellars, or his city, at all.

Something was in the wind. Something big, or perhaps many
things. The trip to Constantinople had its practical purposes, to
move wine and ale from the cellars of a prosperous city to the
thirsty throats of one recently in ruins, but Torquato suspected
there was more to it than that. Any driver, or group of monks,
could have made the journey as easily, and many of them were
more experienced at both travel and the world. There was
something happening that Jacobo hoped to hear of, and so, he
had sent Brother Torquato, hoping that the monk's half-human

countenance and ability to blend into a crowd would allow him to bring back the information that was desired.

If only he could discover what that was.

It was a long time before his second sharp knock was answered. The man who stood inside the doorway glared at him in open hostility, and Torquato bowed quickly, taking half a step back to show he meant no harm.

"I did not mean to disturb," he said, "but I have a wagon laden with wine and ale from the cellars of Venice standing at the end of the alley. I have been directed to deliver several barrels of each to you, and have come to make good on that bargain."

Torquato watched the man warily. There was something more than normal caution in that craggy face, and it wouldn't do to walk into trouble with his eyes closed. The man glared at him again, then swept his gaze up and down Torquato's plain brown robes. Balding, slightly portly from the sampling of his own wares over the years, the only indication that the monk might be more than what he appeared to be, a pale, ugly little man, was the almost grayish pallor of his skin. In the darkened alley, this was not something the man could make out, so he made a mistake. He assumed that he faced nothing more than a simple monk with a wagon, and he sneered.

"Come back in the morning," he said gruffly. "We're open now—there's no time to unload a wagon."

Torquato stood his ground, and smiled. "Perhaps if I were to unload myself?" he asked, keeping his voice steady. "I have to be out of the city by morning, and on my way to Adrianople for another delivery."

The man scowled. "I said come back in the morning," he repeated. "We aren't taking deliveries tonight. We had some trouble yesterday, and there's no one to spare."

"I'd be happy to unload myself," Torquato insisted. I can bring it in and load it wherever you ask. In fact, if you are short-handed, I'd be happy to help out for a while. It's been a long trip, and I haven't had much company."

The man looked as if he were about to slam the door and go about his business, but he hesitated. Once again, Torquato felt the man's gaze sliding over him, appraising. Then the door swung wider.

"All right, then," the man said. "I'm Lucius. If you need me, I'll be in the front. Bring the ale and wine in and stack it here by the stairs. We'll take it down later. Whatever you do, if you see anyone around this door, or in the alley, close up, and come and find me. Like I said, we had trouble yesterday. We don't want any tonight."

Torquato bowed slightly, and turned toward the wagon without a word. The quicker he got his goods inside and the wagon to a place of greater safety, the sooner he could relax. Besides, this would be a perfect opportunity to listen. He wasn't certain what kind of trouble the man spoke of, but whatever it was, it might prove of interest to Jacobo. Any way you sliced it, it would be of interest to Torquato himself. He'd not spent much time outside the walls of his order, and even inside he was most often found alone in the cellars, poring over recipes acquired from other vintners and working out ways to improve his wine.

The order had been for three barrels of ale and four of wine. It wasn't a huge order, and for a fleeting moment Torquato wondered why, if this were all they desired, the tavern's owners didn't order from local vintners. Surely, they could find such small amounts at a much cheaper cost than that of shipping it in from Venice. More to consider. More questions, no answers.

As he moved up and down the alley, rolling the barrels slowly, not wanting to give any indication of his true nature unless the issue were forced, two sets of eyes watched his movements carefully. On the roof of the building directly across the alley, Arturo and Leonid waited. They watched as he worked, sensing what he kept to himself and wondering at his presence.

They also watched the front of the tavern, those coming, and those going, waiting. Half the night had passed, and what they sought would not be long in coming, if it came at all. They sat cross-legged and swathed in shadow like two blonde gargoyles, watching the alley and the street beyond.

Torquato did not see them, and when he'd unloaded the ale, and the wine, he returned to his wagon, moved it a few streets down, into another alley, drawing a covering over it and tying it securely. When he was done, it looked like any other wagon of the quarter. Dingy and half-abandoned. He unhitched the horses, leading them back down the street, and tied them at the head of the alley by the tavern. They might have belonged to a customer, or the tavern itself. He hoped they would be there when he returned, but there was nothing to do for it. He had to speak with the owners of the tavern before he could depart, and that meant returning to the back and inside, where he could lend a hand where it was needed.

As he stepped in through the back entrance, he heard a soft sound and glanced up and behind himself. He saw nothing in the shadows, and the sound did not repeat itself. Uneasily, he entered the back of the tavern and closed the door behind himself, locking it securely.

Chapter Fifteen

Inside the tavern, Ian and Pasqual had moved their game board to a table near the rear. The pieces were arranged to appear as if they were in the midst of a game, but no moves had been made in some time. They were waiting, and watching. It was unlikely that those who had made the attack by daylight would he back tonight. In fact, judging by the manner in which the pair had apparently left the building, it was unlikely they would ever return. Still, they might not be working alone, and those allies might try another attack. So, Ian and Pasqual watched, and they waited, and as the evening progressed, the room filled slowly, then more quickly, all hint of trouble forgotten in the easy flow of liquor, blood wine, and the prospect of a night's entertainment.

"How long do we have to put on this show," Ian asked at last, staring at the mock game between them and toying with one of the pieces. "I'm ready to be out of here and back at the camp."

"Not yet," Pasqual replied. "There is time. It won't take us long to make the journey, and if there is anything to be learned here, and we let it slip away from us without trying for it, it won't be a happy reunion when we get back. Surely you have the patience to sacrifice a single night?"

"We are wasting our time," Ian growled. "If there were anything to learn in this God-forsaken place, it has been lost in the wine and the ale. There are only a couple of others here who aren't mortal, and neither of them is any threat. The bartender is new, but he is our man, and the new watcher is in place in the kitchen. What could happen that would require us to be sitting here, wasting our time and watching vermin crawl over and around the tables?"

He punctuated this last by snaking his fist out and bringing it down hard on a roach that had flicked its antennae up over the table's edge, then drawn itself up to search for food.

"Arrogant little bastard," Ian frowned, wiping his hand on his cloak.

Pasqual laughed. "Impatient, even with the bugs," he snorted. "You would make a poor spy, I'm thinking. An even less inspiring priest. I can't imagine your reaction to a long, involved presentation of some poor man's sins."

"I would relieve him of his misery," Ian asserted, sitting back and scanning the room in obvious boredom. "That response would empty the pews quickly enough. Perhaps I'd explain to him about Caine, deliver a short sermon on the coming darkness and how his weak, worthless life would soon devote itself only to my pleasure. I certainly would not sit, hour after hour, as he poured out a string of nonsense that I was to answer with a dose of Hail Mary's and penance."

Ian rose. "I'm going to take a walk," he announced. "I'll check around the alley in back, and then the street. No sense in both of us wasting our time in here, and there are a couple of people watching us and beginning to wonder why we play this game, hour after hour, without making any moves."

Pasqual did not answer immediately. He was troubled by something, it was obvious in his expression, but on the surface there was nothing wrong with Ian's suggestion. They had had no indication that anything was amiss in the crowd. There were a couple of Alfonzo's men in the tavern, trying to appear as if they were regulars and passing well enough, except among those who were watching for them. This was to be expected. When something out of the ordinary happened in the quarter, Alfonzo's people were bound to show up sooner or later.

Pasqual nodded, at last. He was clearly not happy, but he couldn't come up with a viable reason to hold Ian back. The younger Cainite was uncomfortable with inaction. There was some wisdom in watching the exterior of the tavern, as well, and Pasqual knew he could handle anything that might take place in his partner's absence.

Ian drifted away from the table, skirting the tables where

Alfonzo's men sat, making loud, boisterous conversation and pretending to drink too much ale. He didn't want to be dragged into that conversation, or to draw any unwanted attention to himself, or Pasqual. The two of them operated in a wholly different fashion from the boisterous Raphael and his ill-tempered friend, Gradin. Ian slipped out the door and into the shadows, relieved to be on his feet and moving. He glanced down the street, then back the other way. He saw a man tying horses at the head of the alley. Short, portly and bald, wearing the robes of a Dominican. Ian hesitated. There was something odd in the man's presence, particularly with a pair of horses.

Ian watched and waited as the figure turned into the alley behind the tavern. The monk, if he was indeed a monk, did not reappear, and Ian's curiosity got the better of him. He moved to the head of the alley, glanced around at the street in either direction, then slipped into the shadows of the alley himself.

There was no one in sight. There were no side entrances to the alley, the only way out was the way he'd come in, and the far end, which was a long block away. There had been no time for the monk to make his way to the far end. Ian glanced at the rear entrance to the tavern. It was closed, as it had been when he'd last seen it upon their arrival. Could the monk have gone inside? What did it mean, if he had, and why—the question nagged at him—did the man have *two* horses?

Ian moved down the alley, splitting his concentration between the far end of the alley, and the door to the tavern. If someone had entered this way, then he and Pasqual had better find out who, and why. This was the sort of information they'd been sent to gather, and it wouldn't do to let something important slip right out from under his nose.

If Pasqual had been with him, he would possibly have pointed out that Ian was learning too slowly. He was focused on the immediate and unaware of the larger scope of the moment. He was in danger of sudden checkmate and too blinded to take notice. The twins watched him from above for a moment, then, at a nod from Arturo, they launched silently from the roof and into the alley. Ian heard the whoosh of their bodies slicing the air, and spun toward the entrance to the alley, but it was too late. Leonid landed easily, directly in front of him, and as he launched himself at that blond-haired, grinning threat, a heavy weight hit him from behind, and he found himself pinned beneath Arturo. Ian fought, but he was no match for the two, and before he knew what had happened, he found his arms manacled tightly behind him and a leather hood drawn over his head to cut off both sight and the ability to call for aid. He was hoisted roughly onto the twins' shoulders, and they were off, moving swiftly down the street to where others waited with a cart. Ian was dropped, struggling madly, into the back of the cart and quickly covered with a tarp.

The twins spoke a few terse commands to the driver, then spun away into the night. The cart jostled off down the street toward Alfonzo's mansion, and the street, once again, fell silent.

Inside the tavern, Brother Torquato had found Lucius, rushing about behind the bar and shouting orders at two other men, who appeared ready to snap and break his neck. The place was packed with all sorts, some obviously Cainite, others mortal—a rough crowd. Brother Torquato had seen enough drunks in his time, but never so close-packed and full of energy. He touched Lucius lightly on the arm as he passed.

"I have finished unloading," he said calmly. "How can I be of service?"

Lucius stared at him for a moment, uncomprehendingly, then grunted. "Oh, yes." He thought for a moment, then snapped, "Grab one of those barrels of ale you just unloaded and roll it out to the front. We're halfway through the barrel I opened an hour ago, and it's flowing like water. I've never seen such thirst. When that's done, meet me in the back, and we'll stow that wine. I don't want it getting uncorked and sampled before I have the chance to collect its cost."

Torquato smiled and nodded, spinning back to the rear of the tavern. He gripped one of the barrels, started to lift it and take it to the front, then remembered where he was, and that no one, so far, knew him for more than he appeared—a mortal wagon driver. He tipped the barrel on its edge and rolled it slowly toward the front of the tavern, making a show of manipulating it carefully, as if it were a great burden that taxed his strength.

As he worked, he thought. He took in the crowd, watched each table from the corner of his eye, fascinated. It was so different from his own world, the quiet cellars, the long hours with parchment and pen, worrying over inventory and aging, vintner's recipes and savoring the silence of his brethren. Here, there were no boundaries, it seemed. Some were so drunk they staggered, their faces reddened and their voices loud. Others slumped, the wine, or the ale taking control of their thoughts and speeding them away to some far place, beyond the walls of tavern and city. The end product, he realized, of his own art.

Also, there was the blood wine. Torquato had only recently become fascinated with the subtle and specialized art of making blood-laced wine the undead could consume. He wondered which method had been employed in its creation, longed to test the quality. He himself preferred the newer method, that which required a young, strong mortal and half a barrel of wine. One plied the subject with glass after glass, cajoling, teasing, then taking firm control of the mind. Once this was accomplished, an inordinate amount of wine would pour, the subject unconscious by this time, but still controlled. When just the perfect balance had been reached, before the subject could void the contents of bladder or blood, or die from the consumption, they must be lain back on the table and drained, quickly—catching every drop through a stone table with a funnel and a drain, and corked. This was essential. The product had to be stored in the coldest of the cellars and consumed quickly. There was no good way to age the output, so it had to be combined with well-aged wine from the start.

It did not take Torquato long to get the barrel in place behind the bar, and one of the two men helped him muscle it into place. It was none too soon. The first barrel was drawing its last, and the bartended deftly unplugged the new barrel, popping the wooden spigot into place and drawing a mug to test. He sipped, smiled, and nodded at Torquato, who smiled. He knew that it was good; he'd brewed it himself.

This done, he returned to the back, where he found Lucius

leaning on a wall wearily. The man sized him up, nodded, and started toward the back stairs. Torquato grabbed a wine barrel and tipped it carefully on its edge, but Lucius, who was watching him now, shook his head.

"None of that nonsense," he said with a wink. "Your act may fool those in the front, but with enough wine or ale, you could convince them you're their mother. I know what you are, so heft that barrel and be quick about it. If I'd wanted someone to roll them down the stairs to burst and be spoiled, I would have called one of the boys from the front."

Torquato blinked, nodded, and hefted the barrel easily. There were six in all, the seventh having been the one he took to the bar, and Lucius stood aside, watching him, obviously with no intention of carrying any barrels himself. Torquato didn't mind. It was easy, familiar work.

"This your first stop?" Lucius asked, suddenly more friendly. Away from the bustle of the tavern, his features had softened a hit. Torquato imagined it was a relief to be out of the pressure-packed environment, even for a few moments.

"First in the city. I've been at Hadrian's Rest for the past few nights."

"Oh?" Lucius asked. "You came from Adrianople, then. It seems like everyone is coming through there these nights. I've heard some stories about that place now, good ones, I might add. Strange goings on in those camps. Caine himself has been seen, you know? And others. I'd dearly love to see what goes on there, but those who dwell there aren't fond of outsiders."

Torquato laughed. "I have no sign of Caine," he replied, "but I have met others. It seems these camps really are a nexus of activity."

Lucius followed him down the stairs. "You might want to keep your visit to the camps to yourself," the man said, almost conspiratorially. "There are those in the tavern tonight who are seeking information, and they might be willing to use methods that would he less than pleasant to drag it out of a man...or other."

"I'm sure I have nothing they would be interested in," Torquato replied. "I did not speak to this Malachite, and only saw him for a few short moments. He was speaking with another, and she was no Nosferatu. I didn't want to impose."

"She?" Lucius asked. Torquato glanced at the man. He certainly was the curious sort. Still, there was no reason to distrust him. Beyond a few sharp words at the door, the man had offered him no ill will.

"Yes," Torquato continued, placing the first barrel and starting up the stairs again. He gave a quick account of the meeting between Gabriella and Malachite. Lucius listened attentively, making encouraging comments now and again, but mostly listening. Torquato was happy for the opportunity to hone his conversational skills, and to test his newest tale before taking it home and presenting it to his brethren.

"You say he offered her support?" Lucius asked when Torquato was finished. "Very strange times, indeed. That must have been the Lady Gabriella. She is out of Genoa, and well thought of in the city, but certainly not in the context of being a friend to Malachite."

"They did not seem to be friends." Torquato commented.

Lucius laughed. "In this city, and near it, it is best to trust later and question earlier. Everyone has their own stake in what is to come. I've heard the rumor before that the camps would empty. Now you say they will move toward France. This is a new twist, but better news than to hear that they intended to return here and try to carve out a corner of the Latin Quarter for their own. The city has room for only so many leaders."

"That is true of any city," Torquato said, hefting the last of the barrels to his shoulder and beginning the descent to the cellars. "Who is the leader here?"

The question was innocent enough, but it got a start out of Lucius. A short, guilty expression flitted across his rough features, then was gone again.

"There is no prince in Constantinople," he answered. "There are many who may step forward and claim such a position, but that is the game, you see. None wants to stake a claim he or she cannot back up, and none is certain enough—yet—of their control.

"There is the Bishop Alfonzo, very likely the strongest and

best connected, but with difficulties of his own. There have been recent attacks, and distractions. There is the Lady Gabriella, she whom you saw in the camps. Rumor had it that Malachite would return and set about the job of rebuilding the city in its own image, but that appears to be a false report. There are a couple of others."

Torquato placed the final barrel. He turned with a quick smile. "Well, I will leave you to your customers, your tavern, and your many leaders," he said. "I have a long journey still ahead of me and I have only barely enough time to get out of the city and find a place to shelter for the night. It has been interesting talking with you."

Lucius nodded, his gaze far away, as if other thoughts had suddenly intruded. "Thank you for your cargo, and your assistance," the bartender said, glancing up with his smile back in place. "Have a good journey, and may you continue to avoid Dark Caine on the roads."

They both laughed at this, and moments later Lucius was holding the door for Torquato, who stepped into the alley, and with a wave was gone. He found his horses at the end of the alley, just as he'd left them, and led them off down the street toward the alley and his wagon.

As he trotted away, he chided himself for surrendering so much information to the man. But, after all, he had spoken only of local matters and he owed this Gabriella woman nothing. He had kept his message from Markus Musa Giovanni secret and that was all that truly mattered. Malachite would soon he gone for France and, assuming the news he'd conveyed was welcome, be meeting Giovanni on the road.

Lucius watched for a long moment as Torquato left, then glanced furtively over his shoulder into the gloomy interior of the tavern.

Seeing no one, he stepped into the alley and quietly closed the door behind himself. He gave a short low whistle, and moments later, Arturo dropped through the shadows from the rooftop once more, slipping up beside the bartender so quickly and quietly that the man nearly screamed at the hand on his shoulder.

"What is it?" Arturo asked. "You were not to call us until you knew something important. If they find that you speak with me, they will kill you."

Lucius nodded, glancing about nervously. "This is important," he said. Then, breathlessly and with as few words as possible, he passed on what he'd learned of Gabriella's meeting with Malachite, and of the coming exodus from the camps. Arturo listened intently, particularly the part about Prince Licinius of Adrianople. Then, without acknowledging the message, or the messenger, he was gone. He scaled the wall and slipped over the roof like a shadow, joined instantly by his twin, and the two streaked off across the city, leaving Lucius standing alone in the alley. He watched a moment longer, glanced up and down the alley, then slipped back into the noise and jumble of the tavern. The door closed behind him with a solid thud.

On the street, the soft clatter of horse's hooves and the creak of a wagon's wheels ushered Brother Torquato toward the gates and beyond, whistling softly to himself, already mulling over the favors he might ask of the Giovanni traders when he returned to Venice. The tavern, and its curious bartender, fell away behind him with the wind.

Chapter Sixteen

Lucita and Anatole headed for the camps once again, but the tension was thick. Something had changed with her companion, and Lucita wasn't absolutely certain what it was. She didn't want to confront him, because she wasn't certain what the confrontation would entail, and there were things she needed to accomplish. She didn't want to be out of the city any longer than was absolutely necessary, but this trip couldn't be put off. Anatole had been her companion many times in the past, but each time there had come a point when they parted. She had not anticipated that it would be so soon, but she could sense that he was pulling away from her, distracted by something beyond her understanding.

Anatole was a good companion, and he could be an invaluable counselor, but he had his own road. Sometimes it was easy to push this aside, focusing on herself and her goals without considering that he might not agree. Anatole hadn't openly challenged her, but she suspected that there was more to his silence than introspection.

They were making for Hadrian's Rest, a rest-stop on their road, when Lucita caught sight of activity ahead. There were fires lining the road, and many voices floated out to them. "What's this?" she asked.

"Our destination," Anatole answered.

"What? But the camps are several nights off still.

Their heart is here," Anatole said. "Here is the thing has stirred them."

Lucita nodded, but did not reply. The voices were growing louder, coming from a large clearing just off the road. She stopped the carriage and descended. Before she headed toward the small crowd, her hand slipped to the hilt of her blade, as if testing to be certain it rested where she'd left it.

"I do not believe you will need that tonight," Anatole said. "They are concentrated on another. I can hear his voice from here."

She turned and glanced at him, then returned her attention to the voices. As they approached, she could make out that there were murmurs in the clearing, but only one voice speaking aloud. It was a strong voice, speaking in powerful and compelling Greek. It rang through the streets and drew the attention of all who were gathered. Lucita understood the language well enough, but her ear was more used to Latin and the *langue d'oc*, so it was one of the murmurs she caught first. "Malachite has returned," one of the gathered souls said.

Lucita stopped for a moment, bewildered. "Malachite is here?" she whispered.

Anatole did not answer, but neither did he stop at her side. The monk continued on toward those who were gathered, and Lucita hurried after him, falling into step at his side just as he reached the rear of the small crowd.

"The time has come," Malachite intoned, "to move on. The city is behind us. The Dream? Michael's dream of a great city is just as it has always been. It is behind us *and* ahead. We carry it with us, and we can rebuild it in any image we can imagine, and many that no single one of us could imagine. There are leaders to show the way, and there are roads that lead to better times.

"I ask you," he said, "are the camps our, your future? Is that the end of those who ruled the greatest city in the world? Will that be the end of our road, or the beginning? I will go there to bring my message and then leave that place. I am going on a journey that could end a thousand ways, and all of them better than the ruin of Constantinople and the camps of Adrianople. War nips at your heels. The city you loved rejects you, the city you have latched onto ignores you—for the moment.

"You are the disowned. There is power in the camps, among those of us disowned. In numbers, in wisdom and years. We believe strongly enough to deliver yourselves from the fall of Constantinople. Let that belief carry us to something new. Something even more grand, more powerful. Let that belief lend us wings. It is time to fly."

The words were overblown and grand, but Lucita could see that they were being gobbled voraciously by the gathered throng, and she knew how well it would all play in Adrianople camps. Even here, on the road, there were other Nosferatu, hanging on Malachite's every word. There were small bands of Toreador, bedraggled and wide-eyed, ready to map such a journey in drama and song. Ready to rebuild the finery they remembered and to leave this nightmare pit they had called home for too long.

Malkavians dotted the small crowd, here and there, disheveled robes and stark features rigid. Among them, Lucita was startled to see the two who had joined Anatole and herself on the rooftops. It seemed that some of the questions were being answered.

"They have heard him before," she whispered, turning to Anatole. "You knew this?"

"I knew that he's been to the camps and would come to his city's very door to carry his message," Anatole replied. "I knew that the camps would empty, and that it would happen soon. I did not know all the details, nor do I know them now. You indicated before that you would be happy if those in the camps would move on, so I did not think you would be upset to find out it was happening."

"I did not know it would be Malachite," she replied. "Has he found the Dracon? Is he here alone?"

"The Dracon's location is as much a mystery as it has been since he departed the city," Anatole assured her. "Malachite is on his own quest. He has received visions, and he will not remain here for long, whether they follow him, or not. Many have already decided. Others join them daily. The only real task left to him is to decide how to control them. It is one thing to convince them all to leave here, where they don't wish to be in the first place. Once they are moving, however, or once they reach France—that is where I understand he would lead them— it is another matter."

"It isn't a task I would set for myself," Lucita agreed. "I wonder why he bothers. I wonder why he doesn't just take those who would go willingly, and leave the rest to rot here."

"I told you," Anatole replied almost smugly, "he acts upon a vision."

Lucita restrained the urge to roll her eyes at this. She had heard Anatole speak of visions many times before. Sometimes they seemed to be honest glimpses into the future. Other times she was certain he had cloaked thin suspicions and lightly veiled intuitions in the language of vision for his own purposes. To many, wisdom could take on the trappings of divine knowledge with no great leap of faith, and it was to such as those that "visions" appealed most strongly. Lucita was fonder of hard fact and action.

They watched a few moments longer, then moved along the side of the crowd, trying to make out faces. Lucita saw few that she knew, though there were some. She had known at least a portion of each of the great houses in Constantinople before the fall. She knew there were others would be in the camps, those who had already been convinced, or those who kept to themselves, preferring to remain in their dens and hideaways, seeking their own answers, or just waiting to decide whether to stay, or to go, when the time came and the pilgrimage began.

Malachite had disappeared from his makeshift stage, and the crowd dispersed into smaller groups, surrounding fires, or retreating into doorways and beneath the street.

The words that had been spoken would be contemplated, spread to those who had not been present, discussed, argued, and remembered. That was the purpose of such a gathering, to stir the coals in the fire and fan it to a blaze. Malachite, it seemed, had a particular talent for this.

"He will have them ready to leave within a month's time," Anatole commented. "The time is here. If it had not been Malachite, it would have been another. They cannot leech off of the side of Adrianople forever, and there is no place for them any longer within the Empire."

"That is their own choice," Lucita replied. "We choose our place in the night, then we deal with those choices."

"I hope that you will deal so easily with the bedfellow you have chosen," Anatole said. "I am not so certain of your choice."

"You mean Alfonzo? I thought you supported him as prince."

"I supported you, and whatever you chose, but Alfonzo is a different matter. He may see the strength in cooperation, or he may turn on you the moment this business with Gabriella is concluded. He will support himself, and no other, in the end."

"I would expect no less, old friend," she smiled suddenly. "Surely you don't believe I would trust him? I do what I do to create the lesser of evils, or possibly to geld the greater of them. Gabriella would be a problem, were she to rule, and given free reign, Narses might well have gotten Alfonzo into power without my assistance. Even if I fail, I will have severed, or severely damaged, Alfonzo's ties to Venice. Mongada should be pleased."

"Let us hope your sire sees the wisdom in this that you do," Anatole commented dryly. "I assume you lied when you told Alfonzo you had sent word to Madrid?"

"Actually," Lucita smiled, "I sent word *after* we spoke. No sense in being rash, but I don't want to appear to be acting too independently. I'd rather that Mongada continue to trust me, as well."

"A wise choice," Anatole nodded.

Suddenly, a tall, slender figure melted from the shadows, and the two stopped.

Malachite watched them in silence, studying them intently.

"Surely," he said at last, "you have not come to join me, Lucita of Aragon. Do not be surprised I recognize you, you who came to our lands to help bring Byzantium down in flames."

"You see what you wish to see," Lucita countered, barely controlling the urge to grip the hilt of her sword. "Perhaps you sell me short. Still, you are correct. I have not come to join you. In truth, I did not know you were here."

"I have not announced myself, except in small gatherings," Malachite replied. "I prefer to let those within Adrianople's walls and in fallen Constantinople believe the reports of my arrival are similar to the sightings of Caine, and Calomena. Rumors, myths. I would rather they believe I am running about the globe in search of the Dracon."

A hint of melancholy echoed in these last words, and for the briefest moment a flicker of something akin to sorrow flitted across the Nosferatu's hideous countenance. Lucita caught it, even though it was fleeting, and he was still cloaked in shadows.

"I am leaving soon for the West," Malachite continued. "I have traveled far, been through many adventures, and seen a great number of things that can only be considered as signs. I believe that we will be welcome in Paris, and so, I will lead those who will follow. There is nothing for them here, and destruction is close at hand. Licinius might have taken them in, but this is a troubled group, and they are more restless than that. They don't wish to be taken in, but to rebuild, to find a new dream and make it their own. When wanderlust strikes, it is a hard thing to control."

"The old ways are passing," Lucita said. "The old dream is faded, as all dreams must. If half the tales they tell of you are true, then you should be wise enough to see this. The dream your people knew is gone. The perfect city, the work of the trinity of Byzantine elders, is no more. Two of those three are no more. The Dracon flees, and if I guess rightly, has no more desire to return to Constantinople than these who would follow you west. It is over."

"Endings and beginnings," Anatole chimed in, "have a way of blending and twisting until it is difficult to separate one from the other."

Malachite nodded at these words.

"I will travel your road with you for a time," Anatole continued. "I have been too long in the city, and I sense something here—something important. I will not follow. I follow no one but myself, and my vision, but I will go west. It is time."

Malachite nodded again, not seeming surprised. Anatole knew that his own people had been circulating through the camps. Those who followed him were dedicated beyond thought. They would not follow if he remained behind, but it was obvious they wanted to leave. The very ground beneath their feet seemed to groan with the weight of the camps, as if it would heave up and cast them along their way to be rid of them.

There is a sensation you get when you belong somewhere. That sensation had left the camps. It could be seen in the eyes and heard it in the voices of all who surrounded the three. The time had come for action, for motion. This place had gone stale, and it no longer felt like a settlement at all, but instead like a trap. It would not take long for it to become an empty husk. And for all Lucita's scoffing, stories of Caine were not something Anatole could ignore.

"What of Gabriella?" Lucita asked. Malachite started slightly, and her expression said that she knew she'd hit her mark. "She has spies throughout the camps. Will they follow, do you think?"

Malachite had regained his composure. "I don't presume to speak for Gabriella," he answered. "I don't know what she plans, but I do not believe she is ready to leave the city. She still has her connections, and unlike many others, her home is not destroyed. She is comfortable enough, for the moment, but I do not believe she will leave any here. There would be no purpose."

"Gabriella," Lucita said, "is not a follower. I am not surprised she will not follow you, but I wonder. If she is to stay in Constantinople, will she follow another, or will she try to take control?"

"That is an issue to be taken up with those of the city," Malachite replied stoically. "It is no concern of mine." Lucita watched him carefully, but he gave away nothing. It was obvious he knew something of Gabriella, but what that might be, he was not going to reveal. Lucita turned away.

"I see nothing further to be learned here. I am returning to the city," she turned to Anatole, "will you be joining me?"

Anatole shook his head. "I will not return to the city," he replied. "There is nothing further I can accomplish there, and the best support I can be to you is to remove the tension between myself and the bishop before it can become an obstacle."

Lucita watched him for a moment, bit her lip and almost asked him to reconsider. There were many times the two of them did not see eye to eye, but in a rough situation, there was no other she would prefer to have at her side. This was certainly shaping up to be a rough situation, and though she'd been angry with him, she found she was also loath to see him depart.

"Are you sure?" she asked. "There is so much to do."

"For you, yes," Anatole smiled, "and you are more than adequate to the task. We will meet again, you and I. Perhaps we will travel again, as well. For now, I must go, and you have your own roads to travel. I wish you well." Giving in to the moment, Lucita stepped close and embraced the monk. "You as well. And watch this one," she said, nodding toward Malachite. "I'm not certain what motivates him, but I'm certain that whatever it is will come before any momentary alliances he might make."

Both Malachite and Anatole laughed at this, and Lucita began to grow angry, then let it go with a shake of her head. The two of them were cut from similar cloth, even if the weave were drastically different. Neither would trust the other too far, but their minds were set, and nothing she could do would persuade them otherwise.

"I must go," she said, turning back toward where they'd left the carriage. "I have to reach the city before nightfall. Until we meet again, old friend," she said, smiling at Anatole a final time. He nodded in reply, and she turned away, already thinking of what she would tell Alfonzo, and the report she must make to Madrid.

The two watched her depart, then turned away, both from her and each other. Malachite returned to whatever underground burrow he'd chosen for himself, and Anatole took to the streets to gather those of his following who were already present.

Lucita mounted the carriage, took up the reins, and made as tight a turn as the narrow, dusty road would allow, angling back out of the camps and onto the long road to the city. There was plenty of night left to her, and she intended to make the most of every moment of it. She whipped the horses to a gallop and roared back down the road.

Chapter Seventeen

Arturo and Leonid had lost no time in reaching Alfonzo with what they had learned. They were back at the mansion long before the wagon carrying Ian could arrive, and when it did, Alfonzo had a hand-picked crew, including the twins, waiting for him. The bishop had listened carefully as the two reported what they had learned.

Since that moment, Alfonzo had paced the corridors, walked along the balconies, and cursed loudly at any who came near. His anger was spectacular, and none wished to give him another opportunity to vent it. He sent Matteo for Lucita, but the young man returned, greatly agitated, reporting that she was not to be found. Alfonzo ordered Matteo to walk with him, turned on his heel, and started toward the balconies once again, retracing steps he'd walked a dozen times that night.

Matteo hurried in his lord's wake, uncertain whether he should be honored at the opportunity to accompany the bishop, or in fear for his life at being the only living thing close at hand to smite.

"It is too much," Alfonzo growled at last. He'd been stalking up and down the length of a balcony that overlooked the street leading toward the city gate. "Are there none to be trusted anywhere in this forsaken cesspool of a city? Everywhere I turn, I find betrayal. Venice sends assassins to kill my childe—wanting, I am certain, only to protect me. Gabriella sends her minions skulking about the Latin Quarter, bribing tavern owners and plotting to take over the city—and with a Nosferatu. I take a new childe, and now I am threatened with the same treatment over her that I suffered for Isadora. Lucita, who claims to support me, heads toward Adrianople at the worst possible time," Alfonzo rounded on Matteo quickly, "and has been seducing my closest assistant from beneath my very nose."

"She will return," Matteo replied, blushing, but not denying what his lord could clearly see.

Emboldened by the fact he was still standing, Matteo continued. "It is not too late to turn what you have learned of Gabriella to your advantage, milord," he said, speaking quickly so he could get out what he had to say before Alfonzo flew into another rage. "She does not yet know what you know. Why not send a messenger, immediately, to Licinius? You could tell him about Katrina yourself. He didn't want her and if Gabriella is given no opportunity to make it seem as if you stole her from behind his back, then there will be no quarrel. At the same time, you could tell him of her plotting, directly outside his own gates, with the Nosferatu. A fast rider could catch Lady Lucita and the monk as well, tell them to return to your side."

Alfonzo stared at him, concentrating. Then, the bishop turned away and glanced down at the street below so that Matteo would not catch him smiling. The boy had promise. He had the mind for intrigue, and he was showing more courage than Alfonzo would have given him credit for. Perhaps Lucita had been good for him.

Just at that moment, the clatter of horses' hooves on the street below announced the arrival of a wagon. Close on its heels, another carriage whipped around the corner, coming from the city gates.

"Send a messenger to Licinius," Alfonzo said quietly, not turning. "Someone who is fast, and can be trusted. Not the twins. I have work for them here, and I need someone who will not be hampered by the sunrise. I will feed him my blood and more to the horse, so they may make fast time over the road. It is imperative that the message reach Licinius before Gabriella has a chance to be heard. I will pen the message myself. Send your messenger to me within the hour."

Matteo bowed and backed away, hurrying back down the corridor and center stairs toward the kitchen. He knew who the carriage belonged to from sound alone. He could sense her, and he knew that Alfonzo had sensed her as well. Why had she returned so soon?

As he neared the kitchens, he saw a man he knew only as Luis lounging against the door frame. Luis was one of the captains of the mercenaries that Alfonzo employed to assist in keeping order in the quarter. They were seldom visible by day, when the citizens of the city might seek the good graces of the bishop, or leaders of church and state were abroad. It was a thin veneer of respectability, but as long as Alfonzo was willing to perpetuate it, those who walked in the daylight seemed only too ready to accept it.

Luis was a good man. He'd been with Alfonzo since he was a boy, and if it were not for the fact he hailed from a small city in the mountains, and not Constantinople itself, Matteo might not have considered him a mercenary at all. Matteo hurried up and greeted the soldier, outlining his need of a messenger as quickly and concisely as possible.

"Can you do it?" he asked at last. "I would ask for one of your men, in most cases, but this time the bishop has requested someone who will he fast, someone who will be listened to when they arrive—and someone he can trust. There are not many to whom this description can be applied."

"I will go," Luis replied, draining a flask of ale he'd been nursing. "I've been itching for a reason to get out of this place. There is nothing I hate more than sitting inactive."

"Good," Matteo sighed with relief. "He is waiting for you now. This is a very important task, my friend. Be certain that if it goes quickly, and well, the reward for this success will not be a small one."

Luis nodded, dropped the now-empty flask on top of the barrel and turned toward the stairs.

"Then I'd better not keep the bishop waiting," he said with a laugh, clearly anxious to taste his master's favor.

Matteo watched him go and was suddenly, deeply aware of just how much he would have wanted that mission for himself only a few weeks ago. Luis and his steed would both drink deeply from the bishop's veins so that they could ride without rest, making Adrianople in a day and a night when it took others a week. The beast would have to be killed—for the blood would eventually make the animal unmanageable to all save the bishop himself—but the man would rise in status if he did his work well. To taste the bishop's blood again would become the center of the man's existence, as it had once been the center of Matteo's.

Before Lucita.

Snapping out of his reverie, he went through the doors to the kitchen, headed toward the stables. He wanted to be there to greet her, and he wanted to be there to help supervise the unloading of the prisoner. It was important that as few as possible among the staff witnessed the transfer. It was not outside the realm of possibility that there were some among them who might take the risk of sending word out to Gabriella, hoping to win favor. Better to get the thing over with, perhaps he and the twins would be enough, and get back to Alfonzo as quickly as possible.

That was surely where Lucita would be heading, and that was another reason for haste. Matteo chastened himself, but could not contain the shivers of anticipation brought on by the thought of her presence. He felt like one of the old men in the alleys, punch-drunk on the rot-gut remnant at the bottom of barrels thrown out by the taverns, unable to pull free of the draw of it, despite the dangers and consequences. He was encouraged that Alfonzo had not killed him as a traitor, but he had no illusions. The issue was far from dead—perhaps a great deal farther from it than he himself.

He reached the street, and found that Arturo and Leonid had arrived before him. The driver was holding his horses steady, and the twins stood beside the back of the wagon. They were watching Lucita, whose carriage had pulled up behind them. The distrust on their features was blatant, and Matteo hurried to intercede.

By the time he'd reached her carriage, Lucita had dismounted and stood beside the street, returning Arturo and Leonid's cold stare. The situation was on the verge of a disaster that Matteo was not equipped to handle.

"The bishop has asked to see you the moment you arrive,"

he called out to Lucita, breaking the silence. He knew, also, that though his words weren't exact truth, they were enough to add a warning to the twins. They might not trust Lucita, but they knew better than to intercede in something Alfonzo desired.

"I will see to your carriage," he continued, slightly out of breath. He glanced behind and around her. "Where is the monk?"

"Anatole will not be returning," she replied. "Are you disappointed?" She stepped closer and reached out to trace her nails across his cheek. "I thought I would be enough to keep your interest."

Matteo gulped. He had no control of the wash of red heat that flushed his features. He knew that the twins would see, and that they would be angry. They had never liked him, sharing time with Alfonzo between themselves and a mortal. It had been bearable for them when Isadora was there to share, but now that they had only one master, they were very protective, and very jealous. Only Alfonzo stood between Matteo and destruction, and if Lucita continued as she was, he might lose that favor as well. He had no illusions about his relationship with the bishop. If he ceased to be of use to his lord, he would simply cease to be. He knew far too much of his lord's affairs to be allowed to escape.

He didn't even manage to answer. She handed him the reigns and stepped away from the road, heading toward the rear entrance to the kitchens. Arturo and Leonid watched her go, then, as she disappeared inside, they turned as one to face Matteo.

"She is not for you, little dog," Leonid hissed. "Don't get your heart set on things that will drain it."

Arturo remained silent, but the hatred that seeped from the darkly beautiful depths of his eyes spoke eloquently. This was to have been their moment. They had gone, as instructed, and they had returned with what they sought. They had given counsel, and now, they had their prisoner. It had been a flawless operation, and it should have been the focus of the evening. They should be inside, with Alfonzo, receiving the praise and reward they had earned.

Instead, Lucita would be at his side, and this sniveling mortal piece of flotsam would join them, eventually. The twins would be consigned to the dungeon, the prisoner, and one another. It was a cycle that wound tighter and tighter, and sooner or later Matteo knew that it would unwind like twisted rawhide, snapping out to strike. He hoped he would be able to avoid that strike, or that some other would be the one to finally put them over the edge. They were cunning, there was no denying that, and they were good at what they did, but there was something floating beneath the empty surface of each of their stares, something identical in each, and unique from anything else Matteo had experienced. They were dangerous, and they frightened him almost as much as the thought of what Lucita's teasing and taunting might bring him if and when it tempted Alfonzo's temper beyond its limits.

Matteo stepped up onto the driver's seat of the carriage and shook the reins, driving around the corner and down the alley to the side of the mansion. Two large wooden doors swung open as he approached, and he turned the horses down the slight incline and into the stables below. He brought the carriage to a halt almost immediately, stepping down and handing the reins to the stable master. There was a small troupe of half-guards, half stable-hands that inhabited this lower level. There were several ways to enter the main building from below, and they were all guarded, after their own fashion.

Artemis was the name of the current stable master. He was a tall, dark-haired man with eyes even darker than his hair, if that was possible. The man had a constant stubble of beard, not long, but not well-trimmed either. Matteo often wondered if the horse master trimmed it with his dagger on long, boring nights.

He had been in his position for six months, which was a good deal longer than the term of his predecessor, who'd run afoul of Leonid one dark night, allowing a horse to void itself too near the twins, splattering the floor at their feet and the tips of their boots. He hadn't lived long enough to fall on his knees and brush the leather clean. The horse had lived slightly longer, but had died in more pain. After that, Alfonzo had barred the twins from the stables, except on his direct order. They rarely traveled by any other means than their own limbs, speed, and agility, and they had no patience for the animals. The decision had been very helpful in obtaining a good stable master, and keeping him.

None of this registered as Matteo hit the stairs, stumbling up toward the main hall in a jumble of clumsy limbs and jittery nerves. He didn't know how Alfonzo would react to Lucita walking in unescorted. He knew his lord wanted to see her, had in fact been worried that she would not return, or that she was planning some sort of deceit, but the bishop had not actually requested she come straight up to see him.

Now, with the immediate threat of the twins behind him, he was faced with the different, but equally threatening proposition of explaining why he had spoken as if he were in command, and the possibility that he had chosen wrongly.

As he passed the hall leading to the kitchen, he heard shouted orders, and he knew that the twins had unbundled their captive and were escorting him below. Whoever it was, Matteo knew he would bear the brunt of his captor's anger, and that it would not be pleasant. He gave silent thanks to whatever god of the living or dead had delivered the poor wretch into their hands. He had no time, nor stomach, for facing down the twins.

When he reached Alfonzo's chambers, he hesitated. The doors were closed, and Lucita was nowhere in sight. He had assumed that she would ask directions and find her way, that she would be deep in counsel with his lord by the time he could make his way to their side and offer his services. Now he hesitated. What if she'd entered, gone on to the hall below, where they'd met twice before, and stood waiting—alone? What if the twins rose from their morbid duties with the prisoner and found her there? What if Matteo entered, was set to some task that forbade his interference?

In the end, it didn't matter. He could not risk waiting longer to report. Alfonzo was waiting for Matteo, whether or not he was waiting for Lucita. The bishop did not care to be kept waiting under the best of circumstances, and the past few days had proven far from ideal. Matteo knocked sharply, then entered the outer door and let it close behind him. He pressed forward into the curtains and before he could knock again, on the inner doors, they swung wide. Alfonzo stood framed in the doorway, his expression one of impatience, rather than anger.

"Where have you been?" he demanded. "Lucita has been here long enough to give me a full report from the camps. We have much to do, and very little time to do it, if everything is to go our way this night. It would be nice, Matteo, to have things go my way. Where are the twins?" Matteo was grateful for the direct question, and he answered in a rush of words, entering the room and catching site of Lucita, and of Katrina, talking quietly together by the window. He had not seen Katrina since the night she'd tried to make a feast of him, and he took an involuntary step backward, but Alfonzo stopped him with a hand on his shoulder.

"You have nothing to fear here," the bishop said, "unless you fail me. What I have for you is possibly the most important task you have performed in my service. If you succeed, then you will be rewarded."

Matteo lowered his eyes, heart slamming in his chest. "I know I have made promises in the past," Alfonzo said, "and I won't even pretend that I regret any action I may have taken. I am giving you my word, this time. If you complete this one simple task, quickly and without error, then I will grant you what you have wished for all these years. Better—I will grant the lady you so admire the right to grant that wish."

Matteo stiffened at this, but even the sudden, biting fear of the reminder that he had been disloyal, at least in mind and heart, to the one he'd followed so many years, was not enough to dampen his spirit.

"Anything," he whispered. "I would do anything. But you know this."

"I do," Alfonzo agreed.

In terse, simple terms, Alfonzo outlined his instructions, and Matteo nodded, though his blood ran colder with each word. He steeled himself. This was the test, the moment that would decide his eternity—the short, painful life of a man, or the blood. When he had finished, Alfonzo slapped Matteo on the back and shoved him on his way, nearly pounding him through the inner doors in his haste. Matteo didn't hesitate. He slipped through the outer doors, down the stairs and through the first outer door and courtyard he reached. He didn't want any other to see his departure, or to follow. He had one chance to get through, and didn't intend to let it slip through his fingers.

On the balcony, far above, Lucita caught site of his form as he slipped away down the darkened street. She didn't let on that she'd seen. She and Katrina had been talking for the better part of half an hour. The girl was young, very naive, very pretty. She might make an ally at some point, but at present she was little more than a toy, and so she was losing Lucita's interest. Alfonzo joined them, and, relieved, Lucita stepped back, including him in the conversation.

"Where has he gone?" she asked, not wanting to seem too curious, but also unable to resist testing her limits. She had begun to tease Matteo for a single purpose, and now was the time to make use of the result. She needed to know if Alfonzo would trust her, not in his words, but in his affairs as well. She'd needed a way to test that, and Matteo had offered himself up without a whimper. Alfonzo had as much as admitted the boy knew more about the workings of the mansion, and the bishop's own plans, to be trusted to anyone outside his immediate circle of influence. Yet, he had allowed her to toy with his trusted servant, and had intimated it might go further, both the toying, and the trust.

"If he does as I have asked," Alfonzo replied, "then I will tell you the entire story. If not, it won't matter, and we may find ourselves with a much more difficult task than we have anticipated. I sent a messenger to Licinius, but I have no way to know how he will react. He may remember Katrina—fondly," Alfonzo laid an arm across Katrina's shoulders, and she smiled up at him. Her eyes were filled with empty adoration, and hunger. She was so new to the blood she could think of little beyond his control of her, and feeding. Lucita wanted to say something. She wanted to point out that the simplest means to their end was to stake her for the sun or feed her to pyre and then find someone to blame it all on. She said nothing. She smiled, and she nodded, waiting to see if Alfonzo would give away any further secrets.

"We have taken one of Gabriella's followers," he said. "I have him below, ready for questioning. I assumed that you would want to be present. You and the lady Gabriella seem to have your differences."

"I find that I have differences with almost everyone I meet," she answered cryptically. "It is a character flaw, I admit. I like power. You like it, as well. I can sense this in you—could sense it from the beginning. I sense the same in Gabriella, but there is a difference. Gabriella is emotional. She will allow herself weaknesses that I do not believe you would indulge in." Lucita smiled, but the expression lacked the warmth to carry it through. "For instance, she will not wish to sacrifice one of her own. I assume you have prepared for this?"

"Of course," Alfonzo replied. "I am actually looking forward to her arrival, or to that of those who serve her. I have no intention of killing the one I hold. There are a great number of ways to assert control. One is to kill everyone and everything that opposes you. This method, I admit, has its merit. It leaves few loose threads to trip you in the future, and it sets a marvelous example for others. Still, it is not necessarily a popular method of ruling, and it tends to limit one's circle of trusted allies."

"I can see your point," Lucita murmured, hiding her smile. "So, you will show mercy to this captive?"

"I don't know that I would call it mercy," he replied. "I will not destroy him, and I will not allow the twins to destroy him, but they have other pleasures. It may be that when this one returns to Gabriella's service, he will be a bit less useful for a time. I doubt that he will be quite so eager to invade the territory of another, for instance." Lucita turned to the window, and the balcony beyond. The moon had risen high in the sky, the night was half alive and half dead—a perfect balance. "There are lessons that all must learn, in time," she said softly. "Gabriella has been hurt before, and I suspect her nature will cause this not to be her last. She chose her allies, but I think, this time, she chose with less prudence than she might have. I wonder how Licinius will react to the knowledge that Malachite schemes just beyond the walls of his city."

"I am not so certain that Licinius is unaware," Alfonzo replied. "Basilio has been in that city a bit longer than I am comfortable with, and my sources tell of a great many comings and goings that have little to do with the normal affairs of the city. Things are happening there, things beyond our control, or concern. I would not be surprised to find Licinius' hand in that pilgrimage, as well. I would be even less surprised to find that he knows of Gabriella and her followers, tucked up against his walls and ignoring his influence. This is a tide that could turn either way."

Lucita turned back to him. "You may he right," she said. "I have spoken with Basilio myself. I wonder if you would he surprised at the counsel he gave."

Alfonzo stared at her, caught off guard. "When? When did you speak with him? Why didn't you tell me?"

"It was before I came to you," she said, turning back to the window. "Anatole took me to Adrianople by ways I was not familiar with, inside the walls of the city. Basilio was there, and he gave me counsel. He said that there was one who might make a prince in Constantinople, and he suggested that I work toward that end."

Alfonzo was staring at her back, but he did not speak. "He told me," Lucita said, turning to meet the bishop's gaze, "that I should come to you."

At that moment, a cry rose from below, and Alfonzo actually smiled.

"I believe," he said with a short bow, "that we have company."

He turned toward the door, and Lucita followed. Katrina made as if to fall in behind them, but Alfonzo turned and warned her away with a glance. "I will be back for you," he said, "soon. It is not yet safe for you to be seen. When this is over, you will walk freely. A second promise, for a remarkable night."

Then, with a flourish, he ushered Lucita through the large, ornate double doorway of his chambers and into the halls beyond. The shouts from below had grown louder, and Alfonzo began to laugh.

Chapter Eighteen

The lower level of the mansion had been sealed again. This time, however, rather than trying to keep a small chain of naked women captive, the doors were barred against those attacking from the street. Alfonzo knew, of course, that these precautions were only a temporary measure considering that the attackers were Cainites, and angry Cainites at that. It was only meant to buy time.

He led Lucita down the stairs, passed by the kitchens and descended the stairs toward the dungeon below. There were cries at their backs, but this only seemed to fuel Alfonzo's mirth. He hurried down the steps, turning into the stone corridor below and following a new set of sounds.

As they came into sight of the cell where Ian had been tossed, still trussed like an animal, the shadows of the twins loomed. In the light of flickering torches, the shadows had grown longer, elongating to eerie long-lingered shades.

"You are ready?" Alfonzo question had the feel of a statement, so apparent was his confidence in the two, and Lucita was glad for it. After the near confrontation on the street, it was good to see the bishop showing his support to his followers.

Arturo slipped from the darker shadows beyond the cell, eyes gleaming in the torchlight. "We have always been ready," he replied testily. "There is little time, milord."

Alfonzo nodded. "Bring him," he said brusquely. "We will take the private stairs."

Leonid had stepped up beside his brother, and he frowned slightly, glaring at Lucita. It was obvious that he wanted to say something, to question the wisdom of taking someone so newly included in their affairs by a way that none knew.

"We can't make it otherwise," Alfonzo said sharply. "There is no time for questioning. You will do as I tell you to do, and quickly. If you do, we will turn this tide nicely, and by the end of the night have entertainment such as we have not seen in a very long time. If we stay here too long, though, we will be caught like rats in a trap, and while I suspect that I would escape with my skin, I can't say the same for us all. Gabriella is angry, and those who follow her are not weak."

Without further speech, Alfonzo spun on his heel and headed back the way he'd come. Lucita fell in beside him, not wanting to be left behind as a distraction to the twins. There might come a time when that confrontation would have to take place, but this was not it.

Behind them, she heard the grate of metal on stone. The cell had been opened, and moments later there were footsteps behind, following them down the hall and up the stairs. As they reached the hall above, they heard shouts from near the front of the mansion. There was the clash of weapons, and Lucita's hand slipped to her own blade. She was not afraid of a fight, but she wondered what Alfonzo hoped to gain from this one. Defeating Gabriella and her followers was hardly a foregone conclusion, but even if the bishop and she did prevail, where was the gain in it all?

Then, to her surprise, Leonid pushed past her and raced to a spot on the wall near the stairs leading upward. He pressed his palm in a quick sequence against what seemed to be solid stone, and a panel slid to one side, opening on a dark doorway. Leonid stood aside, and Alfonzo ducked through the entrance and out of site. Lucita followed, and as the sounds of battle behind them grew louder, and closer, the twins brought their burden through and the panel slid closed behind them.

The hidden stairwell was dark, but this posed little problem for any of them. They climbed rapidly through the walls, the twins taking perverse pleasure in cracking the head of their captive into stone walls at every opportunity. Lucita ignored them. She had no particular concern for any follower of Gabriella's, and it was certainly a lesson that might increase the length of one's existence, the helpless sensation of being dragged, bound, and blindfolded, to a fate you could only guess at.

Alfonzo paid no attention to any of them. He moved quickly, anticipating each turn in the stairs as they wound upward. Lucita knew that they must have passed several floors, but Alfonzo didn't hesitate. They didn't slow until the steps ended at what seemed another solid wall.

"Now," Alfonzo said with a short laugh, "the real entertainment begins."

They stepped through the doorway and into open air. They stood on one of the battlements, far above the streets. The wind caught Alfonzo's hair, blowing it wildly about his head, and he walked the edge of the roof easily and without fear. Lucita stepped to the wall behind him and followed. Behind, the door was closed with a bang by the wind, and the twins were on the wall alongside Lucita, Ian's body hefted to their shoulders and borne between them.

They moved around to stand on a larger, flat slab of stone from which an intricately carved gargoyle jutted outward, its eyes scanning the streets below in eternal vigilance.

"This will do," Alfonzo said with a nod.

The twins, already aware of what their master was planning, lowered Ian to the stone. Leonid pulled a length of rope from his pocket, and Arturo began to unbind Ian's arms, careful not to allow him a chance to escape or retaliate. Ian was dazed from the beating on the stone walls as they'd ascended. He posed no threat. "You know what to do?" Alfonzo asked.

Arturo gazed at the bishop for a long silent moment. He clearly wanted to say something, but he held himself in check. Alfonzo stood silent, waiting, knowing the struggle that was taking place and not fearing it. The twins were powerful and headstrong; it was natural that they would chaff under too tight a control. Lucita's presence added to the tension of the moment, but finally, Arturo nodded.

"You know that we do. This is a simple thing, easily completed."

Alfonzo nodded. "I do not doubt you, Arturo," he said, his voice soft, but somehow echoing about the rooftop. He drew himself up, and as he had at the party, he took on form, substance as dark and empty as shadow, and as dangerous as impending storm. Though his voice was the same, his appearance shifted to shadow. His eyes glowed with flickers of red and the air near him took on an impossible chill. "If all goes as planned," he said, "you will not be disappointed in your place in the order of things to come. I do not forget those who serve me well. Nor those who fail me."

Lucita shifted nervously for just a second. It was easy to forget how powerful the bishop was. Alfonzo was old, and powerful, and in such a form his presence was overpowering. She shook her head, fighting to concentrate.

Arturo turned back to his brother, and the two set to work, binding the separate ends of the rope to Ian's shoulders and winding them down his arms, securing them tightly. Satisfied, Alfonzo turned to Lucita.

"They will complete what must be done here," he said. "It is time for us to greet my guests. If the sounds we heard before climbing up here were any indication, they are impatient. I would hate to keep them waiting."

It was Lucita's turn to laugh. For all her guile, she had no idea what he was planning. She felt the exhilaration of the moment, the wind in her hair, the streets far below, almost calling out to her to leap into the night sky and drift to their embrace. The sounds of battle rose from beneath them, and it was impossible to tell from those sounds who prevailed.

Alfonzo was touched by none of it. He stood watching her for a long moment, then turned back to the doorway through which they'd come and opened it, slipping back onto the shadowed stairs. Without a glance at the twins, Lucita followed, pulling the door shut behind her.

On the main level of Alfonzo's mansion, Gabriella had forced entrance through the front by brute force. She'd brought all of those she could muster, knowing she would get one shot, and one shot only at pulling Ian out unscathed. It was obvious from what had taken place at the tavern that her influence there was known, and through that, probably everything she'd planned,

as well. There was no way to know to what lengths Alfonzo's
people would go to drag information from Ian. He was strong,
and would likely hold out to the end, possibly beyond, but
there was no way to know it for certain.

So, they'd come. She had managed to draw together a size-
able force, though a great deal of them were mortal. Most were
mercenaries, those gathered from the tavern and the Genoese
Quarter, lured in by a quick handful of gold and an incomplete explanation of where they were going and why. Her own
people were spread thinly, but they were good.

When the break had happened into the main hall, she'd
quickly conferred with Raphael and Gradin, who'd slipped off
down the street in the blink of an eye. Pasqual stood at her
side, and he fought like one possessed. For all his teasing of
Ian, the Frenchman worried more about his chess partner than
he would ever have let on. Also, the younger Cainite had been
taken while under Pasqual's supervision, right out from under
his nose on a night when both had been warned to be on their
guard, and to exercise extra precautions.

Those inside fell back from the door, and Gabriella hesitated. This was too easy. She knew that there were flaws in
Alfonzo's defenses, but he was not a fool. This was happening
far too quickly, and she nearly called her men back, retreating into the streets. Then Ian's scowling face popped into her
head—eyes intent on the chessboard before him, seeing a part
but not the whole, and frustrated by his lack of vision—and
she gave the signal to move ahead.

They would go inside, and they would get Ian out, one
way or another. She wasn't looking forward to locking horns
with Alfonzo, but neither did she fear him. There was more
at stake than a simple argument, or even the control of the
city. She had lost those close to her many times in the past,
to a number of different enemies, and once—one very dark
moment in time—she had lost the one closest to her heart to
another she had trusted. This was not going to become another
such moment.

With a feral growl, she leaped through the damaged doorway, cut out and down with her blade, felled a man who'd tried

to come at her from the side, and dodged nimbly into the hall. She could see only half a dozen of Alfonzo's servants, armed and ready, squared off against her. It wasn't right.

They were no match for her, or even for the least of her followers. These were no hardened soldiers, nor even time-tested mercenaries. They were servants, kitchen workers and clerks, and they fell back rapidly, as though the job at hand were not to repel invaders, but instead to merely remain alive.

Pasqual leaped through the doorway to her side, and she pulled him back hard against the wall. None pressed the attack once the first to do so had fallen, and moments later Gabriella's entire troop stood in the hall. The defenders watched a moment longer, making a brave show of brandishing their weapons and glaring at the invaders, then as if on a signal, they cut and ran back down the hall. They never looked back to see if they were pursued, or if they would die. They ran, and dumfounded, Gabriella and Pasqual stood in the hall, their small force gathering behind them, wondering what had just happened.

"It seems," Pasqual said softly, "that we play someone a bit more skilled than young Ian this night."

Gabriella said nothing. With measured footsteps, she set out down the hall, her weapon held loosely to her side. She watched the shadows for an ambush, but her instincts told her it was wasted effort. There was no one. None stood between her and the rest of the mansion, and the only thing that remained to itch at her mind and steal her thoughts was the absence of a defense. Moving ahead into such a void was foolish. She had watched Ian make such a mistake time and again on the chess board, and she could tell by the wary expression on Pasqual's face that he recognized it too.

It stank of a trap, but for all of that, she could not sense the specifics of the danger. The hidden pieces remained obscured, and none stepped forward to call the check.

With a shrug that meant nothing and everything all at once, she continued. Just down the hall was the great double door leading to the hall where the bishop had held his party. It had been an eternity since she'd last entered that room.

"He will be waiting," Pasqual whispered.

Gabriella nodded. "I know, but this time, old friend, I don't intend to sacrifice my knight."

Pasqual nearly smiled, but repressed it, and they moved on, measuring their steps in shadows and listening intently for the slightest sign of motion, or retaliation.

Alfonzo had dropped down the steps like a dark bolt of lightning. Lucita followed easily, and they were at the base of the stairs in moments, standing on the opposite side of the stone door that led to the hall by the kitchen. Alfonzo did not use this exit, but turned into a deeper shadowed passage and continued on. Lucita still did not question. She knew he had a plan, and she knew that, if his trust was to be won this night, it would not be because she questioned his actions, or his judgment.

They reached another wall, and Alfonzo turned to her, bringing a finger to his lips to indicate she should continue in silence. Lucita nodded, and Alfonzo pushed against the wall, sliding another panel open. He glanced through, listened intently, then gestured for her to follow once more. They entered the great hall, and as they passed along the wall, Alfonzo reached out, plucked a wine bottle from the great racks lining one dark section of wood, and in the next second had managed to add four long-stemmed goblets to his take without the slightest break in stride.

He turned to the center of the room, and when they reached the raised platform in the center, he nodded for Lucita to precede him up to the table. He leaped nimbly up beside her, placing the goblets on the table and quickly opening the wine bottle by pressing one long-nailed finger into the cork hard and fast, popping the cork inside. He poured until the four goblets stood full and gleaming in the dim reflected light of torches in the hallway beyond. Turning, he tipped the bottle up, took a long pull of the blood-soaked wine, and smiled.

Not knowing how to react, or why she wasn't fleeing this place, Lucita returned the smile. There had been the faint clash of weapons in the hall, but this had passed, and there were retreating footsteps drawing ever nearer.

"It is nearly time," Alfonzo said softly. He pulled back a chair for her, and Lucita seated herself at the table. Alfonzo joined her, taking the seat opposite and picking up one of the goblets, watching the doorway in what appeared for all the world to be no more than idle curiosity. With a shrug, Lucita picked up her own goblet, as well, and leaned back, watching Alfonzo as he watched the door.

The sounds in the hallway beyond grew louder. There was a crash of wood, and a single scream. Immediately following this, the sound of footsteps pounding the floor grew nearer. It seemed to Lucita that whatever defense Alfonzo had prepared was buckling. She wondered at his calm.

Moments later, they saw a rag-tag group hurry by in full retreat. They were followed by another group, weapons at the ready, which stopped as it drew abreast of the door to the great hall. Even from that distance, Gabriella was clearly visible. Alfonzo raised his goblet, tilted it slightly in the invading group's direction, and took a sip. His smile had not wavered.

Gabriella stalked into the room, Pasqual pacing nervously at her side. Her mercenaries fell in behind, and they moved slowly across the floor to the raised platform, and the table, where Alfonzo and Lucita sat waiting. Lucita's hand had drifted to the weapon at her side, but she made no move, taking her cue from Alfonzo. He was obviously planning something, but what it could he she could not guess.

"So nice of you to drop by," the bishop said in greeting. His voice boomed out across the room, taking on that surreal quality that seemed to echo it from every board and rafter, bringing it to those within hearing from every direction at once. He lifted his glass again.

"Where is he?" Gabriella asked, ignoring his greeting. "What have you done with Ian?"

"Your spy?" Alfonzo asked, raising an eyebrow. "I would think that by now you would understand that when you place someone in a precarious situation, sometimes they fall. I'm certain the chess master there would agree." Alfonzo acknowledged Pasqual with another nod. "It is not a peaceful world," he added. "Come, drink with us. The night is young, and we have started it off with such excitement."

Gabriella drew into herself, growing very cold, and very pale. She was shaking with the effort of controlling herself. Pasqual put a warning hand on her shoulder, but she shrugged it off. Alfonzo was taunting her, but she was no fool. As Lucita had done moments earlier, she'd realized that something was not what it seemed.

"You are wondering," Alfonzo said at last, "why I would sit here, calmly, as you invade my home, hopelessly outnumbered and putting myself—at least potentially—at your mercy."

Gabriella did not reply.

"That would make me," Alfonzo went on, "either confident of my control of the situation or a fool. Which do you believe, my friend? I am here, if you believe you can rush in and take me. I do not think that you will. The one you call Ian's very existence is in the balance, and only I can solve the mystery of the outcome. I wish you would reconsider. Sit, talk, have a drink."

Gabriella stood, uncertain and wavering, and suddenly, the bishop clapped his hands. The room lit on all sides. Torches leaped to life in a huge circle, held aloft by twice a hundred hands. Men, Cainites, everyone that could be dragged in at short notice and up through the doors from the stables had been summoned. They closed their ring, leaving Alfonzo, Lucita, and their attackers penned into the center.

"You might escape," Alfonzo conceded. "There are many among them who fear you outright, and not many here could stand before you if you desired them to fall. Still, you would be departing without that which you came here for, and I don't believe you want that. Sit. I promise, for once, that I shall be brief." He hesitated, then smiled again. "The wine really *is* excellent. The blood is from an eighteen-year-old swordsman who fell in battle. He was dying when he was drained, slowly, and he fought very bravely. It has a strength to it—a vigor that many other vintages do not. I know not everyone enjoys this particular Venetian specialty, but you really must have some."

Gabriella sheathed her sword in a sudden, violent motion. She continued her stalking, angry walk to the table and stepped up. Pasqual joined her, but the others, overwhelmed and certain they were breathing what might be the final breaths of their lives, fell back into a tight knot to one side.

"I admire your courage," Alfonzo said pleasantly, as Gabriella dropped haughtily into one of the free chairs. "I have to question the logic of such a frontal assault, but I admire the spirit behind it. I might have acted the same, when I was younger."

"Where is he?" Gabriella repeated. She made no move to lean forward, engage Alfonzo in conversation, or to take the wine. Pasqual sat easily, poised on his seat for whatever might come, but with an expression more of curiosity than of fear.

"Your spy is safe," Alfonzo said, more brusquely, "for the moment. The outcome of his days depends entirely on yourself, and your reaction to the things I'm about to explain to you. I am not fond of destroying our kind, particularly if it can be avoided. There are better uses for power, uses I'm both aware and fond of, as well you know. For now, you will he silent, and I will speak. I will tell you how things are now, and how they are going to be. You will agree, and then we will part. Your follower will be returned to you. It is simple, yes?" Gabriella glared at him a moment longer, then nodded. Alfonzo continued.

"I have given a great deal of thought to our city, of late," he said, carefully choosing his words. "I have remembered how things were in the past, and I have looked out over the way things are now. While this has been a good time for myself in many ways, it has not been good for the city itself. Those who were decadent before the fall are worse. Those who were noble, or trustworthy have turned to intrigue.

"I will be the first to admit that the Latin Quarter, where my own influence has been strongest, has been a cesspool of such behavior all the nights of its existence. I have ruled over that, understood it, embraced it and made it my own. Still, it does not feel complete. One can only spend so many years as the ruler of the taverns before becoming enamored of the ballrooms. This was a great city, and whatever such as we may do, it is destined to be great again.

"Those who ruled have fallen or are gone. There are a few who believe the Dracon will return, but I am not one of those few. He left Byzantium behind long before either of us arrived here, and I believe that rather than thanking his followers for tracking him to the ends of the earth, he may well destroy them for their arrogance. This city is a new city now, and it needs new rulers. *One* new ruler," he corrected. "I have decided that this one must be myself. That is why I have summoned you."

Gabriella bristled at this, but Pasqual barely contained a smile. "Check," he whispered under his breath. Lucita heard it and winked at the old Cainite, enjoying the show now that it was finally underway, and admiring Alfonzo's style. He had a way of doing everything extravagantly that lent the air of importance to things that might otherwise have seemed trivial.

"Do not be deceived," Alfonzo laughed softly. "You were summoned. I had no other reason to capture your whelp at the tavern. I could have easily had him destroyed and his dust returned to you in a box. I knew that you would come. I would have been disappointed if you had not."

"Then return him to me," Gabriella said, less certain. "I have not come here to attack you, but only to win him free."

"You will be given ample opportunity for that," Alfonzo replied. "You will remove yourself, your followers and any interest that you currently possess in the Latin Quarter and keep to the Genoese Quarter across the Golden Horn. Failure to do so will result in the destruction of any and all I find in violation of this. The quarter is, was and shall remain mine. You are free to traffic, travel and conduct business in your own quarter, but you will do so openly and on my leave. I will not have spies skulking about my doorstep."

Gabriella was silent. She listened, but she acknowledged nothing.

"You will withdraw your agents from the camps at Adrianople, but this should not be too difficult for you as I do not believe they will exist for much longer. I have been in contact with Licinius, and I believe he grows tired of the hovels leaning on the walls of his city. I expect that he will agree with me that they should be emptied. In fact," Alfonzo whirled the goblet in his hand, took a sip, then went on, "I hear that your ally Malachite will be leading them all away soon. Have you considered, Gabriella, the wisdom of following him?"

"This city is my home, for now," she said. "I will not follow a fool on a fool's quest. Not for him, and not for you. Nor will I," she said evenly, "give over domain of the Genoese Quarter."

"Then," Alfonzo replied, slamming the goblet suddenly onto the table and leaning forward, lifting slightly out of his chair to loom over Gabriella's smaller form, "you will remain here under my rules. This will be a great city once again, and it will be my city. You can be a part of that, or not, but you will not hinder it."

"You mean," she sneered, "it will be a pawn to the powers in Venice. Archbishop Narses will rule here as surely as he has ruled everywhere else he has sent you."

"Narses knows nothing of this," Alfonzo laughed softly. "When he finds out, I am certain he will be displeased, but then, what is a family without its disputes? I have other allies than Venice," he cut his gaze to check Lucita, who nodded at him coolly. "I have also come to some personal conclusions. Let those erstwhile refugees play at being pilgrims and preachers of Caine. As I'm sure you'd be happy to indicate, Narses himself has shown the difficulties of reconciling being a bishop and a prince. Heresy is an ill-fit for me. I believe that I will trust in what I am, and who I am. I am darkness. Let the mortals of this city be my herd and my domain, but I do not need to make them my flock.

"If damnation is what they fear, I will become their fear. I will be Prince in Constantinople from this night forward," he said with finality. "I have sent messengers to the various houses, those who joined you at my party. I have heard back already from a third of them with their support. That is more than enough to carry the day should any have other ideas. You see, Gabriella, I did not call you here to warn you I was about to take the city you so covet for your own. I called you here to tell you it was already mine."

Gabriella remained silent. At last, she bowed her head, just for an instant, as if gathering strength from somewhere deep inside. "You have made your point," she said at last. "I will abide by your rules, for the moment, because, as you well know, I have little choice. I will remain in the city. Where is Ian?"

The night had steadily slipped away from them, and just the faintest hint of glowing light had painted the edges of the skyline beyond his walls. Alfonzo knew the sun would still be a bit in rising, but it was imminent. He felt the pull of the earth and the faint uneasiness that accompanied each new day.

"Go," he said quietly. "You will find him on your way. I will send for you soon, and we will take counsel, not just the two of us, but all the houses." Gabriella rose quickly, still uncertain.

"Where will we find him?" she asked, still focused on her follower. She ignored everything else, and Alfonzo watched her, giving Lucita the impression of a great black spider watching a moth squirm in his web.

"Go," he repeated.

Gabriella whirled and leaped from the platform. Pasqual was at her side, and her other men fell in behind. No one stood in their way as they departed, hitting the hallway at a run and heading for the broken doors beyond.

"Where is he?" Lucita asked while Alfonzo watched Gabriella's departure with an intensely satisfied smile.

"Where we left him, more or less," Alfonzo answered. He stood, gestured for her to follow, and ran for the stairs leading upward, toward the quarters where Isadora had been slain. It did not take them long to reach the rooms, and Alfonzo stepped quickly through to the balcony beyond, leaning out over the edge and looking up. Lucita followed his example.

Far above, where the gargoyle jutted from the side of the building in the path of the rising sun, not so far in the future as it had been moments before, a figure swung violently, suspended by a length of rope. The twins had looped the rope over the neck of the gargoyle and kicked Ian's still-bound form over the edge. He could not break the bonds, and within short moments, the sun would break free of the horizon and he could be fried, crumbling to dust.

Below, there were shouts from Gabriella's men. They had spotted Ian, and several of Gabriella's men had returned to the broken doors, trying to fight their way inside and up to where Ian hung. The doors were closed to them, a small group of Alfonzo's mercenaries having secured it.

Then, with a cry, Pasqual drew back his arm. Lucita watched in wonder as that arm whipped forward with the speed of a striking snake. Something silver and glittering whistled past the balcony, and both she and Alfonzo shied back away from it. There was a crack, metal glancing off stone, and moments later, with a hoarse, muffled cry through his gag and the ruffle of cloth in the breeze, Ian's form shot past, falling toward the ground below.

He struck a small stand of trees, one of the many gardens, and bounced violently from branch to branch. Lucita watched, wondering if he would pierce his heart on a tree branch. Now that would be an entertainment worth seeing. He did not. Moments later, Ian's crumpled form lay on the street below, and Gabriella was directing others to lift him and carry him. They had little time to get off the streets, or they would all suffer the fate their now broken and battered companion had so narrowly escaped.

Lucita leaned out, glanced up at the gargoyle once again, then down to where the dagger still lay in the dust of the street, blade broken.

"You knew he could do that?" she asked, turning to Alfonzo.

He looked thoughtful. "No, but it is a good thing to know. Amazing, really." He turned to leave the room, then turned back.

"You will stay here tonight. There is no time for you to get safely to your own quarters. When Matteo returns, I will have further news. Important news. For now, we both must sleep."

Lucita nodded, and smiled. "I will stay here, then," she said. "It seems fitting, since in a way this is where all of this began."

Alfonzo nodded slowly.

"Rest well, Lucita of Aragon," he laughed. "The new night may bring more than we have bargained for." And he was gone. Lucita slid the triple panels of dark mahogany across the balcony exit, sealed the sleeping chamber tightly, and made herself comfortable.

Beyond the walls of the mansion, the sun rose over Alfonzo's Constantinople.

Epilogue

Matteo staggered down the street. He was chilled. Every inch of him felt as if he'd been dipped in an icy stream and held up to a stiff breeze, whirled and slapped to increase the stinging pain. He pulled his cloak about himself more tightly and went on. He had only a short distance to reach Alfonzo's mansion, shorter hours before he must present himself.

His mind was awash in anticipation, fear, longing and hunger, but despite all of these sensations, he could not stop the crawling of his skin. He felt awash in tiny feet, as if vermin squirmed through his clothing and into his hair.

He made it as far as the doorway to the kitchens, and he fell against the wood heavily, managing to turn so that his back struck with a loud thump. Moments later, the doorway was opened from within, and he was dragged inside. He was vaguely aware of being lifted and lain on something soft. He remembered the scent of food from the kitchens, and little else before exhaustion dragged him away into its clutches. He slept for hours.

When darkness had fallen, Matteo was awakened by the shake of a strong hand on his shoulder. He gasped and sat upright, catching the scream before it could escape and shaking loose from a very dark dream. In the dream, he fled through the streets of the city, heart pounding, and behind he could hear the laughter of the twins, and that of Alfonzo, mocking him. His skin was coated in sweat, and even as he shook off the dream, he wondered if it held more truth than nightmare.

He rose and quickly cleaned himself. There was no time to change, he strode into the hall and up the stairs with purpose.

Alfonzo would be awake, and likely Lucita would be with him. Matteo noted the repairs underway on the great front doors, but he did not pause to hear the story of how they'd been broken.

He knocked firmly on the outer door of Alfonzo's chamber, pushed it open and stepped inside. He let it close behind him completely, sealing off the light, before he parted the curtains and stepped to the inner doors, heart pounding. No one opened the door, and, with another knock, he pressed on the latch. It opened with a soft click, and the door swung wide.

Matteo gathered his courage, sucked in a long, rasping breath, and stepped inside.

He saw Alfonzo immediately. The bishop—no, the prince—stood at the far wall, leaning back against the polished wood and watching Matteo's entrance. In a chair to one side, Lucita lounged. She had one leg up and over the chair's leg casually, leaning back to expose a good portion of flesh at her throat. Her eyes were dark and without emotion. She watched Matteo as well.

"I have seen him," Matteo said without prompting. "Myka Vykos. I made my way to the place you told me of. I passed through, though his guards—they are..." Matteo hesitated, then continued. "They are ghouls. They were not gentle, and they were not easy to convince that I had business with their lord."

"And your business went well?" Alfonzo asked. There was something in the tone of his voice that removed the question from the words. Matteo only nodded.

"I told him what you asked," the servant replied softly. "I told him what had transpired here, and what you plan." Matteo turned and bowed slightly to Lucita. "I told him of you, as well, lady. He was very intrigued to hear that you were here."

Alfonzo watched Matteo for a long time. The prince remained silent, and Matteo stood firm. His knees felt as if they'd been replaced by soft bread dough from the kitchens, and he felt as if he might faint from terror, but he stood very still. If he were to die now, at least he would do so with courage.

Then, very suddenly, Alfonzo laughed. The sound was full and deep, echoing through the chamber, not dulled by the heavy curtains and rich tapestries.

"He has already been here," the prince said. The moment that daylight failed, he came, unannounced. We have spoken, the three of us. It seems that Vykos has plans of his own, and an interest in my own.

"The greatest threat to my own rule here might be Malachite and his quest for the Dracon, who is the progenitor of Vykos' own line of Obertus monks. If that Nosferatu fool ever manages to bring the Dracon back to this city, there could be trouble. It seems, Matteo, that Vykos himself has plans to eliminate that possibility." Matteo gulped in more air, fighting for the strength not to cry out in relief.

"There is more," Lucita cut in. "I have arranged for Vykos to meet with my own sire in Madrid. It seems a great number of the powerful have suddenly found themselves walking parallel paths. There could be great things in the future. There has never been an alliance between my clan and the Obertus, but who knows? When the future of a city, or a world, hang in the balance, fate can choose odd bedfellows for the powerful."

"And so," Alfonzo continued, "you have done as I asked. You have done me a great service, Matteo, a service I'm not sure another could have done in so swift a manner. Vykos and Moncada have also agreed to help smooth things with Licinius and Basilio in Adrianople, relieving us of potential tensions between the cities. It would appear that I am in your debt."

Matteo dared not speak. He dared not meet the prince's eyes, nor Lucita's, so he kept his own fixed on the floor, where richly designed rugs formed a soft, plush carpet.

In the corner, a shadow moved. Katrina stepped into the dim candlelight. She was smiling, but her smile was for Alfonzo alone. Matteo watched as this former living noble of Adrianople slipped up behind the new undead Prince of Constantinople, slid her arms around his waist and teased the flesh of his throat with gleaming fangs that glittered wetly.

"We will hunt," Alfonzo said. "When that hunt is done, you will both be gone from here, I believe, and that is well. I will expect to see you within a few nights. You, Lucita, because we have things to do—things to plan. You, Matteo, because though I do not believe you will carry on my affairs during the daylight after this night, I do expect you to carry them on as you can. You will remain with me, afterwards. You will be my...collateral."

Lucita smiled, rising as well. Matteo nearly took an involuntary step back. The moment was overwhelming. Fear crept in to join a rising elation. He raised his gaze to meet Lucita's and the fear washed down and away. He was trapped. She moved with deceptive speed, one moment directly in front of him, the next behind, a long nail pressed into the base of his chin, lifting and tilting. Matteo trembled and leaned back against her.

He never knew when Alfonzo and Katrina departed. He knew only that first, sharp bite, the grip of her hands, so strong he might have been clamped in bands of metal. Matteo closed his eyes, and he was surprised. He had expected visions of darkness, of blood and deep shadows, of Lucita's dark eyes taunting him and her lips pressed tightly to his flesh, but that was not what was granted.

As Lucita ushered him into the night, Matteo saw a final vision of the rising sun.

It did not take long to fade to dusk.

About the Author

DAVID NIALL WILSON has been writing and publishing horror, dark fantasy, and science fiction since the mid-eighties. An ordained minister, once President of the Horror Writers Association and multiple recipient of the Bram Stoker Award, his novels include *Maelstrom, The Mote in Andrea's Eye, Deep Blue,* the Grails Covenant Trilogy, *Star Trek Voyager: Chrysalis, Except You Go Through Shadow, This is My Blood, Ancient Eyes, On the Third Day, The Orffyreus Wheel,* The DeChance Chronicles, including *Heart of a Dragon, Vintage Soul, My Soul to Keep, Kali's Tale* and the stand-alone spinoff *Nevermore – A Novel of Love, Loss & Edgar Allan Poe.* His novels in the O.C.L.T. series include *The Parting, Crockatiel,* and the novella *The Temple of Camazotz* He is also the author of the memoir / cookbook *American Pies: Baking with Dave the Pie Guy.* David can be found at http://www.davidniallwilson.com and can be reached by e-mail at david@davidniallwilson.com.

Printed in Great Britain
by Amazon

31667799R00136